Washington Spring books

A Horse of a Different Color

ROBIN ARCUS

Copyright © 2021 Robin Arcus
All rights reserved

The characters and events portrayed in this book are fictitious. Any similarity to real persons, living or dead, is coincidental and not intended by the author.

No part of this book may be reproduced, or stored in a retrieval system, or transmitted in any form or by any means, electronic, mechanical, photocopying, recording, or otherwise, without express written permission of the publisher.

ISBN-13: 979-8-51-260772-5
Cover design by: Art Painter
Library of Congress Control Number: 2018675309
Printed in the United States of America
All rights reserved.

DEDICATION

For all readers searching for the truth.

WASHINGTON SPRING

On September 18 a horse appeared on the property of Washington Spring. After multiple unsuccessful attempts to locate the horse's owner, the community voted to sell the horse. We enlisted the help of Jerry Wagner of Fortune Farms, Richmond, Virginia. Mr. Wagner paid for the horse and removed it.

–Washington Spring Archives, Mary Gray Walterson

A HORSE OF A DIFFERENT COLOR

1

HALIFAX

The storm began as a distant rumble, audible only to an animal's ears. Through her feet, the horse felt the subfrequency begin to intensify, the smell of sulfur and approaching rain rankling her nostrils. Birds began collecting in the barn, nestling in protected corners and perching on rafters. A screech owl hooted, with no reply, then tried again. Outside, treetops began swaying. Under the barn floor the ground trembled causing the horse to stamp her feet. She was tired from the day's ride, wanting to sleep, dreaming of sleep, but now wide awake, fear forming in her belly. A crack split the air, close and brutal. Thunder followed. The barn shook. A barn cat jerked, unable to feign disinterest. Wind whirred and the shhhh of heavy rain began. Crack! Now nearer. Electrical currents frayed the animals' hair. The horse bucked her head and shook her shoulders.

Crack!! Sizzle. Roar. Lightning tore through the barn roof, white and terrible, seeking ground. A mouse leapt. The horse whinnied fretfully. With a mighty jerk she jumped her stall, and bolted through the open door into the rain. Water sliced through the air beating down on the horse. Now free, instinct directed her. She galloped through the pasture, vaulted two

A HORSE OF A DIFFERENT COLOR

fences, and kept going. The forest beyond the open fields would provide protection. She ran in that direction.

Damp grass glistened in the late morning sun. After a night of rain it would be food and water. Hunger drew the horse out from the woods and into the unfamiliar field. She gorged herself. With hunger and thirst satisfied, the horse's mind turned to her surroundings. The land's strangeness unsettled her. She preferred the customary smells and sights of home. But where was home? And the boy who brushed her, gave her carrots to eat, and read to her?

That month the boy had begun coming to the barn regularly. The woman in charge, the boy's grandmother, told the boy that he was old enough to learn the ropes, which meant cleaning the stalls, filling the food troughs, brushing the horses, and in time learning to clean the horses' hooves. He did this with only half interest. He was sometimes lazy, preferring to poke around the barn without accomplishing much. But his grandmother would come and survey his work, gently reminding him of his tasks. She never scolded. She made suggestions, which were helpful when he took them.

The boy was unwilling to ride any of the horses. He feared these large, unpredictable creatures. He had seen his older sister on one of the ponies prancing around the paddock near the barn. By the time she was ten, she had already been riding for a year. Being ten himself, he did not want to ride. He had seen his sister thrown from a horse. The first time it happened she cried desperately as their grandmother rushed over to check for broken arms and legs. Fortunately, she was uninjured except for a very sore tailbone. On subsequent rides after she fell again and again, the boy vowed never to mount a horse. It was enough to feel these falls as if they were happening to his own body as he watched his sister from a distance.

A HORSE OF A DIFFERENT COLOR

The boy and girl lived an hour and a half from the barn in a suburb of Baltimore. They attended boarding schools, she an all-girls school in the District of Columbia, and he an all-boys school in Baltimore. He disliked school. If asked, he might have said that school was where people made fun of you and gave assignments to make you feel even worse about yourself. His school had recently started a year-round policy, which distressed his mother because it interfered with her involvements and didn't match his sister's schedule. His father wasn't concerned because it didn't affect him.

When the time approached for the boy's first three-week break, he texted his mother from school to ask if he could stay at his grandmother's house. His mother furrowed her brow and responded, Why? She didn't mean for her reply to seem curt. It was simply the fastest way to ask. He responded that he liked being there. In truth, it was because he would be far from his parents who pressed him with questions about his progress at school. At the farm he could be alone, or mostly alone.

His mother asked if he had homework to do over the break. He said he had a project from his English teacher, which he assured his mother was in his backpack. The assignment was to read three books, biographies, autobiographies, fact or fiction and to write a summary of each one. He had stuffed into his pack three books that he had checked out of the school's library. Some of the boys laughed that he was even using the library, yet that's what the teacher had said, to use the school library, not to read online. The boys joked that the teacher was "old school" and how would he know what they used, anyway. Intent on following the teacher's directions, the boy wandered through the library stacks glancing at titles. Nothing lured him. He ended up choosing three books because of their covers, never bothering to open them to see if their contents were legible to him.

A HORSE OF A DIFFERENT COLOR

At his grandmother's house no one checked on his school progress; however, he did follow a schedule. He was expected to be up, dressed and downstairs for breakfast by 8:00 a.m., after which he had barn duty, which meant cleaning the stalls after the horses had been let out to pasture. At noon he was to return to the house for lunch. At 3:00 p.m. he was required to be at the barn for the horses' return, to groom and feed and do the day's remaining chores. His life there fell into a predictable routine.

At the beginning of the third day he remembered his assignment. That morning, after cleaning the stalls, he returned to his room, flopped onto his bed and opened the first book. The print was tiny. Squinting at the first paragraph the words made no sense. It may as well have been Latin.

Tossing that book aside he pulled out the second book. It was all pictures, a series of photographs of a man's journey along the Amazon River. The centerfold image showed a straw-hatted man poling his way in a small boat through jungle waters. That same photo was featured on the cover. Its provocative image had enticed the boy to choose it. However, this book had very few words, only captions explaining the pictures. The boy read the words as well as he could, and then heaved the book aside. He knew that he was a poor reader. He had been faking his way through most of his assignments. He had learned to listen intently to his teachers, to absorb their instructions. This was half the battle of getting passing grades—to do what the teacher asked. Other boys seemed to be whizzes at this. He felt like he was blindly groping in the dark, only sometimes getting to the right places. His mother had him tested for glasses--which he did not need, for Attention Deficit Disorder--a popular condition among his classmates, and dyslexia—not his problem. He simply did not like reading. Nothing interested him. Nothing concerned him. It seemed like a waste of time. He would rather spend his time with his games. These were where he

A HORSE OF A DIFFERENT COLOR

felt competent, where he belonged as master of a universe. His grandmother let him play his games at night, but only after they had finished the day and had cleaned up from their last meal. She sat and read. He played his games, an easy silence passing between them. He wondered how his grandmother could find so much pleasure in reading books, but then to him she was old-fashioned.

On his bed the boy opened up the third book. It was a collection of word problems to be solved. This was the worst thing possible. Other people were able to reason out the answers, whereas he could never see the way through. He could do math calculations as long as they were straightforward, but word problems were different. This would never do. He flung the third book across the bed and sat up straight. One out of three, and that one was just pictures, not much of a book.

Back in the barn, he brushed the horses. This was his favorite chore. He leaned into their flanks and felt their warm muscles. Most of the time the horses let him do his work. One of the horses, a gray-dappled mare would turn her head and gently bump his hand with her nose to encourage his grooming. He liked her best. Sally May, his grandmother called her. Sally because she liked to sally forth, which was a way of walking with determination, his grandmother explained, especially when one knows he or she is special, and May because she may--or may not--walk as asked.

That evening the boy and his grandmother sat together in her quiet living room, she in a faded floral upholstered chair with her feet propped up on an ottoman and he lying on the soft-cushioned sofa. He ventured to ask if she had any books that he could read. She put down her own book and looked at him curiously with a smile spreading across her crinkled face. Yes, she did. Would a horse story do? He nodded. She rose from her chair and crossed the room to a bookshelf that reached nearly to the ceiling. In a moment she handed him a

A HORSE OF A DIFFERENT COLOR

hard-cover book *Misty of Chincoteague*. He took it, noticing its worn edges. His grandmother told him it was her favorite book when she was his age. He turned it over in his hands, then opened it from the back. He started to read the last page. His grandmother chuckled and asked if he wanted to know if it had a happy ending. She assured him that it did. She told him it took place not far away on an island off of the coast of Virginia called Chincoteague. She said the word carefully so he would know how to pronounce it. And then she returned to her chair to resume her own reading.

The boy skeptically opened to the front. The first four lines were okay, he could read those, and the illustrations helped, but the story, though dramatic wasn't like his games that had a clear purpose from the first moment. He put the book aside and picked up his iPhone, instead.

Two days later when he awoke, panic set in as the boy realized that he had to read two additional books and write three summary reports. He had flipped through the Amazon River book re-reading all the captions. He could write about that book, but where would he find two more? He was uncomfortable reading his grandmother's book in front of her. He wondered if she could tell that he wasn't a good reader by how slowly he turned the pages. Probably she wouldn't notice, but he was self-conscious enough not to bring the book into the living room at night. She didn't ask him one way or the other.

He decided to stuff the horse book into the pocket of his grandfather's old barn jacket that he wore on the chilly mornings. Maybe he could find a place to read. When he reached the barn, the horses were out to pasture as usual, which signaled the start of his work. He used muck buckets and hoses to clean out the stalls. Six horses lived in the barn. After an hour he decided to sit down on the fresh bedding in Sally May's stall. He had removed his jacket to do his barn chores because it was always warmer in the barn than outside.

A HORSE OF A DIFFERENT COLOR

But now he thought of the book in his jacket pocket. He pulled himself up and retrieved *Misty of Chincoteague*, then returned to the stall and sat back down. Settled in, he opened the book and began to read.

In the afternoon, when the horses returned and he had completed his late day chores, he paused at Sally May's stall. He handed her an extra carrot since he liked her best. She took it with her usual friendly nuzzling. He spoke to her as she ate. He asked if she knew the story of *Misty of Chincoteague*? The horse chewed. She looked at the boy, listening. Her ear twitched. The boy backed up to the stall wall and slid down onto the floor. Near a corner where he had brushed a large amount of hay, he pulled out the hidden book and began to read. He said the words out loud so the horse could hear him. It seemed that the horse understood. So he kept on reading. She didn't mind when he misread a word or skipped one here and there. She seemed intent to hear the story. On he read. When his grandmother rang the bell for dinner, the boy bolted up from his place, surprised that so much time had passed. He announced to Sally May that he would be back to read more the next day. He placed the book back under the pile of hay and went out the barn door.

The next day when the horses had returned to their stalls and the boy had completed his work, he returned to reading. Now the story grew darker. Would the little foal, Misty, make it across the channel of foaming sea water? The boy thought that Sally May was intent on knowing. His grandmother said the ending was happy. He would be disappointed if it were otherwise. The boy sat in the stall and read aloud, his back at the wall, his knees drawn up as a book rest. On Saturday he wasn't ready to stop the story when the dinner bell rang. He told Sally May that he would try to come back to the barn in the evening, that he would find an excuse. He started to leave, then, thinking that he might not be able to come up

A HORSE OF A DIFFERENT COLOR

with a plausible reason, he ran back to the book's hiding place and snatched it up before rushing out the door, leaving it unlatched behind him.

At dinner, his grandmother said the weather was going to turn. She could tell by the gathering storm clouds and because her bones ached. She asked if the horses had enough hay and grain in case he couldn't get to the barn the next day. He thought they did. She nodded and kept on with dinner.

When the two sat in the living room that night, the boy waited until his grandmother was involved in her book, and then he exchanged his iPhone for his book. He had placed *Misty of Chincoteague* between the sofa cushions so it wasn't clearly visible. Now he slowly pulled it out and placed it in front of his iPhone.

Adding to the drama of the book, the boy saw a flash of light outside of the living room window. His grandmother kept reading. More light flashed, and then thunder. His grandmother made an off-handed comment that the storm was finally on its way. She said that from the feel of it, it might get strong. Since she wasn't alarmed, the boy felt no need to be worried either, and so he continued to read. In his book, a great storm raged. Outside, a great storm seemed ready to descend. He could hear the wind in the trees and then rain pelting the ground. Thunder rumbled. Lightning cracked. His grandmother sniffed the air, for what the boy didn't know. She rose from her chair and said she would get some candles just in case. He considered following her into the dining room so he wouldn't be alone with the storm that sounded as though it were breaking on top of them. Trying to be brave, he remained on the sofa and looked at his book. He knew there were words on the page, but he couldn't absorb them. His own real-life story was taking hold with a real-life storm descending. Great gusts of wind shook the house. He heard it creak. Lightning cracked again. Close. Very close. Thunder boomed. He could feel it in his feet. Just as his

A HORSE OF A DIFFERENT COLOR

grandmother returned to the living room with two lit candles, they heard a sizzling crack. It jolted the house so loudly that his hands reflexively shot up to cover his ears. His grandmother was telling him to get in the kitchen broom closet. She kept saying the words broom closet. She chased him into the kitchen, and into the closet. She shut the door, then opened it, handed him one of the lit candles, told him to stay, and shut the door again.

From inside the closet he heard his grandmother exclaim something, then heard her say that the barn had been struck by lightning. It was on fire. He realized she was on the phone, repeating her location. He heard her swing open the back door and run out into the rain.

Suddenly all was silent except for booms of thunder. The boy became acutely aware of his close surroundings lit by the candle, and the smell of dust and furniture polish. His every instinct insisted that he help his grandmother. But would she be angry at his leaving the closet? He felt frightened, uncertain what to do. He remembered a boy in school calling him a coward. But he was following her order. Nauseating anxiety roiled in his gut. He remained enclosed, alone, waiting. Piping hot wax slid down the shaft of the candle and touched his fingers. The boy jerked his hand away and dropped the candle. The light died as it hit the floor. Now he was in the dark. He began to cry.

Ten minutes later he heard noises. The closet door opened and his grandmother stood before him with water dripping from her nose and ashes clinging to her hair. She announced that the horses were out and that fire trucks were on their way. She told him to get his coat on and be ready to help. His belly did flip flops as a new fear took hold. What work would he be asked to do? She tossed him one of her outdoor hats. At any other time he would have felt silly wearing it, but tonight he simply did as asked. She said they would wait inside for the fire trucks. He could hear the

A HORSE OF A DIFFERENT COLOR

approaching sound of their sirens. For the first time, the boy could see the fire. Flames licked toward the sky from the barn roof. He and his grandmother stood at her backdoor, side by side, peering out the same window. It was a most terrible, intimate feeling, watching together such total destruction and being unable to stop it.

Two fire trucks arrived. Six men jumped out of the first engine and four from the second. Most of the men began unfurling thick water hoses, while two others ran around the barn, each in opposite directions. At their arrival, the boy's grandmother pulled two umbrellas from the backdoor peg, handed him one and took the other. She led him out into the rain toward the trucks, then stopped within a few yards. It seemed to take forever for the men to unload and start their streams of water on the hungry fire. The two stood silently watching, each under an umbrella. Rain sliced down from the sky. The boy wondered how a fire could burn in the midst of a downpour.

At last the hoses filled with water pressure and began shooting spray onto the barn. First one hose, then two more. They attacked the blaze from opposing angles. The water formed graceful arcs, performing a beautiful ballet of motion. Smoke began blowing toward the boy and his grandmother with sparking bits of ash. They ducked under their umbrellas. One of the firemen trotted toward them. He wore heavy gear, an oxygen mask at the ready below his chin. He asked if all the animals were out. She told him yes. Then pointing, he asked the pair to go to the field motioning that he would be ordering the men to direct water on the house to prevent the fire's spread. The woman nodded and tugged at the boy to follow her. From the near side of the field they watched as a fourth hose unleashed a spray of water onto the house. It was a broader projection than they used on the barn. Smoke continued to billow from the barn, black and thick. There was nothing for the two to do but to watch. Thinking of the

A HORSE OF A DIFFERENT COLOR

horses, the boy turned toward the field. He thought he saw them and nudged his grandmother, telling her to look. It satisfied him to think that the horses were safe, although he hated that they were suffering in the rain. In the dim light it was too difficult to make out who was who, but he felt better simply seeing their figures.

Mutely the boy and his grandmother stood watching as the barn's skeleton began to fall apart. A beam crashed to the ground. They could feel the earth shake. As the rain and hoses doused the fire, the diminishing flames produced a thicker smoke. The boy covered his nose and mouth with the back of his coat sleeve. He sneaked a look at his grandmother. For all the time they had been observing this horror, he had not been able to look at her. It was as though if he didn't look at her, the full truth of the event would be held at bay. But now he looked. And the appearance of her face made him want to cry again. Water streamed down her face which he took for tears, although it could have been rain. Under her umbrella, her hatless head was a mop of strewn grey hair. Her eyes stared at the sight of her whole life's labors going up in smoke. On her face was a look of utter defeat, an expression he had never before seen from her. Always the optimist, determined to see the good in every circumstance and every person, she lived by the rule that if you couldn't say anything kind, then not to say anything at all. Now she was totally silent, shattered.

Neither slept much that night. It took three hours for the firemen to put out the barn fire. The house remained safe. After an additional hour the men reloaded their trucks, rumbled down the lane and back toward the distant fire station. At midnight the pair came inside, soaked by the storm. The grandmother insisted that they each take a hot shower, the boy first. She put water on to boil for hot mint tea, and waited her turn for the bathroom. After mugs of tea they went to bed. He wished that his grandmother would let

A HORSE OF A DIFFERENT COLOR

him sleep in her room. He felt full of fear and worry and many other emotions for which he had no words. He knew that the fire had been bad and that the horses were out in the rain that still came down. The thunder and lightning had stopped, but what would the horses do for protection? The boy pulled his bed covers closely, wrapping himself like a cocoon.

When he woke, his first thought was of a barn on fire. For a moment he reasoned this was part of a bad dream. Then he remembered. The storm. The lightning. The closet. The barn. The horses. The horses! He flung back his covers, noticed the grey daylight, and dressed in his nearest clothes. The house was silent. He thought he smelled smoke. There were no signs of his grandmother. His first stop was the back door. Even before opening it he could see the charred structure across the yard through the door window. The barn wall closest to the house appeared almost untouched, but the roof was nearly gone with the few remaining beams now black. Rain still came down, less of a storm, more of a misty shower. He wondered again about the horses. Reaching for his barn jacket from the peg where he had placed it the night before, it felt damp and smelled of smoke. Grimacing, he pulled it on along with his barn boots. He grabbed an umbrella and headed outside.

He saw his grandmother at work in the nearby field. She had a posthole digger and was sinking holes into the wet ground. The boy could see that the horses were gathered in the adjoining field under a small overhang by the trotting ring. He counted five. Who was missing? He looked again, and realized that Sally May was not among them. The boy ran toward his grandmother. When he reached her he could see that she was sweating from her labor. He wondered whether he should help her? But his concern for Sally May took over and he blurted out, where is she? His grandmother, not stopping her chore, said that she didn't know. The boy

A HORSE OF A DIFFERENT COLOR

wondered how that could be. His grandmother knew everything. He announced that he would look for the horse. His grandmother advised against it. Locks of hair hung out from under her hat. She had no umbrella to keep the rain from reaching her. The boy suddenly felt ashamed. He shoved his umbrella over his grandmother. She stood up straight and told him she needed to get a temporary shelter built for the horses and if he wanted to help, he could carry the aluminum poles and tarps from the back of her pickup truck. He obliged by bringing the supplies and laying them near her feet. She said this would be a meager means of protection, but it would do. Thankfully, the rain stopped and made endurable the slippery work of erecting the make-shift shelter. By noon they had created a sizable space with green tarp walls and roof, with six stalls delineated inside. The boy fetched items while his grandmother loaded in straw and wood shavings for bedding, and hay and grain pellets for eating. The real test would be bringing the horses into this unfamiliar space. The grandmother said their hunger might be enough to persuade them.

More easily than expected, the two led the horses inside. There were no places to hook or hang things, which made all the barn chores difficult. However, the animals were out of the weather. The boy and grandmother toweled off the horses, laid blankets over their backs, and set out the hay and grain. It was well past 4 o'clock by the time they were done.

The grandmother suggested going inside the house for their own meal. She fried up potatoes and scrambled a mountain of eggs while the boy toasted bread. He lavished butter and jam on each piece. At his grandmother's order, he poured steaming mugs of mint tea. Mint had healing properties, his grandmother said. The mint she used came from a huge patch that grew each summer by the back of her barn. He wondered if it would still be there. When they sat down, they said their customary grace, but this time, his

A HORSE OF A DIFFERENT COLOR

grandmother continued to pray, thanking God for keeping everyone safe from the fire, for the men who saved their house, and for energy to do their day's work. She hoped that God understood their decision to work on the Sabbath. The boy added his own prayer, to bring Sally May home. They said a joint Amen and then dug into their feast.

Without a proper barn, the daily chores tripled. To reestablish the routine, feed and hay had to be fetched in smaller amounts and more frequently, and from farther way. Inside the shelter, the grandmother strung ropes and attached rigs to better secure the horses' stalls. She brought in tall buckets to store long-handled tools. Using smaller buckets and lumber planks she crafted shelves for bits, bridles, brushes, combs and scrapers. For ventilation she had snipped the tarps to create openings on two sides, and similarly had cut a hatch for a door. It would do, at least for a little while. For the rest of that week, dinner came only after dark. Daytime had to be used for all the work of getting the horses out and in, groomed, fed, and watered. There was no horse riding for his grandmother, which she otherwise enjoyed most days. And in the evenings the two didn't linger in the living room after washing and drying the dishes, but instead went directly to bed. By 8:30 p.m. both were fast asleep.

The boy forgot entirely about his book assignment, but he did not forget about Sally May. Each day he asked his grandmother what he could do to find her. She said that horses had an instinct for home and that Sally May would certainly return soon. He kept an eye out for her, always surveying the farthest field, believing that would be her path home. The sad site of the barn loomed over their work.

An insurance man arrived to speak to the grandmother and take pictures. He used words like insurance value versus replacement value. Several neighbors and church members came by carrying casseroles. One person brought flowers, saying that something pretty might be the right thing to set

A HORSE OF A DIFFERENT COLOR

their eyes on. Everyone rejoiced that no one was injured. The boy always asked if they had seen Sally May, but no one had.

A HORSE OF A DIFFERENT COLOR

2

WASHINGTON SPRING

"**D**amn!" Mary Gray Gabriella Walterson exclaimed as the lights flickered with the increasing storm. "Not now."

She grabbed her reading glasses from atop her head and swiftly placed them on the end of her nose so she could read the dial on her stove. She maximized the heat thinking she better get her pot boiling while she still could.

A tropical storm was pressing in, and she was in a hurry to finish her potato salad for tomorrow's luncheon reception for the new bishop. He—and it was a he in spite of a capable woman candidate with a resumé more impressive than the man elected—would be visiting and presiding over Holy Communion at tomorrow morning's worship service. Mary Gray had more to do than time allowed, even in perfect weather.

To her, the whole affair seemed ill-conceived, the bishop-elect's hastily-scheduled visit to her parish, St. James-in-the Wood, and she having to organize the after-service reception. Her duties on the altar guild and her tithing were her reliable

A HORSE OF A DIFFERENT COLOR

contribution to St. James and to the Lord's work, but the priest had telephoned and asked her to step in for the parish's events coordinator who was called away for the weekend.

"If St. James wants a saint, then don't ask me," Mary Gray mumbled. The lights flickered again and her world went black.

"Damn. Damn. Damn!" Mary Gray fumbled and felt her way across her kitchen, through the hallway and into her bedroom where she kept a flashlight. She clicked it on, hoping the batteries were still good. In spite of the weather reporter's warnings to stock up on supplies, she had been consumed with church matters. In town earlier that afternoon the long lines at the grocery store irked her all the more because she didn't have time for weather nonsense. Besides, these weather things were always overblown as a way of gluing eyeballs to the TV, paying the wages of men in raincoats who were flown to sites that everyone else was ordered to leave.

A beam of light shot forth from her flashlight. "Good. At least something is working right. What will I do if the power stays off?" she said to no one in particular, except perhaps God. She thought of the altar linens that needed to be ironed, her altar guild duties of laying out the sacred elements and making certain all things were ready. She could count on others to do their part. Bryan Beal, the church organist and choir director always did what he said. He was the saint of that congregation. Bryan would have the scripture lessons marked, the hymn numbers changed on the sanctuary placard, and would have carried the bulletins from the parish office to the church vestibule for the ushers to hand out tomorrow morning. So many thoughtful things that kept St. James-in-the-Wood running smoothly. She wondered if Father Eric realized how much work others were doing without recognition.

A loud knock startled her from her reverie. As she

A HORSE OF A DIFFERENT COLOR

stepped toward the door in the dark, she could hear the wind picking up momentum. The rain's pounding sharpened as she opened the door.

"Can I come in," Jimmy Johnson announced more than asked as he shoved his way past Mary Gray and into her living room, leaving a pink umbrella just outside her door. She hated not having an interior entry way, something she had noted to the building committee when they were drawing up house plans.

Mary Gray lived in an experimental community called Washington Spring which formed when a group of unlikely souls pooled their resources and made commitments—both financial and by written pledge—to develop a community of residents age 60 and older. Each had followed the lead of John B. and Pauline Martin of Annapolis, who publicly invited response to an invitation to participate in an intentional community to be created near the inlet of Paribar Shore, Maryland. As a commercial banker, John knew the value of land and had invested early, as well as inherited properties which he helped to manage. His wife, Pauline, had died of brain cancer three weeks before the group cut the ribbon on the first initiative of their overall plan: twelve 1,100-square-foot one-story cottages patterned after early twentieth century millhouses. Their Washington Spring homes all faced inward toward a community garden and would have had spectacular botanicals, had Pauline lived. It seemed a bad omen that the woman who was a force for good and a visionary like her husband had died just as the community was preparing to live. They had cut the ribbon in Pauline's memory. It had rained that day, too. The press covered the story of Washington Spring, an experiment of baby boomers taking into their own hands caring for each other through the aging process. John and Pauline had put the land in trust for the collection of houses that would include an eventual home-like skilled nursing unit. The idea

A HORSE OF A DIFFERENT COLOR

was to build the additional structure before any of the residents needed it.

Washington Spring required everyone to contribute a skill. Mary Gray Walterson was the community's historian and archivist. With nearly forty years of work at two branches of the National Archives, she felt more than able to document the formation of Washington Spring and begin its written and pictorial history. She was also responsible for all communication that went out to the public about their little community, and acted as secretary for their monthly meetings. In her seventy years she had lived long enough to know that communities don't begin ex nihilo, and that some amount of research about both the land and the people involved would enliven their tale if it were to be told in future generations. When she had more time, she would add to the miniscule research she had begun.

"Do you have any candles? Bryan has his shorts all in a twist. We have no candles next door," Jimmy Johnson said as he stood dripping on her carpet. Carpet, another bad decision by the design team, Mary Gray thought. Jimmy continued, "Bryan said that as a good Episcopalian you should have a bumper supply."

"Good Episcopalian? What about him? He's always carting things to and from the church. Oh, let me look."

Mary Gray turned and took the light with her. She should have candles, but living in 1,100 square feet had meant shedding almost everything she owned. John and Pauline urged that the community should include as much cooperative sharing as possible. If one person had a kettle of canning size, that was enough among all members. John had large serving platters and chafing dishes. Mary Gray kept one of two communal irons and ironing boards, vital to her work on the altar guild. Ruth and Larry Long had lasagna pans and one of two vacuum cleaners. Tom and Tracie Allgood kept large suitcases. Acton Alexander oversaw brooms and mops

A HORSE OF A DIFFERENT COLOR

as well as a master set of keys. He also administered the homeowner's association dues that paid for outdoor maintenance and supplies. The inventory listed everything shared among the members' twelve houses, and meant a cumbersome process for reserving, fetching and returning items, but members were growing accustomed to the arrangement after nearly a year, and it kept their closets and households in reasonable order. Their cottages were numbered in order around the Close, Close being a word Mary Gray and Bryan proposed from their Anglican heritage. The Washington Spring Close, abbreviated WSC, consisted of twelve cottages, a central garden, a shed nearly as large as a cottage–which contained lawn and garden equipment, along with holiday decorations, and assorted odds and ends that each member could obtain as needed. The houses had identical floor plans, a requirement that nearly ran the project off the rails. Two early members mutinied when their design exceptions were not approved. It was rumored they were trying to start a similar community in Delaware. That news didn't bother John and Pauline, since they wanted to spur the development of small, viable aging communities wherever they could survive. John and Pauline's house was located at the start of the Close. They had demurred at the prospect of locating in WSC-1, but everyone insisted, and John and Pauline could act as ambassadors to curious visitors, since theirs was the vision that began the ball rolling in earnest four years earlier, and was now realized, at least by John, and set to celebrate its first anniversary in two months, November 15.

"I think I have candles," Mary Gray said over her shoulder to Jimmy as she pointed the flashlight farther into her open living space. To her thinking, open floor plans were a temporary fad of few walls, walls which to her thinking would have served useful purposes, like places for furniture and divisions of labor. But with 1,100 square feet one had to make concessions. She approached an heirloom cupboard made by her father, a possession she would be loath to release, release being the favored word among clutter-control experts.

"Mary Gray Walterson, you better have candles!" Jimmy teased. "I won't ever call you my favorite Episcopalian again if you do not have the finest beeswax candles hand dipped by some fair-haired English maiden." Jimmy leveled his right pointer finger toward Mary Gray who could not see him.

"Oh stop. I do not have candles, well, except for this one large red thing that was left over from Christmas. It must not have made it into the shed." She took it from her cupboard and started back to the doorway. "Do you have matches?"

"Do I have matches? Of course I have matches. Who do you think lights the wood in the cooker for the annual pig picking here at Washington Spring?" Jimmy said, mockingly.

"Forgive me, Jimmy. I didn't think we had an annual pig picking."

"Yet. That's just because it hasn't happened yet, but it will. And I will be the one to start roasting that pig at least sixteen full hours before we eat it. Just like we did back in Salisbury, North Carolina. You will think you have died and gone to heaven." Jimmy affected his Southern drawl. "Sweet tea, too. You know, Bryan thinks the rector will cancel church services for tomorrow morning, bishop visit and all. He's upset because the choir's been practicing an anthem by Charles Stanford just for the occasion. He says it's the Sunday closest to Stanford's birthday. So if the church service gets canceled, then the bishop will have to re-schedule and you know the music Bryan chose will not work for whatever new date the bishop comes. Bryan will have to start his planning all over again. I don't think this storm is going to be that bad. I think the worst is on us now, and by 9 o'clock tonight, this thing's going to be by us. You watch. The weathermen always make it sound worse than it turns out to be."

"That's what I say. But I am starting to think that if

A HORSE OF A DIFFERENT COLOR

church isn't canceled, there's no way everything will be ready for tomorrow. I have potatoes I'm trying to boil for the potato salad. Thank God I cooked the eggs earlier today. But I have all the china and silver to lay out in the parish hall, the coffee urns to set up, the punch bowl to assemble, not to mention tablecloths I need to iron and altar linens to prepare along with the Communion elements. I need three hours at least at the church before I am ready. At least someone is bringing the flowers. I do know my limits," Mary Gray announced with more certainty than she felt. She handed Jimmy the red candle. "It's not much, but it will get you through. Don't you two have a flashlight?"

"It's in the car and Bryan's gone out for supplies. We didn't think the power would cut off," Jimmy said.

"Neither did I. Maybe they'll get it on shortly. These things are always overblown."

"Right."

"Do you have your cell phone?" Mary Gray began to ask. "Never mind. You have your landline just for occasions like these. I'm glad John insisted that we all have house phones. At least until we're so old that we need those alert necklaces, 'I've fallen and I can't get up,'" they said in unison.

"Well, bye," Jimmy announced. With the red candle in hand he started out the door. "Keep in touch," he shouted over his shoulder toward the closing door grabbing his pink umbrella as he stepped out into the rain.

"Where is the punch bowl?" Mary Gray snapped to the empty church kitchen.

"I think it's in the pantry closet," an unexpected voice replied.

"Lord's sake, Bryan! I thought I was by myself. It's 7 o'clock in the morning. What are you doing here?"

Mary Gray was standing in the St. James kitchen with her hands on her hips, glasses on her nose and an exasperated

A HORSE OF A DIFFERENT COLOR

look on her face. Bryan Beal approached her, looking handsome in his grey Sunday suit. He kept a trim frame and his shining, hair-free head seemed to enhance his look at sixty-plus years.

"Thanks for lending us the candle. Jimmy said it was your best Christmas leftover. Good that the power came back on last night." Bryan removed his suit jacket and started pulling water glasses down from the kitchen cabinets and placing them on trays.

"I was up until midnight making potato salad and ironing altar cloths. All in the name of Jesus."

"That's whom we serve. To whom every knee shall bow and every tongue confess."

"I'm confessing, but not necessarily the name of Jesus this morning. Hey, did you happen to notice if John's car was still in his driveway this morning?" Mary Gray asked.

"John B's car?"

"Yeah. I had reserved a couple of serving platters from him thinking that I would pick them up last evening but with the storm, I called to tell him I would pick them up later, after the rain slowed down. I could only leave a message. This morning I left in such a rush that I didn't even think to look and see if his car was in his driveway. I didn't expect to see you this early."

"I usually practice on Saturday evenings but with the storm I couldn't get over here, and besides I wasn't sure if there was still power at the church. I had to come in before the 8 o'clock members arrive for the Rite I service."

"You and I are running the same race. We've got to get done what we can before the 8 o'clockers. You can quit setting out those drinking glasses and go practice. I'll have time while the 8 is going on. Thanks for doing that, though."

Mary Gray thought about Jimmy's news that Bryan had gone out in the storm. He had said for supplies. Knowing Jimmy, he probably sent Bryan out to fetch him a carton of

A HORSE OF A DIFFERENT COLOR

filtered Camels that he not so secretly smoked. Living side-by-side meant that all of the eighteen residents of Washington Spring were getting to know one another up close and personal. Mary Gray sometimes wondered what they were thinking about her.

"All things come from Thee O Lord, and of Thine own have we given Thee," Father Eric announced as he raised the collection plates before the central stained glass window that showed Christ ascending heavenward. As if on cue, sunlight suddenly emerged and the window's colors glistened in divine confirmation.

"Amen," the congregation loudly responded.

Mary Gray's mind should have been on the liturgy, but instead she was counting heads and wondering if she had set out enough plates, silverware, glasses and napkins. She had planned for one hundred and fifty. The punch bowl turned out to be cracked, so she had gone with Plan B, which was to serve lemonade in glass pitchers. The luncheon had a leftover summer feel about it, and if someone wanted to take umbrage at the fact that it was long past Labor Day, and why were they drinking lemonade, well, too bad. The Youth Group had three gallons of lemonade from their overnight lock-in that never happened, so Mary Gray commandeered it. She had improvised several serving platters in place of the ones she had planned to pick up from John B. Martin, saying to herself that arranging to borrow items really had its limitations.

The priest began preparing the Eucharist. Mary Gray watched as he made a show of pouring the wine from the fine glass cruet into the Communion cup. He then took a perfect white cloth and daubed red wine droplets from the pouring pitcher, creating the stain that every altar guild member sighed over. From day one of this exercise, guild members were charged with cleaning red wine stains from altar cloths. This was a divine labor of love as well as a confounding

A HORSE OF A DIFFERENT COLOR

situation which could be avoided if the presiding priest just used a little common sense. One of her Pennsylvania friends dared to dab some Super Glue on the tip of the Communion cruet, preventing the dribbles in the first place. Mary Gray sat watching the new bishop, wondering what kind of wine-pourer he might be.

"*Be Thou My Vision* has always been one of my favorites," boomed the new bishop to Bryan, who had been asked to use this hymn to close the 10:30 a.m. service. "I had them sing it at my installation," the bishop went on. "I always thought there should be a place for folk melodies in our church's music." Bryan and the bishop were passing through the lunch line after the service. Bryan refrained from asserting his true thoughts toward the new bishop, which were that last minute music changes showed flagrant disrespect of the church musician; after all, the church musician would never dream of asking the priest to substitute a different sermon for the one he prepared. And for *Be Thou My Vision* to be the closing hymn. Clearly this bishop had no sense of liturgical movement. A closing hymn should be a musical summary of the complete intention of the service and provide for corporate dedication, not some personal heartfelt "me and you and a God named Boo." What tripe, thought Bryan, in place of Ralph Vaughan Williams' *By All Your Saints Still Striving*, with a soprano descant on the hymn's penultimate stanza and an organ re-harmonization on the final verse. Now back in his suit coat from his choir robe, Bryan drew a hard breath and stiffened his resolve of silence.

"Yes, 'Heart of my own heart, whatever befall, still be my vision, O Ruler of all.' Now that's true testimony!" The bishop quoted the final line of his beloved hymn, punctuating his remark by plopping down emphatically in the center seat.

"How did it go?" Jimmy was all questions as Bryan

A HORSE OF A DIFFERENT COLOR

entered their front door at Washington Spring. Soft strains of *You'll Never Walk Alone* from the Broadway musical *Carousel* lofted throughout their living space of bold colors and clean lines.

"Fine," Bryan said dismissively. He slid his shoulder bag heavy with music onto one end of their persimmon-colored sofa.

"You can't tell me it wasn't a rush to meet the new bishop. Go on. Tell me all about it," Jimmy patted the cushion on the other side of the sofa where he sat shoe-less with a newspaper in his lap. He was dressed in plaid socks that clashed with the plaid of his shorts and a bright pink shirt. He removed his oversized black-rimmed reading glasses.

"Not much to tell. God help the state of church music under his campaign. He insisted on *Be Thou My Vision* in place of a Ralph Vaughan Williams hymn arrangement of *By All Your Saints Still Striving*," Bryan explained as though simply stating the facts.

"He didn't! That dog." Jimmy was all emotion.

"And, he had the ladies eating out of his palm by the end of the luncheon. Poor Mary Gray. She looked ready to tear him up when he commented to her and everyone within earshot that summer still seemed in bloom at St. James-in-the-Wood. He thought the lighter fare was chosen in favor of a summer theme. He must think that congregations are created to cater solely to their bishops. What I really need is a drink." Bryan started for the kitchen and grabbed a glass.

"What you need is an AA meeting, young man." Jimmy paused. "Let's take a drive and put the top down and visit the Chesapeake Bay. You've had a hard day already, and I know you have to be back in three hours for your Youth Choir rehearsal."

"So why are you telling me we should go for a ride with the top down?" Bryan snapped, now aggravated remembering that their icemaker was broken.

"Oh, just use your imagination, then," Jimmy sniffed. "Besides, I thought you once told me that Ralph Vaughn Williams *loved* folk melodies."

3
HALIFAX

Sally May was a light grey pony with a dark tail, dark ear tips and dark face. She didn't know that she was prized not only for her looks but for her unusual bloodline. She simply knew herself to be. At night she retreated into the woods, instinctively preferring not to remain in the open field. On the third day, she began to widen her grazing area. No familiar scents led her home. She preferred home, but with nothing to lead her, she wandered farther and farther away.

A HORSE OF A DIFFERENT COLOR

4
WASHINGTON SPRING

John? John?" The last light had left the sky when Mary Gray knocked on John B.'s door. The door of WSC-1 stood silent and unanswered. John's car was in his driveway, but no sound came from inside the house. Odd, thought Mary Gray. By the light of the Close's tall, black ornamental lampposts, she walked along the central garden path across to WSC-10 and knocked at Sue and Sandy Cantelli's door.

"Hi Mary Gray. How are you?" Sue answered the door wearing a thin smile and a heavy blue and gray sweater with a sailboat motif. The gray set off the silver in her bobbed hair that framed her round face.

"I'm fine, thank you, but have you seen John?" Mary Gray asked politely, aware that she felt wary of this woman she was still getting to know. People were still feigning politeness when seeing one another around the property. The monthly meetings were another matter, however.

"John B? No. Why?" Sue chirped.

A HORSE OF A DIFFERENT COLOR

"He doesn't seem to be home, yet his car is in the driveway. Did he say anything about leaving?"

"Not to me. Sandy, did John tell you he was leaving town?" Sue shouted over her shoulder into the house where her husband, Sandy, was lounging, watching television.

"John? No, I don't think so. Why?"

"Mary Gray can't get him to answer the door. His car is still here."

Sandy got up and came to the door. He wore jeans and a t-shirt in rainbow colors that said, *Myrtle Beach*, hardly something he would have chosen for himself since his wardrobe leaned more toward brown and black. "Hi, Mary Gray."

"Hi, Sandy. It's not like John to leave and not say something. Will Acton know where he is?" Mary Gray asked.

"You can try," Sue answered.

All three walked over to WSC-7, Acton Alexander's house, and knocked on the door.

"Yes?" Acton asked, opening his door. At age 67 he appeared vital and fit. His dark skin set off his white collared shirt and tan slacks, both crisply ironed. Acton had served in the military for twenty years. He was John's prize choice from the residents' candidate pool since Acton had administrated VA medical facilities after his time in the armed forces.

Sue spoke first. "Mary Gray says she can't get John B. to come to the door. Do you know if he's home?"

"I don't know. Do you think something's wrong?"

Mary Gray jumped in. "I tried calling last evening before the storm and left a message but I never heard back. Then today after church I was going to stop, but I had a car full of stuff to unload, and only now went over to see about him. He's not answering the door."

"And you think he's in there?" Acton asked.

"I don't know. His car is in the driveway," answered Mary Gray.

"This is why we should have a buddy system. Every day

A HORSE OF A DIFFERENT COLOR

we should check in to say that we're okay. It's part of best practices in Continuous Care Retirement Communities, CCRCs," Sue said.

"Why don't we go over and check?" Sandy asked.

"We need a key if we're going to go inside," Sue announced.

"Do you think we need to do that?" Acton asked.

"Yes, I think we should do that," Sue affirmed.

Acton left everyone standing at his front door crowded under the tiny overhang, another poor design choice to Mary Gray's thinking. The stoop fit one person comfortably, and so the three stood shoulder to shoulder each trying to avoid touching the other.

"He'll have to get the key from the safe," Sue pronounced.

Mary Gray wondered if Sue loved stating the obvious, as if it put her in charge somehow. Sue was a triage nurse, comfortable issuing orders. Mary Gray often thought of Sue as Hot Lips Houlihan on M*A*S*H and tried to feel compassion for her, reminding herself that even Hot Lips got lonely from time to time.

In a moment Acton was back. "Okay. Let's go." Acton joined the group and the four set off to John B.'s house.

"We should knock first," Sue said as they walked across the Close.

Mary Gray rolled her eyes, hoping no one could see her in the dark.

John and Pauline had seemed the perfect couple. At ease with themselves they made others feel comfortable in their company. When they interviewed the Washington Spring candidates Pauline enjoyed telling the story of how they met.

"It was at University of Maryland in chemistry class. So I guess you could say it was chemistry that brought us together!" Pauline explained, always with a twinkle in her eye.

When the two interviewed Sue and Sandy, Pauline

A HORSE OF A DIFFERENT COLOR

disclosed that she admired Sue's resume since she herself had wanted to attend nursing school. Pauline mentioned that John had also thought about medicine, but his father persuaded him to go into banking, the field that had been so lucrative and satisfying for him.

In fact, it was John's father who arranged for John to spend his summers interning in his hometown, Annapolis, at Maryland Bank and Trust, which held a major portion of the area's high dollar investors' money. With the Vietnam conflict escalating, John's father had taken a relatively silent stand on political matters, especially the War, keeping their television quiet during the evening hours, getting his news through the daily Maryland Gazette. John's mother had been a direct descendant of Jonas and Ann Catharine Green, 19th century publishers of the Maryland Gazette, through whom her family could trace their legacy to the earliest Pilgrims. John's mother's family all maintained clear allegiance to their Congregationalist roots, thus John and his sister were baptized and raised in the Congregational church.

Pauline had been from Baltimore City. Her mother was a Catholic from Irish descendants and her father was also Catholic, but he had lapsed in his faith and left such matters to Pauline's mother who determinedly took the children to church. Pauline prayed the rosary every night and went to Mass on Sundays, even during college, and she held no objection to Protestants, which was why, when she and John met, chemistry could have its way. Pauline's mother, however, was not pleased that her daughter was marrying a non-Catholic, even if she did come to love John over the years. Their wedding was another matter. Having to get a special dispensation for a Catholic-non-Catholic marriage embarrassed Pauline's mother, and for a while Pauline's family was the talk of the parish. However, it was also clear that Pauline was marrying up, into a family of means and legacy. And so the families tolerated one another and, after

A HORSE OF A DIFFERENT COLOR

two shared grandchildren, came to an agreeable fondness for each other. Pauline had watched her mother suffer for six years with dementia in a facility that could hardly have been called attentive. Pauline exhausted herself juggling her own affairs with frequent trips into Baltimore City where her mother resided in Sunny Acres which was anything but sunny or on sprawling acres, which is what spurred her to declare to John, "We do not want our lives to come to this one day," and the first seeds of the Washington Spring community were sown.

When their first child was stillborn, Pauline left the Catholic Church entirely. The local priest, a new man out of seminary, though well-meaning, explained that this was God's will. Pauline took him to mean that the death of her child was punishment for her marrying a Protestant, which was not at all the young priest's intention, but in her heightened state of grief, took his meaning for something far more sinister and cruel. Pauline knew why the child was stillborn and it had nothing to do with religion. So when John's kindly Congregational minister visited and prayed openly with them, equally full of grief, Pauline decided to attend church with John thereafter. Her mother said she always knew it would come to this, that Pauline would leave the Church, but in truth, it was simply the evolution of Pauline's faith. Pauline had watched women be marginalized by male priests who guarded their lines fiercely and since Pauline was college-educated and was intent on appearing well-bred in this new family, she knew from her Congregationalist mother-in-law that women should have an equal say in matters, and so her leap across the great Christian divide was more like skipping over a mere puddle.

John and Pauline's two subsequent live-birthed children were twins, which Pauline took as an affirming gift from God. These were fraternal twins which they named Ward for Pauline's mother's father and Samuel for John's mother's father.

A HORSE OF A DIFFERENT COLOR

Most of their next twenty years were spent growing family and fortune. Pauline oversaw the family and John, the fortune. When John's parents grew to retirement age, they entered Ginger Grove, a CCRC whose opulence drew the attention of all who visited. For John's mother this was not an easy decision. The blood coursing through her veins protested the French silk curtains and five o'clock cocktail hour. She was no Episcopalian relishing small talk over late afternoon sherry. She was a hard-working inventor of free literacy classes, teacher of phonics to under-privileged children, and a political action committee member that lobbied for non-development, or at the very least, responsible development of the ever-shrinking natural shorelines of their state. However, John's father as a prominent banker sometimes crossed purposes with his wife's passions. He marveled at her energy while questioning her need to get so involved. Several of his clients' land deals were held up due to unforeseen environmental clearances that suddenly arose just before closing. That these transactions nearly fell through and in one case did derail was attributed to the new ordinances championed by a group called MSPS, Maryland Shoreline Protection Society, of which John's mother was a founding member. This defunct deal fell squarely into John's father's lap. John's father could see that the MSPS hold up would not be sustained and that the eager buyer who impatiently pulled out, unable to bear high interest rates in floating his money for a length of time, would not be returning, so John's father formed an LLC that patiently pursued the derailed land sale. It took time, but his patience paid off. In 1981 he had bought a large swath of prime real estate which included waterfront property. He neatly tucked this into his personal portfolio along with multiple other holdings throughout the state of Maryland.

John, being groomed by his father, watched all these events, both admiring and fearing his father's business

A HORSE OF A DIFFERENT COLOR

acumen. Had John's mother known the full picture, she might have left her husband for his traitorous actions.

John's parents' first introduction to Ginger Grove happened when John's mother required knee replacement surgery. She was sent to Ginger Grove for rehabilitation. "This is way too much," she protested, signaling the opulent furnishings. But she never once complained about the staff who nursed her back to health. And having heard far less glowing reports of other places, she later consented to her husband's idea to sell their two-story Colonial and buy a cottage at Ginger Grove. "But do not ask me to attend cocktail hour!" she retorted. It was 1989 and John's parents were among the first residents to live in the property's newly constructed semi-detached homes.

Three years later John's father had a massive stroke. He was sent home from the hospital to Ginger Grove's skilled care unit. John's mother sat with him around the clock during his sixteen final days. She hosted neighbors and visitors who came with cheerful conversation and garden flowers. At night, by her husband's bedside, she opened a novel and picked up where she had left off, reading not just aloud, but loudly, to be sure her husband knew what she was reading. In their forty-eight years of marriage they had read novels aloud to one another as a way of keeping interesting ideas before them, and as John's mother joked to Pauline, "Sometimes I think I would have divorced him, but I kept on with him because I wanted to know how the story turned out!"

She had chosen James Michener's *Chesapeake* because it had held special appeal to them both since so much of it took place not far from where they lived. For all she knew, the very land upon which Ginger Grove sat might have once been the forested playground of the peaceful Choptank Indians. She read loudly and slowly, as though the sheer length of the novel would suspend death for him, as it had suspended divorce for her.

A HORSE OF A DIFFERENT COLOR

After sixteen days, John's father died, placing John in the unsavory position of deciding whether to reveal to his mother the catalog of properties his father had amassed. His father had always managed their portfolio and all things money. John's mother only handled the grocery budget and personal shopping. John estimated his father's holdings to be worth many millions of dollars, which included commercial properties, undeveloped land, as well as several unexercised options on land that John could see might easily double the family's fortune.

John told Pauline in rather vague terms the problem he faced. Pauline, a woman who typically saw things in black and white, took an unexpected route through the middle and said, How about not saying anything to your mother unless she asks, which is what John chose to do. John offered to continue to manage her affairs, although with every visit he expected his mother to ask for an accounting. She never did.

In May of 2009, seventeen years after her husband's death, at eighty-eight years old, John's mother lay down to sleep and never woke up. No one could have been more shocked than John. His mother had kept up her literacy and environmental efforts until she stopped driving at age eighty-seven and nearly then convinced the environmental council members to hold their meetings at Ginger Grove so she could continue to attend. She had migrated to an apartment inside Ginger Grove, but had in no way given up her independence. She had taken to writing Letters to the Editor of the Maryland Gazette, mainly in support of race relations efforts and the preservation of land and tidewaters. John could hardly write his own mother's obituary for in doing so he realized the full value of his two parents who had taught him everything that mattered, each enlivened by righteous passions but from very different sides of the aisle. As far as John knew, his mother never did attend cocktail hour at Ginger Grove.

A HORSE OF A DIFFERENT COLOR

"John? John?" Sue knocked and shouted as though John were deaf, which he wasn't. "Use your key, Acton. He told me once that his mother died in her sleep and his father died of a PE, pulmonary embolism. That's a stroke."

Acton was turning the key in the lock and opening the door when the headlights of a Toyota Prius glanced off the party of four squeezed onto the little landing.

"That was Tom and Tracie," declared Sue. "They went to Wilmington to visit Tom's son and daughter-in-law." Sue was a fountain of knowledge.

Acton swung the door open into darkness. "John?" Acton called out. No reply.

"Well, someone switch on the lights." Sue declared as she groped for the wall switch. "Hmm. The switch is already on. No lights. What's wrong with this?" Sue's switch flipping sounded loud in the empty room. "Does anyone have a flashlight?" Sue continued.

Mary Gray was already pulling her cell phone from her pocket as the group moved inside.

"Here," Mary Gray said as she used the light on her phone to locate the switch in the kitchen.

"I wonder why the wall switch didn't work," Sue complained. "Sandy, can you look into that?"

Sue and Sandy had been invited to join Washington Spring because of Sue's medical training and Sandy's construction skills. Sue continued to work at Mission Hospital in Baltimore, a 45-minute commute on a good day. Sandy had retired when they moved into Washington Spring. He was asked to keep his electrical and plumbing licenses current so he could perform maintenance at Washington Spring. Sue urged him to start a little side business from their Paribar Shore location, but thus far he found reasons not to.

"John?" Mary Gray called softly as she walked down the hall to the bedrooms. Both bedrooms were dark. She flipped on the wall switch of the master bedroom, bracing herself for a difficult scene. The bed wasn't made, but everything seemed in place. From the master bedroom she turned and went into the second bedroom, John's office.

"John?" she called quietly. From the hall light spilling into the room she could already see that no one was in the office. Mary Gray let out a huge breath she didn't realize she was holding.

"He's not in here," she started to say when she turned and bumped into Sue who had crept up behind her. "Oh, sorry!" Mary Gray said to Sue.

"I knew he wouldn't be here," Sue announced.

"What do you mean?" Mary Gray queried.

"I just mean that I had a feeling that Ward or Sam must have come by and taken him out, maybe for the weekend."

"But you would think he'd have let at least one of us know," Mary Gray reasoned.

"Which is the whole point of the daily check in. That way we can say if we're going away. We really should have a sign out sheet."

"Oh come on, Sue. That's overdoing it, don't you think?" Sandy parried.

"Look, I am telling you here and now while the four of us are wondering what we're doing in the middle of John B's house that this all could have been prevented. If we had a system for keeping track of each other, we wouldn't have to go through all this. What if John were to come home right now and find all of us standing here? Don't you think he would feel embarrassed? I feel embarrassed looking at this man's personal things."

"You've been in this house ten times before now. What could you possibly mean?" Sandy asked.

"I mean with him not here. I don't want to notice his dirty laundry and his unwashed dishes or those broken bits of pottery over there, I don't." She gestured toward the kitchen. "I will say he isn't the best housekeeper in the world and

A HORSE OF A DIFFERENT COLOR

maybe we need to offer a little help."

"I think we should all go home," Acton offered. "I'm sure there's a good explanation."

"Why don't we call his cell phone?" Mary Gray asked.

"Well, why didn't you ask that before we all crowded into John B's house? I thought you had called his cell phone and no one answered." Sue stated.

"I said that I called his house phone and no one answered. I didn't think to call his cell phone. This escalated so fast, I just didn't think of it."

Sandy whipped his cell phone from his belt holder. "I've got the number. Let's see if I can get him." Sandy dialed. "John? This is Sandy. Are you okay? We didn't know if you'd left town and, well, we wondered. . ."

"Tell him the storm had us concerned about him," Sue added.

"The storm had us concerned and we didn't realize you weren't here. We were checking on everyone. . . No, no damage that I can see. Seems like it was just a bad few hours of wind and rain--Uh, right—I see—"

"Ask him when he's coming home," Sue ordered.

"When did you say you're coming home? Tomorrow night? Okay. Well, let us know if you need anything. Right. Bye." Sandy turned to the group awaiting answers. "He's with Ward for the weekend, seeing some properties upstate," Sandy explained.

"Did you tell him we were all standing in his living room because he didn't tell us he was going away for the weekend?" Sue snapped.

"You heard what I said. And no, I did not say that. I didn't want to embarrass him."

"Or us," said Acton. "Thank you, Sandy. I think we can go back to our places now."

"I feel terrible," Mary Gray declared. "If I had only thought to try John's cell phone I wouldn't have created all this confusion."

"Don't you feel bad, Mary Gray. This just goes to show that we need a system in place to deal with our comings and goings so we can all feel secure. I will put this on our next Community Meeting agenda for discussion," said Sue.

They turned off the lights, watched Acton lock up, and each headed home.

A HORSE OF A DIFFERENT COLOR

5
WASHINGTON SPRING

"**D**o not forget to check on John's wall switch," chimed Sue before leaving for work the next morning.

Sandy heard Sue's car roar to life and then fade into silence as she drove toward the main road to Baltimore. Instead of getting onto the task, Sandy flipped on the television in WSC-10 and slid into his lounge chair. He resented his wife's meddling personality which grated on him by a much larger degree now that they were living in 1,100 square feet and he was no longer working. She wanted him to get some side work. But that took energy, and energy was not something he had. He wasn't sure what had changed, but he knew he wasn't himself. He attributed most of his fatigue to the move they had made, downsizing from 2,200 square feet to 1,100, exactly half, and that meant tossing out half of what they owned. He and Sue had argued over what to keep and what to get rid of. Most of her things somehow made it inside the cut line, while he gave up the majority of his

A HORSE OF A DIFFERENT COLOR

possessions. In the end, they kept way too much, regardless of whose stuff it was. She still felt like she needed to have her high school yearbooks, letters from girls she met at Girl Scout camp, paper Valentines and love notes from old boyfriends. He couldn't exactly blame her. If he had had those things, he might have wanted to keep them, too. He didn't have any high school girlfriends, and he had never joined the Boy Scouts. In fact, he had not finished high school, a detail about himself he kept secret. Sue knew, but on applications he always listed himself as attending Monroe High School in Boyertown, Pennsylvania, which was his old school, but he had never graduated and as far as he knew, no employer ever actually checked.

In 1969 Sandy's older brother Pete landed a job working for a paint contractor and during that summer, between Sandy's junior and senior years of high school, Sandy asked Pete if Mr. Metzer would take him on, too. During June, July and August, both brothers worked for Alvin Metzer's Paint Company. They both became good at exterior painting projects. When it came time for Sandy to return to school, he started back, but in October his science teacher made a fool of him in front of the class. Sandy, whose given name was Samson Underwood Cantelli, went by Sandy because that's what he was called by everyone in his family. When the science teacher handed back the first tests of the new school year, he handed Sandy his paper saying, "That's right, Samson Underwood Cantelli, your work is just like your initials." Although the teacher didn't say it, kids whose minds moved fast pieced it together. S-U-C. Snickers erupted across the classroom. Sandy felt all the air leave his body while a flush rose like fire to the top of his head. He was so deeply mortified he sat there in complete silence, trying not to hear the jibes from others in the class. At the end of the hour, Sandy slunk out of the room and out of the school, vowing never to return. He walked for four hours before coming

A HORSE OF A DIFFERENT COLOR

home at approximately the usual time. After dinner that night, Sandy told his brother what happened. Pete was indignant and offered to slash the teacher's tires. 'We have to do something,' his brother had said. Both wondered how the teacher even knew Sandy's full name. Teachers know everything, they finally concluded.

For a few days Sandy got up in the mornings and acted as if he were going to school, but instead he milled around, avoiding places his parents or their friends might be. That was relatively easy since both of his parents and most of their friends worked in the flag factory at the edge of town. His father was a mechanic and his mother worked as a fabric inspector. One afternoon Sandy found his brother high up a ladder painting a house. Sandy asked Pete if he needed help, and when Pete said he did, Sandy took a paint brush in hand and that simple act turned the tide and there was no going back.

Sandy timed his announcement to his parents about quitting school for Friday after dinner. Friday was payday, so his parents' mood would be lighter, and Friday after dinner was when everyone felt as good as they were going to feel after a long week of hard work. What Sandy didn't know was that the Cantelli's paychecks had both been held up that particular week, in fact the entire factory's checks were late. The boss had put it down to a problem on the bank's end, and the employees were left to wonder if that was the truth or whether they should fear for their jobs. When Sandy made his announcement to his parents about leaving school, he rushed to include the information that Mr. Metzer was willing to hire him for $1.65 per hour, which was high wages. His mother made $1.70 per hour and his father $2.95, and that was after years of working for the same company. His parents' anger cooled when their son reasoned that he would contribute his entire weekly pay to the household, if only he could keep the job with Mr. Metzer. Fearing the worst with their own jobs,

A HORSE OF A DIFFERENT COLOR

the Cantelli's gave a tentative okay, with the agreement that Sandy should reconsider at the Christmas break and try to return to school in January. Mr. Cantelli's logic was that outdoor painting work would soon cease altogether and perhaps Mr. Metzer would run out of projects, prompting Sandy to go back to school. However, when fall weather turned to cold, Mr. Metzer moved both Pete and Sandy indoors to interior painting. And when the Christmas break ended for those in school, Sandy and Pete kept picking up their paint brushes and heading off to work like they were born to the profession. Sandy didn't mind giving his paycheck to his parents. He understood the cost of room and board as he considered what it would mean to move out one day. For now, he was happy just to be doing work with his hands. As spring rolled around and with it, exterior projects again, Sandy and Pete started to learn carpentry. Often houses that needed painting also required repairs. Until then, Mr. Metzer either did small repairs himself, or if they were more extensive, told the homeowner he would have to get them done first before Metzer could bring in his paint crew.

Pete and Sandy learned basic carpentry and before long, they were using hammers as skillfully as paintbrushes. Mr. Metzer treated the Cantelli boys well and with their reliable help, he expanded to projects as far away as Reading. The Cantellis had been to Reading once to pick up their uncle at the Reading Railroad station. That day the boys nudged each other in the back of their parents' 1948 Buick saying they were going to take a ride on the Reading Railroad, "That'll be 25-dollars, please," they said, thinking of the Monopoly game. Now under Mr. Metzer's employ, they went to Reading frequently, by company truck, always on residential painting projects.

One of their assignments during the summer of 1972 was a large house owned by a doctor near the Reading Hospital. Pete and Sandy were both on ladders one hot July afternoon.

A HORSE OF A DIFFERENT COLOR

The date was July 5th which Sandy could always remember because the smell of pitch was in his nose from the blacktopping everyone did to their driveways on July 4th, the one day guaranteed to be hot, and most likely dry. Sandy was up and down his ladder multiple times just to cover the east side of the house, which seemed like the largest house he had ever painted. When he was on the ground resupplying his bucket, he looked up to see a group of girls pointing at him. One of them smiled and pointed again. They all giggled and started down the sidewalk away from him, except for the girl who smiled.

"What's your name?" she asked.

"Sandy," he replied.

After a few moments of silence she asked, "Don't you want to know my name?"

"Okay," Sandy said. "What's your name?"

"Susan Young."

"Pleased to meet you, Susan Young."

Sandy started to turn back to his work.

"What's with your white pants?" she asked.

"What do you mean?"

"Why are you wearing white pants? And a white shirt? You're white all over, except where you're not." She giggled.

"It's a painter's uniform."

"I'm going to be wearing white soon," she announced.

"Congratulations on your wedding," Sandy proffered.

"No, not my wedding, silly. I'm going to be a nurse!"

"Oh, a nurse." Sandy could hardly match this girl's enthusiasm.

"And I've been promised a job right here at the Reading Hospital. I've been in the Reading School of Nursing for the last three years and at the end of this summer, I will be graduating. I've been working so hard to make this dream come true, and, as long as I pass my boards, I will be a full-fledged RN, that's a registered nurse."

A HORSE OF A DIFFERENT COLOR

"Well, congratulations on your—nursing," Sandy said and turned back to his bucket once more.

"See you around Mister, Mister--?"

"Sandy," he said.

"Sandy. Right." she repeated. "Hey, where does a name like Sandy come from?

"Samson. They just call me Sandy."

"Why not Sam?"

"Don't know. Just didn't stick, I guess."

A long silence passed.

"Hey, we are having a party this Saturday night. Would you like to come?"

"I don't think so," Sandy answered.

"It's going to be a lot of fun. Minny, Nancy and Brenda are going to sing this song they've been working on. I don't sing, but they have the prettiest voices. And Minny's boyfriend is going to accompany them on his guitar. It's going to be over there." She pointed to a building off in the distance. "I think a hundred people might be coming. A swell time. Do you like music?"

"Ah, sure." Sandy wasn't sure where this line of conversation was going and the sun's heat was intense at the zenith.

"They say that Bob Dylan is our generation's greatest troubadour. Do you like him?"

"Ah, yeah." He had no idea who Bob Dylan was.

"And we are going to sing some of his songs. You really should come. In fact, I won't take no for an answer." She walked closer to him. He could see her pupils which appeared larger than normal in her gray eyes.

"Oh, look. You are sweating. Here, let's continue our conversation under the tree." She pointed to a large oak in the yard of the doctor's house. Sandy slid a lid over his bucket and followed her to spot in the shade.

Everything felt more intimate and immediate now that they were under the tree. They were also closer to one

A HORSE OF A DIFFERENT COLOR

another and, as Sandy noticed, about the same height. Sandy secretly resented his small stature that always put him toward the end of any pick-up team.

"How about you tell me all the reasons you won't come on Saturday and I will tell you all the reasons you should come?" She waited.

"I don't have transportation," he blurted, feeling stupid the moment he said it.

"Okay. What else?"

"I don't have the time." He wasn't sure if this were true. He figured that he would be painting on Saturday. In fact, he might still be painting this very house, especially if he didn't get back to it. There was no way to know for sure where he would be working on Saturday, although it was possible he would still be here.

"Okay. What else?"

"That's it. And I guess I don't know you very well and ..."

"That's the whole point!" She interrupted, "It's to get to know each other."

"Well, I appreciate your asking me but I really need to get back to work." He removed his hat and pulled a red workman's handkerchief from his pocket to wipe the sweat from his brow.

"Look, I know this is sudden, but the truth is, I told everyone I was coming with a date, but no one has asked me, and so I'm asking you. Would you do me this one favor? I mean, you don't have to like me. Just do me this one favor, and I'll find a way to repay you."

Sandy considered her offer. What would it be like to be in the company of someone his age of the opposite sex? His two sisters were so much older than he was and were of no use to his understanding the female mind. His brother had started to date a girl in Boyertown, but he gave up precious little information about what they did or where they went.

"Don't dither. Just say you'll come."

A HORSE OF A DIFFERENT COLOR

"Alright," he said, wondering how he would make this work. "What time?"

"Eight o'clock. We'll be in the cafeteria, music playing, dancing probably. You don't need to bring anything but your cute self." She looked giddy at his agreement.

"What time does it end?"

"No time," she announced. "Or, when the cows come home, as my friends like to say." She glided past him out into the sun, across the lawn and onto the sidewalk which pointed her toward the place he was to meet her three days later.

Their first date was far more consequential than either of them had pictured in their minds in the days leading up to it. Sandy started to tell Pete but stopped, and then only later confessed that he had made this arrangement. Pete told Sandy he should go, to take his car. Pete said that he and his girlfriend would find another way to see each other.

The party had been loud and full of sweaty people drinking and smoking and laughing, mostly outside because alcohol was not allowed inside the building. In fact, alcohol wasn't permitted at all on hospital grounds, which is where they were, but the party-goers invented ways around that, and before long, no one tried to hide their bottles.

Sandy felt odd about the whole affair, but when he found Sue, or rather she found him, they didn't spend much time inside or outside with the party crowd. She had made a point of taking him by the arm and introducing him to her friends, but then led him away from the crowds and music.

They talked for three hours, sitting on a grassy knoll that looked across to the lights of the Reading Pagoda flanking the mountain that overlooked the city. Mostly Sue talked, but Sandy did, too, surprising himself with his own answers to her probing questions. No one had ever asked his opinion of the war, of the President, or the state of world. Until he said it, he didn't even know that his favorite color was red, like the

A HORSE OF A DIFFERENT COLOR

lights that outlined the Pagoda, Reading's landmark. She insisted that as a painter he must know color intimately, and that it must be satisfying to take something that was torn up and ugly and make it beautiful again, which is what she said she was trying to do with sick people, make them lovely and all put back together. She made it seem like the two of them were on an equivalent quest and that what they did mattered enormously to the infinite universe. She kissed him there on the hill, and for the first time in his life, Sandy felt his spirit soar. Someone wanted him, perhaps even understood him. And so he kissed her back, and from those moments on the hill a partnership was forged.

Sue and Sandy married in 1972 during which time Sue worked at the Reading Hospital. She urged him to purchase a home but all he could afford, even with their combined salaries, was rent for the west side of a duplex in a hamlet between Reading and Boyertown. By 1973 Sue was pregnant. Their daughter was born March 1, 1974. The Reading Hospital attendants were ill-prepared to treat the newborn for the infant was born with a critical congenital malformation of the heart.

The hospital immediately ordered the baby transported to the Children's Hospital of Philadelphia. But when the newborn failed to thrive within 48 hours, Children's Hospital referred the baby to Johns Hopkins Research Hospital in Baltimore where a leading cardiology team was experiencing better outcomes. Sue and Sandy followed their baby to Philadelphia and then Baltimore, where, for nearly a year of delicate surgeries and experimental treatments, she lay languishing in the newborn nursery. If only God would let little Lisa live. On February 14, 1975 Lisa Lee Cantelli succumbed to her birth defect. This child had required every ounce of Sue and Sandy's energy, prayers, time and treasure. But she died, and with her, all Sue and Sandy's hope of a

A HORSE OF A DIFFERENT COLOR

happy life together.

Although they were still loosely tethered to Pennsylvania, and their kindly landlord had allowed their rent to slide for a year, once they buried little Lisa in Pennsylvania, Sandy and Sue relocated to Baltimore. During their yearlong stay, Sue had connected with the nursing staff at Johns Hopkins and now knew enough of their system to get a job. She chose the Emergency department because it kept her mind completely absorbed and off the tragedy of their child.

Sandy's skills were easily transferrable and he picked up work at a large outfit that did mainly commercial painting. The company's other divisions contracted to do electrical and plumbing work, a one-stop-shop enterprise. After a year of painting, Sandy asked to train on the plumbing side. And then after a year of laying pipe and digging sewer lines, he requested training in the electrical department. In another year he had both his plumbing and electrical licenses. At home, he and Sue had a tolerable marriage, although she never became pregnant again, a mystery they never talked about. Each found an outlet in work, which paid the bills and even gave them a little extra for travel, which Sue loved to do. Sandy preferred to limit his traveling to Boyertown to see his remaining family. His father died at age eighty of lung cancer and his mother, still living, chose to remain in their original home. She was no longer the woman working at the flag factory, but Sandy could see her earlier self emerge each time he returned. She was the only one who instinctively knew his interior space, even without a word. She, too, had lost a child, and that bond crossed all other chasms.

Sandy turned off the television and sat staring into space. The newscaster was covering a story about U.S. operations to quash a terrorist force. Sandy thought about the men who were sent into obscure places on deadly missions, like Vietnam. His brother Pete had died in Vietnam. Pete had

A HORSE OF A DIFFERENT COLOR

stood beside Sandy at Sue and Sandy's wedding, and three months later left for the Army. Pete's basic training was truncated, and he and his outfit were sent into the jungle. It was a deadly mission that should never have been asked of green recruits, but decisions from above determined the operation, and the outcome for Pete, or what was left of him, was to come home in a pine box. The emptiness Sandy felt could not be filled with anything, and it was made worse that he, himself, had gladly been exempted from serving.

At noon Sandy called Acton to get the key to John's house, then gathered his tools and plodded over to WSC-1. In the daylight John's place really did appear messy, things left in mid-stream. This didn't seem characteristic of John. But, it wasn't his business what John did. Yes, they were all to look out for one another, but that didn't include snooping or passing judgment on each others' housekeeping.

Gathering his tools he couldn't help but notice a spread of pottery shards on John's dining table. At first glance they appeared rather randomly scattered, but on a second look Sandy could see they were arranged like puzzle pieces hoping to find their mates. A delicate-looking fabric pouch lay beside the shards, all of it resting on a white pillow case. The September issue of *American Artifacts* magazine lay nearby.

Sue pulled into the parking garage at Mission Hospital. She gathered her belongings and made her way toward the employee entrance wondering what she would see today. It was often the same string of trauma cases, everything from headaches to heart attacks to gunshot wounds. The gangs in the area seemed intent on killing each other, which seemed implausible given the polite, quiet, even docile behavior of the victims' gang member friends who clustered quietly in waiting rooms. She wondered how it was that they could carry weapons, let alone use them.

A HORSE OF A DIFFERENT COLOR

"Hello Frank," Sue said as she passed the security officer at the door.

"Good morning," he replied. "Gonna be a hot one, I guess."

"Might be. Seems like hurricanes always bring heat." She marched into the employee kitchen, stuffed her lunch kit into a refrigerator already bursting with cooler bags, then meandered through the hallway to the Women's locker room. 6-14-16, she spun on her padlock. Some days this felt like a high school gym stuck in a cruel time warp where everyone had instantly aged.

Thinking of high school reminded her to check on the progress of her high school reunion scheduled for Thanksgiving Saturday. The reunion committee decided that Thanksgiving weekend would be perfect for their gala event since most of the classmates would be already be in town or coming home to visit. It was true that she and Sandy spent most Thanksgivings in her home town of West Lawn, Pennsylvania, but having the reunion at the same time added to the stress she already felt about being with her family. Sue always played the part of the dependable daughter, making every effort to monitor her parents' conditions, even though she lived two hours away, while her sister, Stacy was practically next door to them.

The high school reunion would be a good thing to occupy her mind, although how, in one long weekend she would prepare Thanksgiving dinner for everyone and manage the reunion, she had no idea. She just knew that she would.

A HORSE OF A DIFFERENT COLOR

6
HALIFAX

On Sunday, the start of the boy's final week at his grandmother's, the two went to church. They attended Wesley United Methodist Church, a small, white clapboard building perched at the summit of a hill nine miles from the farm. On the way, they passed by two other churches, a Holiness church about the size of the Methodist church, and a concrete block building with the name *Righteous Word of Jesus*. Neither had ever been inside these churches. Sometimes they would see black people in Sunday dresses and suits gathering by the doors. The boy never thought of differences in race when he was at school, but in the country skin color seemed to matter because people did not mix as readily. At school, people were people. Some of his classmates had parents born in India; several boys were Asian, a number of boys were black, and one was an albino. No one overtly picked on the albino boy, but everyone knew that he was different. In fact, the albino boy was one of the smarter kids and so the other boys couldn't openly disrespect him,

A HORSE OF A DIFFERENT COLOR

although sometimes they tried to use him for their own purposes. The albino boy was in two of the boy's classes for which he was glad because the albino boy was attentive. This made following the lectures easier because of fewer distractions typical with some of the other boys.

Traveling along the country road he saw black parishioners entering the other churches. This made the boy think of school, which suddenly brought to mind his book assignment. He exclaimed this to his grandmother saying that he would have to finish it before Friday. Friday his mother would be coming to pick him up. His grandmother's reassuring voice expressed confidence that he could get it done.

The grandmother felt more concern than she showed regarding the boy's abilities. She kept on the lookout for indications of mental instability. Her son, the boy's father, so far seemed to lack the tendencies that had taken three lives in three generations. Now, arriving to the church, the grandmother looked toward the cemetery where her family was buried. She thought about how the churchyard had been part of the original land titled to her family dating back to the 1600s. The church's property as well as another large part of their holdings had been lost in the aftermath of the War Between the States when her ancestors had to sell because they could not afford the tremendous cost of labor. To narrow the family's focus and make ends meet, the patriarch at the time with a fondness for horses, devoted himself to horse husbandry.

From that patriarch came a son, who, being schooled by his father in the way of horses, came up with an outlandish idea--to revive the all-but-extinct Tarpan pony. When he was a boy, his father had taken him to the Eastern Shore of Maryland to see the wild roaming Assateague ponies. When the boy learned that those fearsome mavericks were the result of the interbreeding of horses who escaped a shipwrecked

A HORSE OF A DIFFERENT COLOR

sixteenth century Spanish galleon, the boy was captivated. From then on he read everything he could on the bloodlines of horses. As fascinating as Assateague ponies were, he discovered that Tarpans were a far more ancient wild horse dating to the time after the ice ages when they occupied the forests of Russia, the German territories, Denmark and eventually England. However, Tarpans were viewed as a nuisance stock that diluted the "better" breeds and over eons were hunted for meat or sport or were simply destroyed.

On the eve of his thirty-ninth birthday during a conversation across the fence with his neighbor, he wondered aloud if it would be possible to revive the wild horse from Europe. He explained that the last Tarpans had been dispersed in 1806 when a Polish wildlife park closed, a last refuge for the wild ponies. The man asked his neighbor, if a stud could be located and sailed to Maryland, would he go in together with him to try their own back breeding? They could use light-colored Assateague ponies and in a few generations have something akin to the original Tarpans. They would be viewed as heroes of the horse world.

On a handshake the men agreed on terms. In a year they had their prize stallion delivered and each acquired several light-colored wild Assateague mares thought to be close to Tarpan coloring. For their equal efforts, it soon became clear that the neighbor's mares were producing more foals. At first, this was a point of humor between the men, but when three years passed and the gap between the two stables kept widening, the humor ended. No proof could be found, but it was likely that the neighbor was interfering with the stallion's duties while boarding at the other's farm. Determined to make his mark on the horse world but now running out of reserve cash, the lagging man took a mortgage on his land. When Year Five came and his mares remained barren, he despaired of losing his farm. One day he went to town, took out a life insurance policy for $1 million, and four weeks later

A HORSE OF A DIFFERENT COLOR

he took the farm truck and drove it off a bridge. His wife knew nothing of the mortgage, or the insurance, but all became clear when the papers were revealed. The land and farm could now be freed of debt.

This was the first of the three tragedies. Knowledge of another suicide rested with the grandmother alone. It was thought that her brother had inexplicably drowned since no one had witnessed his death. After three days his body was recovered in the neighbor's farm pond. When the boy didn't show up to dinner his parents thought maybe he was with his friends, although she, as his sister, could have told them that was improbable because her brother had few friends. As night fell and he did not appear, she had gone into her brother's room where she saw a note on his writing desk. She picked it up and read his awful accusing words. He blamed his parents for their haranguing, that since he would never amount to anything, he would spare them the embarrassment they would endure from their friends. Not wanting her parents to see the letter, she hid it until she could tear it up and throw it away. A sick feeling welled up from her insides. She wondered if he could really kill himself. Nervously looking around his room, she noticed that her brother had taken his swimming bag. She went to her parents, not with the note but with news that her brother's bag was gone.

In the dark of a summer evening the three took kerosene lamps and tromped toward the neighbor's big farm pond. First, they stopped for her father and mother to knock at the neighbor's door to ask if they had seen their son. The neighbors had not, but they offered to go along out to the pond. By the water's edge sat the boy's duffle bag. His shoes rested beside the bag. The two families called the boy's name, making a circle around the huge pond. The lamps would have appeared like beautiful glowing dots of light swinging in the night, had their bearers not been out for such a dismal reason. After an hour of searching without success, the group

A HORSE OF A DIFFERENT COLOR

retreated to the neighbors' house. They entered the side door by the kitchen, a way reserved for family and close friends. The neighbor wife invited the three to sit at the table. The adults sat quietly discussing the matter. The neighbor man suggested that the morning would bring answers, good ones, he thought. The boy's sister felt nauseous, believing that she knew the truth.

The morning brought only more questions and the fact that the fifteen year old had still not appeared. Fearing the worst, the father summoned the sheriff, who came and took his own walk around the pond. The family had left the duffle bag and shoes in place, in case these would bring the boy home. The sheriff suggested that the boy may have run away or camped out with friends. By now, the parents instinctively knew that this was untrue, yet they inquired with other parents. Walking by the water time and again, the father and mother looked at the flat deep pond wondering if their son was under its placid surface.

On the following day, the neighbor took the father in his row boat out on the pond. He used a dredging tool as the father slowly rowed. They worked methodically, making measured passes back and forth across the water. Near the middle at the greatest depth, the neighbor caught on something large. The two men worked the heavy item toward the shore, the neighbor keeping the object in the hook of his dredge, and the father carefully rowing. They dreaded to see what it was. As they neared shallower water, the object took the shape of a body, and closer to shore, the boy's body. It was bloated and green and tangled in pond plants. His eyes, or what was left of them, were open, staring. For the work of getting the task done, the men staved off their emotions of such an impossibly horrid scene. It was only when they beached the boat and both men pulled the body onto the dirt that the father exhaled a low mournful cry and then vomited. The neighbor let go his hold on the rotting flesh and also

A HORSE OF A DIFFERENT COLOR

threw up. To keep from being further repulsed, they crawled away from the fetid stench and willed their eyes not to look back. When they managed a few lungs full of fresh air, the neighbor grumbled that they should call the sheriff. Foul play could be involved. Leave him, the neighbor was saying. Leave him where he is. The father mutely followed the neighbor's orders. Back at the neighbor's house they called the telephone switchboard and asked for the sheriff's office. The operator and anyone else on the party line overheard the conversation.

The sheriff, after seeing the body and deciding there was no evidence of struggle or harm, reported that the boy had simply drowned. The closed-casket funeral was held at Wesley Methodist church. It was a sad affair which drew people from neighboring counties.

Her mother somehow survived the news and lived into her eighties. When she passed away the entire county mourned, saying that a lady of great character was lost to the world. People's opinion of her was based on the other terrible incident. Some years after the drowning, the dead boy's father took a mistress. The two had been recognized at a distant motel. Knowing that he had done wrong, and still tormented by the loss of his son, he threaded a rope through the rafters of his barn and hung himself. A farmhand found him. His wife had been completely unaware of his philandering, and so his suicide had come completely out of the blue. At the funeral the other woman was in attendance hoping to blend in as a local citizen. In the middle of the service that woman's husband appeared at the back of the church in his dark blue machine shop uniform. Interrupting the service he called his wife by name and demanded that she leave. The preacher stopped his preaching. At first the woman didn't move, pretending not to hear her husband. People tried not to turn and look, but some couldn't help it. Glances went from her to him and back again. Everyone knew these two but since the congregation members were unaware of the affair they

A HORSE OF A DIFFERENT COLOR

could only think of this as strange behavior. However, the husband then called his wife a harlot for sleeping with the dead man, and said that she had no business mourning him. With the secret spilled, the husband then proceeded up the aisle, physically pulling his wife from the pew, and led her out the door.

Everyone gaped, including the minister. Not knowing what to do except continue the funeral, the preacher resumed his preaching, a sermon that no one heard.

The family sat stock still, all eyes gazing on them from behind. The dead man's wife never moved. When it was time for her to walk behind her husband's casket being rolled down the aisle and out the door, she kept her eyes level and appeared completely indifferent to the news that burned in her consciousness. At twenty-four, the grandmother was newly married, and she and her husband followed behind, adopting the same countenance as her mother. It seemed that the burden of men's weaknesses were destined to be carried by the women of each generation.

The grandmother shook her head as if to clear away her thoughts.

At church people immediately asked about the fire, and how could they help? The grandmother kept a smile on her face and said little, although she did approach one man to help her create a new barn design.

The church members remarked over the boy. They told him he had grown and asked how he was doing in school. The boy murmured answers about getting along okay. They only ever seemed to want him to say that he was fine, so he did. He agreed that they were fortunate not to have been hurt in the fire and that the horses were safe. That sparked the idea to ask these people if they had seen Sally May, and so after the church service he began making his way around the sanctuary asking if anyone had seen the light gray mare with

A HORSE OF A DIFFERENT COLOR

dark-tipped ears. No one had.

A HORSE OF A DIFFERENT COLOR

7
WASHINGTON SPRING

"**S**andy, could you check our icemaker? Bryan and I will both be out this afternoon if that's when you can come over. Acton will have the key." Jimmy's lilting voice sounded through Sandy's answering machine.

It was turning into a busy day when Sandy checked his messages back home. John's light switch had been an easy fix, a small wiring adjustment. Now it seemed there was an appliance problem. Sandy walked over to Acton's to return John's key and to pick up Bryan and Jimmy's. The idea of a centralized location for keys had been a community decision as both a security and safety measure. Everyone should be able to access everyone else's home in case of needed entry, but it should be through a controlled system. Acton, it was decided, would have the key sets. If he were out, there was a master key on a hook just inside the shed, which negated the security aspect; anyone could access the master key any time and enter someone else's house, but it was agreed that in order to allow everyone their privacy it would only be used in

A HORSE OF A DIFFERENT COLOR

a true emergency.

Acton invited Sandy inside while he exchanged John's key for Bryan and Jimmy's.

"Looks like you get to wear your repairman hat today," Acton said as he handed Sandy the key to WSC-6.

"Yeah, keeping me busy. I may have to run to the hardware store. Anything you need?"

"No, thanks, I'm good."

Sandy turned to go. "Do you want me to let you know if I'm heading out?"

"No. I'll see if your truck's gone."

A few minutes later Acton's phone rang.

"How's my brother?" the voice on the line boomed.

"Fine, Arlen, but I'm sorry to say, I don't have the news you're looking for."

"Come on. I know you can find some piece of history to help me out here. Philadelphia isn't the city of brotherly love it purports to be. And if I want to get this appointment as circuit judge you have to give me something. At sixty-four I'm starting to look like old meat."

"It looks like Granddad Abel got into some trouble. You can use his record of early civil rights activism, but apparently he had some IRS difficulties. That might explain why he and Grandma Rose moved out of their home on Grandview Avenue. I hadn't really thought of it other than what they told us way back then, that they grew tired of looking uphill. It certainly was a grand view for Philadelphia, but apparently it was uphill, whatever that meant. When they moved to their smaller place in the Seventh Ward, it never occurred to me why they moved."

"Do you think he sold the house on Grandview to settle an IRS debt?"

"Appears he was being threatened with incarceration for non-payment of taxes. The Philadelphia Inquirer ran a series

A HORSE OF A DIFFERENT COLOR

of articles on black businessmen who were being leaned on unfairly. Truth is they weren't keeping up with the Pennsylvania Department of Revenue or the IRS."

"Might be he was withholding payments to protest a racist system of government. That would make him a hero."

"You might want to read the articles yourself and make your own judgment. I will send you the links."

"Look, you said yourself that Granddad's claim to fame was inventing the Mouthpieces to further the people's cause. We both know his zest for politics, running in 1937 for the State House of Representatives. I realize he lost, but he was known in the community."

Acton and Arlen's grandfather was Abel Arneson, a well-known black man who operated a barbershop in Philadelphia. Born in 1875 he trained as a barber under his uncle Anderson Arneson who kept a place in the back of his house where men would come every day of the week except Sundays. Anderson had fought in the Civil War by enlisting with one of the first black regiments from Pennsylvania. His company was sent south and took part in the bloody battle at Vicksburg, Mississippi where more than 37,000 men perished. Like Gettysburg, it was the cruelest of engagements, the Confederate soldiers shooting anything and anyone to keep their supply lines open. Anderson's conviction to fight for the Union had taken hold when he heard President Lincoln deliver an address to the people of Philadelphia. He had enlisted with other blacks to defend the country and its cause for unity. On the battlefield at Vicksburg, Anderson nearly died, but not from bullet or bayonet. When a horse and rider fell from a gunshot, they took down Anderson as well, crushing his left leg. He lay in agony under the weight of the horse, waiting on the field for help. It was two excruciating hours before help came and when it did, it took four men to drag the horse off of Anderson whose leg had swollen with

A HORSE OF A DIFFERENT COLOR

blood and appeared ready to explode. A surgeon managed to save his leg, but it was forever damaged leaving him with a severe limp and perpetual pain. Which made his election of barbering a strange choice of profession since barbers normally spend the day on their feet. But Anderson had built a special chair on wheels that allowed him to sit in a perch and rotate around his customer as needed. As a war hero, Anderson had no shortage of patrons visiting the barber shop in his Philadelphia home. He had enclosed the rear porch off of his kitchen. His place tended to be cold in winter and hot in summer, helped somewhat by the windows he kept open to vent the heat, and a small stove that he kept stoked in the winter. Talk of any war, of national, state, and neighborhood politics always filled the air. Some men simply lingered to hear the news. These men with their dramatic conversations fascinated young Abel who lived three doors down. He loved visiting Uncle Anderson's to hear such high-minded talk. After school, Abel would report home and show evidence of his completed school work to his mother, after which he was allowed to spend until dinnertime at his uncle's shop. The smell of shaving cream and hair tonic offered a mystique that was magnified by the endless parade of men with their colorful conversation. Abel loved when his uncle asked him to sweep the floor after he finished with a patron. Abel would empty the hair carefully into a receptacle intended for his Aunt Lizzy, another of his mother's family. Aunt Lizzy used the hair as ticking for pillows and mattresses. On Saturdays after the shop closed, Abel would take the bin to his aunt's place and return with it empty. Then he would collect a nickel or two for his time helping that day, and head home, proud of his contribution.

In this way, Abel learned both the business of barbering and the careful way of handling men, for men in a barber shop were a strange lot; some would become boastful tale tellers, others pontificating preachers, while others reported

A HORSE OF A DIFFERENT COLOR

the latest gossip. Hardly anyone was silent. Had they been quiet, the place would have seemed unnatural. In time, Abel was allowed to learn the art of sharpening the tools of the barbering trade. He felt honored at keeping these in perfect condition, necessary if quality service was to be had at Uncle Anderson's.

By the time Abel finished high school, he announced to no one's surprise that he planned to become a barber and open his own shop. Whereas his uncle had remained tucked in the neighborhood, serving only local men, Abel's interest was to serve more established men, be they white or men of color. From conversations at Uncle Anderson's, Abel heard all about Joe Cassey, one of the great black men of the time. Cassey was a founder of *The Liberator*, the newspaper everyone who could read, did read, and those who didn't read pretended they knew what the newspaper said by repeating lines they had heard others tell. Sometimes these were exaggerated as men misquoted the original ideas. Abel could read well, and knew when men were bluffing, but he also knew by his uncle's keen eye that one did not challenge the man in the chair.

Anderson instructed his energetic young nephew not to cross the color line in his barbering pursuits. Anderson knew that whites were fickle in their loyalties, for his fellow barbers had been left high and dry when Sweeny Todd and similar publications emerged that frightened whites into believing they were at risk in a black barber's chair. To Anderson's mind the way for Abel to make his mark in the profession was to stick with those who would stick by you. Yet, in spite of his own wisdom and because of Abel's nagging, Anderson sent his nephew to a man named Willie Stickler to apprentice with him. Stickler, a fellow black infantryman, had also survived Vicksburg. He had been serving white patrons on Chestnut Street in a location he inherited from Joshua Eddy, one of Philadelphia's most prominent black barbers. Stickler

A HORSE OF A DIFFERENT COLOR

agreed to take on young Abel only because he was Anderson's nephew. However, with an influx of Germans to the city offering their services to whites who were now more comfortable with a white man's touch, it wasn't long before Stickler's well-established business slowed and he had to relocate to the black part of town on South Street near the Seventh Ward. He would be hard-pressed to make a living there because others were already serving the black men in that community. Fortunately, Abel had the bright idea that if Stickler invited prominent blacks to speak formally at his shop, that his place would become a gathering point. Stickler could call these events Mouthpieces of our Sounding Horns. The idea was a hit. Black men always wanted to speak their minds to audiences and audiences wanted to hear these men talk, even if those same audiences came away criticizing the man. It was fashionable to know who stood for what, and in this milieu of change, the timing of these speaking events could not have been better. The wave of southern migration of blacks from south to north meant that men fresh to Philadelphia were hungry to learn all they could and find leaders worthy of their trust. Men such as W.E.B. Du Bois came and spoke at Stickler's, which became such a rallying point that people gathered hours before these Saturday events, sometimes bringing baskets of food. The speaker had to stand outdoors to accommodate the crowds. Women sometimes attended and soon it became clear that Stickler's was now a focal point for the community. This also provided the means for Abel to exercise his skills both as barber and assistant to the cause of men of color.

Abel met Rose following one of the Mouthpieces, MPs, as they were being called. She lived near Stickler's shop on South Street and knew they attracted great crowds. Her mother cautioned her to stay away as this was not a woman's world, nor at her tender age of seventeen should she be getting mixed up with all that talk. Abel was nineteen and full

A HORSE OF A DIFFERENT COLOR

of ideas. Their meeting came by accident the day the speaker's platform broke. It was a slipshod wooden stand hastily thrown together a few weeks earlier when it became apparent that the MPs would need to move outdoors. The day's speaker was William Still, the heroic operator of the Underground Railroad. Still was a robust man of more than two hundred pounds, and the platform collapsed under his weight. He had been animating his speech by hopping up and down to make his point to the crowd, a mix of declamation and admonishment when the wood under his feet splintered and then gave way, causing him to drop nearly two feet, which unbalanced him so badly that he rocked forward as the crowd gasped. When he regained his stance, he was quite a bit shorter and stouter, stuck as he was with one leg in the faulty platform. Young Abel came to his aid by leaping onto the platform and helping the man to an unbroken part of the dais. Not to be undone by the situation, Still made a weak joke that if wood could take the life of Jesus, then it could try to take his life, too. Not wishing to lose his captive audience, Still returned to his speech. Abel jumped off the platform to let the man have his space, but Abel could see that the man's trousers were slashed and rightly assumed so was the man's leg. Abel dashed into the shop for bandages, but returning, he could see that the speaker was so absorbed by his oration that his leg had not begun to register its pain. Able knew in time, it would.

Still's speech went on for 45 more minutes without a stumble in word or body. He gestured with no less vigor to make his points. And when he exited the platform to roars of applause, he waved to his audience, new converts to his moral enterprise. But upon reaching solid ground, his leg presented its problem and the man nearly fell in pain. He quickly collected himself, not wishing to appear diminished before this group of souls he had come to educate. With power he did not know he possessed he turned and walked

A HORSE OF A DIFFERENT COLOR

into the shop behind the dais to remove himself from the pressing crowd. Abel, seeing up close how stricken Still was, followed him into the shop and quickly shut the door, locked it and pulled the shade. Nothing could be done to cover the plate glass windows through which people could peer, but the point was made that the MP was over and that Still should not be disturbed. Abel jumped into action to assist the man who had hoisted himself into one of the barber chairs and was roiling in pain. Abel took a pair of hair sheers and cut away the torn fabric clinging to the man's gash. The man's lower leg was swollen purple and dark red. The wound had pooled blood running down in streaks, now mostly dry. Seeing his own wounds, the man blanched. Stickler suddenly appeared at the shop, quickly opening then shutting the door, and pocketing his key.

"You had the crowd mighty whipped up," Stickler said.

"You have to tell it to them in a way they understand," Still gasped, wincing with pain.

"Abel seeing to you?" Stickler observed.

"Looks like I won't be walking too far today," Still managed.

"Let me see what I can do," Stickler said, and disappeared behind a curtain. When he emerged it was with a cane topped with a carved eagle's head.

"See what you can do with this," Stickler announced as he placed it in Still's hand.

"Mighty nice piece, Stickler," Still said, gripping it admiringly. He winced as Abel did his doctoring.

"The man who owned it is on the other side of the Jordan now. But I believe he would be mighty happy for you to make use of it today."

"Now you wouldn't be meaning Joe Cassey, would you? I understood that he walked with a cane just like this one, carved by his father who fled a plantation on Edisto Island for the promise of freedom in Philadelphia. I heard that he made it for himself when he could no longer walk unaided, and that Joe held onto it as a totem of loyalty to his father and to the cause."

"I came into it when Joe's daughter visited me in my old shop on Chestnut Street, back when I was cutting white heads, not just blacks. The daughter said that not one of Cassey's sons survived the war and while sentiment told her to keep this precious heirloom, she knew that one of her fallen brothers owed me a great debt from the battlefield, and that she could not let it go unpaid. She tried to hand me her grandfather's walking stick. I flatly refused. I told her it held her father and grandfather's spirits and it must remain with her family. But then one day it simply showed up in my back room. I can't tell you how or when. I went hunting some supplies and there that stick stood in the corner tucked behind some shelves. I heard later that the daughter had left town, so I don't know if she put it there or what."

"I would take kindly to using this august stick, knowing it belonged to Joe Cassey and his father. It would be a point of honor and I will return it when I have no further use of it," Still declared.

Abel had bandaged the man's leg and was busy sweeping away the debris as the man struggled from the chair and onto his feet. "I do suggest you build a sturdier platform. People like me are always inventing ways of making our points."

"I will see to it," Stickler said and unlocked the door for Still to greet any hangers-on who might have remained behind.

"How much of that alcohol did you use?" Stickler asked Abel as he turned from closing the door.

"Some. Much as it took."

"We out?"

"Nearly."

"Can't operate without alcohol. Take this and go get two bottles." Stickler handed Abel some cash.

A HORSE OF A DIFFERENT COLOR

At the corner druggist Abel first saw Rose. She was picking up candy to take home to her mother as a show of why she was out, although her real reason had been to catch what she could of William Still's Mouthpiece. She knew by reputation that he could command a crowd and she wanted to hear him. She had only managed to listen to his final five minutes, but even those minutes electrified her and confirmed that he could raise the morale of black people.

Rose was having her candy weighed when Abel walked in. She did not know this boy but he looked familiar. He waited for her to finish her purchase and then requested the alcohol from the clerk. Rose lingered inside the door trying to overhear his business, and then slowly returned to the store shelves as if she had forgotten to make another purchase. As he finished, she made a show of shaking her head as if she really needed nothing more and also started toward the door. He reached the door first and opened it for her to step through.

"Good day," Abel said as she passed by him.

"Hello sir," Rose said. They stepped into late day sunshine so glaring that both had to hold a hand at their brow to see.

"Mighty strong sunshine," he said.

"Yes, it is. Hardly lets you see where you're going," she said.

"Do you have far to go? May I escort you?" Abel offered.

"Oh, I'm fine," she began, and then added, "But it would be kind of you to help me to the next corner."

"Obliged," he said, and offered her his arm. He shifted his package to his other arm and the two set out along the sidewalk, acting fancy and proud.

As they strolled Abel boldly asked, "May I inquire as to whom I have the pleasure of escorting today?" He liked having her hand entwined with his arm.

"Rose Parson," she said.

"Miss Parson," Abel said. They reached the corner where

A HORSE OF A DIFFERENT COLOR

the sun was no longer in their eyes, which also meant that they could look at one another.

Abel said her name once more, then turned to look fully in her face, which made her blush, for she was looking at him, as well.

Their courtship blossomed from those simple beginnings. Everyone in the community celebrated, for during the year of their engagement, Abel rose to junior barber in Stickler's shop with the promise of further promotions. Abel's Mouthpieces drew people and business from wider circles in the black community and connected Stickler with prominent men.

Rose and Abel had four children, all girls, the youngest they named Ophelia. Ophelia was a darling child, spoiled as younger children can be, and was encouraged to set her ambitions high. She fell in love with a man who was finishing school at The University of Pennsylvania and destined to claim a place in the new world of black politics and power. His name was Rockford "Rocky" Alexander and he was the very first black graduate of The University of Pennsylvania's Wharton Business School. His sights were set on law school, Harvard if possible. He came to Wilford Hall to speak as part of a convocation series, an outgrowth of the original Mouthpieces at Stickler's shop. After Alexander's appearance, Ophelia shook his hand and declared to one of her friends that she would one day marry him.

Her prophecy did not come true, for when Rocky Alexander returned the following summer, degree conferred, she overheard him say that he would be marrying his classmate Cynthia Turner, also destined for law school. But remembering the charming Ophelia, Rocky introduced her to his younger brother, Austin. Austin Alexander, like his older brother had similar ambitions, but did not share Rocky's legal interests. Ophelia attached herself to the younger brother,

A HORSE OF A DIFFERENT COLOR

reasoning that the Alexanders as a unit were destined for greatness. When Austin announced his own graduation from University of Pennsylvania, he invited Ophelia to attend the ceremony. Her strict training in elocution and her fashion savvy gave her no pause in believing that she could handle the rigors of such an occasion. And she was right. With her elegance and Austin Alexander's stature they appeared a most handsome couple. Ten months later they married. Their wedding was one of black Philadelphia's most celebrated affairs, second only to Rocky and Cynthia's marriage the prior year.

Ophelia and Austin's lives were often in shadow of the older Alexanders. Rocky and Cynthia had both completed law degrees and were lauded as the first blacks to reach this achievement. And they were all the more beloved when they returned to Philadelphia to serve the black community. Austin, a man of a different mind, had determined his best course was insurance rather than law. He signed on to the Supreme Property, Casualty and Life Insurance Company a black-owned insurer who was expanding from Chicago into Washington DC. This meant a move to the capitol city from Philadelphia's Seventh District, an opportunity Ophelia welcomed since this meant building their own Alexander empire apart from Rocky and Cynthia.

Austin did well in Washington. He excelled in the black social circles, earning credibility when he mentioned his education at University of Pennsylvania and his brother's work in Philadelphia. His lovely wife Ophelia went to great lengths to appear stylish and welcoming. She recommended that they acquire as large a home as possible, even if it meant a high interest rate mortgage, for Austin was showing promise both as a salesman and as a climber in the firm. Ophelia immediately connected with the two organizations that would become the foundation from which she would build their social domain, the most prominent church and the

A HORSE OF A DIFFERENT COLOR

most prominent charity. Serving on committees she could extend invitations to their elegant home. This would display their successful standing in the community, thereby ensuring that they would be seen as integral to the community. Naturally, this also aided her husband's business, for the name Austin Alexander became synonymous with quality insurance. Ophelia was not eager to start a family as this would interrupt her important social enterprising. However, when, in 1949, she discovered she was with child, she took this as a sign that God was providing her a new challenge. By then they had been building their lives in Washington for more than ten years, and she had admittedly grown weary of some aspects of keeping up the rigors of society. Also, she reasoned that with a child on the way they could move into a still larger home. Acton was born in 1950 thus making Austin and Ophelia the first of the two Alexander couples to have a child, for Rocky and Cynthia had not yet produced any children.

Austin and Ophelia's economic standing as compared with the two Philadelphia lawyers equalized when Austin's work in insurance produced robust results. The couples would often spend holidays together, the men talking politics, leaving Cynthia and Ophelia to talk about other matters. The women were sometimes at pains to find comfortable subjects, and since they had no children those topics never came up. With Acton's birth, Ophelia wondered what Christmas of 1950 would be like. As they awaited Rocky and Cynthia's arrival she worried that she and her sister-in-law would have even less to say to one another. Much to Austin and Ophelia's surprise, almost the moment the Philadelphia Alexanders were through the door Rocky announced, "Cynthia's expecting! Looks like we'll be bringing up one not far behind yours." Ophelia drew Cynthia aside and the women fell into easy conversation about what to expect with pregnancy, and Ophelia proudly presented her son, Acton.

A HORSE OF A DIFFERENT COLOR

The tragedy for the Philadelphia Alexanders was that their child, also a son, Brightwood, was born with Spina Bifida, which set their lives on a trajectory far different from what they expected. Visits between the families were often strained as the two tykes were so vastly unequal in their development. The Washington Alexanders often made the trips, rather than straining the Philadelphia family who had to bear enormous burdens of caring for their son. Adding to their sorrow, just after Brightwood's first birthday the boy died.

Austin and Ophelia could hardly bear the news themselves, but adding to the matter, Ophelia was on the brink of announcing that she was expecting again. She hid her news as she did her rounding belly as they attended the dramatic, community-wide funeral for Brightwood Alexander.

A HORSE OF A DIFFERENT COLOR

8
HALIFAX

The boy's heart was heavy as his grandmother drove toward home. When they turned down the familiar lane it was impossible not to see the charred barn ahead. It should not have looked that way. It should have been its usual self, weathered wood walls with an intact roof. On Sundays their custom after church was to eat a large meal, sleep a little and then go visit someone his grandmother knew, either an ancient widow in her home or someone in a nursing home. He didn't enjoy those occasions as he was made to sit and listen to idle chatter and answer the same questions about his school and family. This particular Sunday he was excused from visiting because his grandmother said that she didn't much feel like socializing which was a relief since he desperately needed to catch up on his reading.

The boy reached for his book. He thanked his lucky stars that he had removed *Misty of Chincoteague* from its hiding place in the stall or it would have been lost in the fire.

He opened to where he had left off, with a storm, ironically, like the real-life one they had just had. On the bed

A HORSE OF A DIFFERENT COLOR

in his room he read to learn if the boy in the story would save the pony and her foal from danger. Three straight hours he read. *Misty of Chincoteague* did, in fact, have a happy ending, but not the one the boy would have predicted. He had to admit that this book had captured his imagination. Now came the work of putting the story into his own words. He sat up, pulled his spiral notebook from his backpack along with a pencil and began printing his summary.

In the kitchen, the boy's grandmother stood looking out the kitchen window in the direction of the pasture. She knew that the boy needed help with his reading and writing, but she also respected the child's privacy and ability to recognize that need for himself. His sister was far more gifted, academically and athletically. She took to horse riding with determination. The boy still would not mount a horse and he cut corners in his chores. However, he had a good heart and sometimes made inventive decisions. On the afternoon following the barn fire, he rigged a hose from the house to the temporary barn to make it easier to muck out the stalls and fill the horses' water buckets. She was also worried about Sally May's disappearance because this was a very special breed of horse. Sally May was also the one thing that her grandson truly loved. She overheard him reading to the mare in the barn and knew he spent extra time grooming and feeding her. She downplayed her concern for the horse's absence, believing that the animal really would find its way home. But with days passing without word or sign, she began to fear that the pony might not be found. And that would crush her grandson. She picked up the phone and placed a call. The neighbor she telephoned could not offer any news on Sally May, but he did say that he could be called on to tear down the burned barn to prepare for its replacement. She thanked him and said she would surely need him.

The weekdays sped by full of chores, insurance calls, and draft plans for the new barn. Each night at dinner the boy

A HORSE OF A DIFFERENT COLOR

added to their prayers to bring Sally May home. When he said this, his grandmother's throat tightened as she held back tears.

On Thursday evening, their last evening together, the boy announced that he wanted to show his reports to his grandmother. They had finished their meal and were working on the dishes. He went into his room and returned with a green spiral notebook. He opened it to the first report and handed the notebook to his grandmother. She wiped her hands with a towel pulled from the front pocket of her apron. He didn't look at her, only handed her the notebook and then grabbed his own dishtowel to finish his chores. She took care to treat the notebook with interest, but not too much interest. Darting a look at the boy, who was feigning total indifference, she removed her apron and went into the living room to her reading chair.

At first glance she was surprised by the childish scrawl on the page. Wasn't this boy nearly eleven? He should be writing legibly, in cursive, and then she remembered that penmanship was no longer taught in grade school. Her disdain evaporated as she realized this was the first time she was seeing her grandson's handwriting. Now curious, she began to read.

Report Number One. This was about a man who traveled by boat down the Amazon River. The report said that he was from Jamaica and was fulfilling his lifelong dream. A few sentences listed the animals the Jamaican encountered and that was the end of Report Number One.

Report Number Two was about *Misty of Chincoteague*. The boy lined out the characters, the plot, and the story's outcome. He misspelled words, forgot punctuation in places and could have used help with flow, but he captured the essence of the story. She smiled to think that her grandson had read one of her favorite books when she was his age.

And then she turned the page to Report Number Three. *Sally May of Halifax*. The boy had imagined his own story. He

A HORSE OF A DIFFERENT COLOR

said that *Sally May of Halifax* was about a boy who met a beautiful gray Tarpan pony while staying with his grandmother. He described the storm and the fire and that Sally May went missing. He said that she had been found by a family who did not have a horse but desperately (which he spelled despiritly) wanted one. He said the family had a little girl who had Leukemia (Lukeemea) and that her dying wish was to ride a pony just like Sally May. The family couldn't believe their luck when they found a gray pony in their backyard eating grass. And so they put her in their garage to keep her warm and safe and dry. He said the family fed Sally May carrots and that because of the pony, the little girl got better. He wrote, *This story has a happy ending.*

She put down the notebook, tears spilling from her eyes.

A HORSE OF A DIFFERENT COLOR

9

WASHINGTON SPRING

John and Pauline had in mind a community that was open to nature, which is why the property surrounding the Close included vacant land as far as the eye could see. Their aim was to create a sense of welcome for all; thus, Washington Spring had no fence or gate.

Jimmy Johnson, driving in from errands, saw something completely unexpected not far from his cottage door.

"What in God's name is that doing in our yard?" Jimmy exclaimed. He parked his car and strode over, uncertain of whom he should call. Just then his cell phone rang. Bryan's number flashed. Jimmy answered without a hello.

"You are not going to believe what I am standing here seeing," Jimmy began.

"What? I need you to see if Mary Gray is home. She's not picking up and I have exactly four minutes until noon Eucharist. We can't locate the wine cruet. Is her car in her driveway?"

Jimmy glanced across the Close. "Uh, no. It's not. Listen,

A HORSE OF A DIFFERENT COLOR

do you know there's a--." Jimmy started to say, but Bryan had hung up.

Acton emerged from his front door to carry a trash bag to the common bin near the central shed. Jimmy rushed to intercept him.

"Acton! Did you know there's a horse in our yard?"

"A what?"

"A horse. Come see." Jimmy shadowed Acton to the trash bin. "Over here," Jimmy said, indicating to follow him across the Close. The men walked in silence, cutting through the closely cropped yard and into some tall grass. "See?" Jimmy pointed.

"Where did it come from?" Acton asked.

"Darned if I know. There isn't a farm within fifty miles of here," Jimmy said.

"There must be. A horse doesn't just fall from the sky," Acton reasoned.

"What should we do? Who should we call?" Jimmy asked.

"Sheriff, I guess."

"And report a stray horse?"

"Someone may have filed a missing animal report."

"A missing animal report," Jimmy mocked.

"It happens. People go missing. Animals go missing. I would say to call the sheriff." They both looked toward the animal who was busy eating grass.

"It wouldn't have a tag on it, would it, like a dog? Or a cattle brand?"

"I doubt it," Acton said.

"Well, okay then. I'll file a found-horse report," Jimmy announced, and the two turned to go.

"District Seventeen," a cheery voice answered.

"I need to report a—ah--a horse," Jimmy stated in his telephone.

"A what?" Answered the cheery voice, a little more

A HORSE OF A DIFFERENT COLOR

quizzical now.

"A horse."

"Your location?"

"Washington Spring, Paribar Shore."

"Hold on, I'll transfer you to Sheriff Whiting."

"Whiting," a clipped male voice answered.

"I'm calling to report a stray horse near Paribar Shore. Looks like it may have broken loose from some other location and ended up at Washington Spring. We're the new community off Wellington Road."

"Yeah, I know where you are. A horse, you say?"

"Right."

"Can you describe it?"

"Kind of small. Lightish gray. I would say New England slate gray. Not very large."

"Did it appear to be well-groomed?"

"Hard to say. Sort of a shaggy mane. Might need a hair cut," Jimmy answered.

"Could be an Assateague pony. Have you checked with Jackson stables?"

"I've never heard of them."

"They're at the north edge of the county. Let me give you their number. Call me back if they say it's not theirs."

"Jackson Stables," Hadley Jackson answered.

"Hey. This is Jimmy Johnson at Washington Spring near Paribar Shore. A horse showed up in the field by our property. Could it be one of yours?"

"A horse? No, wouldn't be one of ours. You're twenty-five miles from us and we aren't missing any horses."

Hadley Jackson, who went by Had for short, ran a horse farm on land once held by Maryland Governor Charles Hadley. Charles Hadley himself had purchased the land from a man named Barclay, from the line of the Barclays who originally settled the county. Charles Hadley had been an avid

A HORSE OF A DIFFERENT COLOR

horseman who raised thoroughbreds in the late 19th century, a tradition that continued into the current generation.

"Do you know anything about Assateague ponies?" Jimmy asked.

"Sure. I know all about them. Assateague herds are kept wild on the Eastern Shore, about as far south as you can go. The National Park Service in Maryland manages them. They swim the herds across to Virginia the end of July where the fire department holds an annual auction to thin the herd. Why? Do you think it's an Assateague?"

"Until three minutes ago I had never even heard of an Assateague horse," Jimmy began.

"They're technically considered ponies. Not as large as a horse. Can you describe it? Color? Markings?"

"Light gray."

"The mane and tail?"

"I didn't notice."

"The chance of this being an Assateague is pretty small. It would've had to swim the entire Chesapeake Bay to get to Paribar Shore, or, more likely, it got loose from someone. I could take a drive down to see what you're dealing with."

"Sure, since you know horses."

"I'll throw some hay and grain in the truck and come on down. Take me about half an hour before I can break free. Are you going to be there awhile?"

"Yeah. I'll be here," Jimmy answered.

An hour later a white heavy-duty diesel pickup truck rumbled into Washington Spring. It looked entirely out of place in a community of Priuses and modest-sized sedans. Had Jackson parked in the center of the Close.

Jimmy met him, and the two walked through the same yards that he and Acton had trod earlier.

"I saw it out here," Jimmy announced, pointing to a now vacant field. "It can't be far. I was inside just for a few

A HORSE OF A DIFFERENT COLOR

minutes. Where could it have gone?"

"You say it was gray?"

"Yes, mostly light gray. I saw that it has a dark mane and tail. Seemed like it just wanted to eat grass. I didn't approach it. Do people brand their horses? Should I have looked for some kind of marking?"

"Assateagues aren't branded any longer. We used to get one from time to time. The herd is protected by the National Park Service in Maryland. On the Virginia side they cull the herds by auctioning off about fifty ponies every year. We used to go, make a day of it. Now it's become such a tourist trap. People come from all over--you can't hardly move."

"So you think this was one of those wild ponies?"

"Hard to tell without looking. They tend to be shorter than the average horse, stockier, barrel-shaped. They drink a ton of water. Is there a water source around here?"

"Not that I know of."

"Your horse will be looking for fresh water. If it is an Assateague it didn't swim here, that I can tell you. It's a long way to Assateague Island, a long way."

The men walked the field for twenty minutes looking for the horse. The only animal life they spotted was a wild turkey they spooked and some geese flying overhead.

When they returned to the Close, Had Jackson unloaded the feed, reasoning that if there were a loose horse, it would be hungry and the hay and grain would help lure it so it could be identified and returned to its rightful owner. He also left a halter and lead line for that possibility. When he finished, Jackson gave a tip of his hat, boarded his truck, and left.

"Choir rehearsal was a bust," Bryan announced sadly as he came through the door of his and Jimmy's cottage at 9:30 p.m. "The sopranos complained that their descant for Sunday is too high. And I had no tenors."

"Sounds like a new network drama, *The* Spoiled *Sopranos*,"

A HORSE OF A DIFFERENT COLOR

said Jimmy.

Bryan grimaced and made his way to the refrigerator to pour a cool beverage. "And we never found the glass cruet for noon Eucharist. After searching high and low Father Eric and I gave up. He used a small flower vase instead. Not a pretty sight. We had the usual five people. No one said anything. Maybe they didn't notice. But then tonight when I went to turn out the lights, I went into the sacristy and there was the glass cruet. I swear to you it was not there at noon."

"What was lost is found. Good on you. Look, I have my own mystery to solve. It's called the case of the missing horse."

"Missing horse?" Bryan arched an eyebrow.

"Actually it's the case of the found horse," Jimmy said. He explained the afternoon's events.

"I've been out on the screened porch most of the evening watching for movement." Jimmy held up binoculars. "Got these from Larry," he said. "Did you know there are wild turkeys in these fields? There's a lot of everything out there if you just sit and watch."

"Any sign of the horse?"

"No. It was a strange thing."

"Let's call our meeting to order," John B. Martin announced. The group sat snugly in the living and dining room area of John's cottage. At these meetings, everyone was acutely aware that a central community house should have been built. People had grumbled since their first gatherings at John's place, but now, eleven months later, they remained irked but silent on the subject. John was at his dining table with a folder open in front of him. Adjacent to John, Mary Gray had her laptop perched on the same table ready to go.

"We have a lot to cover. Mary Gray, will you read the minutes from last month's meeting?"

"The August meeting of the Washington Spring

A HORSE OF A DIFFERENT COLOR

Community was held in the home of John B. Martin. All community members were present except for Sue Cantelli."

"I was working," Sue interrupted.

"Waclaw, we appreciate your making the effort to be here," John added. Waclaw, smiled weakly. At eighty-four he was the oldest member of the community. His portable oxygen tank rested on the floor beside him.

"Old business. The planning committee for Phase II was elected as Acton Alexander, Tom Allgood, John Martin and Ray Miller. They will deliver sketches to us in October with the idea that we might have drawings we can display at our anniversary event in November." Mary Gray could see Tom nodding. He was hard to miss with his mop of dyed red hair. Ray Miller sat beside Tom, and fidgeted with the cooler sleeve around his beer can. The sleeve read "Miller Time."

"New business. Anniversary Event Planning. The planning committee will be Jimmy Johnson, Larry Long and Mary Gray Walterson. No other new business was presented. The meeting adjourned at 8:20 p.m."

"Are there any corrections or amendments to the minutes?" John paused.

"Hearing none, do we have consensus to accept these as read?"

Heads silently nodded.

"August minutes accepted. Mary Gray, what old business do we have?"

"The Anniversary Event," she said. Jimmy, as the committee chairman, took his cue and began.

"We are planning for a family-friends-and-neighbors public event on Saturday, November 15, from 11:00 a.m. until 2:00 p.m. We will use the canopy tent stored in our shed and borrow tables and chairs from St. James-in-the-Wood." Jimmy paused and pointed at Sandy.

"Can we ask you to help with tables and chairs? You're the only one with a pickup truck."

A HORSE OF A DIFFERENT COLOR

Sandy nodded.

"I will cook a pig," Jimmy announced, pride in his voice, "and we will request everyone here to bring side dishes. Mary Gray is notifying the press."

"Do you need anything further from us?" John asked.

"A head count of guests the week before," Jimmy sang.

"Fine. Anything else?"

"Not about the anniversary, but I will have some new business when we get to that," Jimmy said.

"So do I," announced Sue.

"Mary Gray, any other old business?"

She looked up from her laptop where she was recording the proceedings and shook her head no.

"All right. New business? Jimmy, let's start with you."

"Most of you heard about the mysterious horse that appeared last week. Has anyone seen it since last Wednesday?" Jimmy inquired.

No one reported any horse sightings.

"Hadley Jackson from Jackson Stables drove down. We were hoping for a look at the horse, but it disappeared before Mr. Jackson showed up. Acton and I both saw it, just so you know I wasn't dreaming."

Everyone's eyes shifted to Acton, who said nothing but through his silence assented to his involvement.

"It could be an Assateague pony. Apparently, there are wild herds out on Assateague Island off the Eastern Shore, but it would have had to swim across the Chesapeake Bay to get all the way to us in Paribar County. Not likely."

"Is there anything you want us to do about this?" Ruth Long asked, leaning in front of her husband, Larry. They wore matching powder blue golf shirts and looked the part of the tanned leisure class.

"Just be on the lookout," Jimmy answered, "and let me know if you see it."

"Thank you, Jimmy," John said. "Sue? New business?"

A HORSE OF A DIFFERENT COLOR

"Thank you, John," Sue began. "It would be a great benefit to our security and safety if we had a monitoring system to know who is coming and going from our community. In fact, best practices among CCRCs mean signing out when going off-property. We should enact just such a policy so we know who is here and who is not. If a house catches fire, we need to know who is home. Also, if someone falls or expires in the night, it might be a day or longer before anyone notices. We should have set this up from the beginning, a system to know each morning that everyone is alive and a sign-out sheet when leaving the Close."

"You mean every time we run an errand or go out of our house we need to record this somewhere?" exclaimed Ray Miller who looked from Sue to Sandy. Sandy peered down at his hands.

"Yes. It's a well-known practice. And, if I might remind you, the backbone of our being here as a community is to look after one another," Sue replied.

"Seems a little like kindergarten to me," Ray said.

A silence hung in the air.

John broke in. "Sue, could you describe how this system would work?"

"There would be two systems. First, a viability check to be sure everyone made it through the night. Each person would have a magnet that they would place on the outside of their front door every morning. A monitor would be assigned to check magnets by 10 o'clock and if someone's magnet isn't out, then the monitor would knock. If there's no answer, he or she would get a key to check. The second system is a sign-out sheet kept on a clipboard at the shed. If someone is needed or there's a concern, the sheet will indicate if the individual is off property. "

"Can't we just tell someone we're leaving?" asked Ray.

"What if *that* person leaves?" answered Sue.

A HORSE OF A DIFFERENT COLOR

"If we are using magnets to show that we're alive—and home—can't we just take them in if we are going out?" Ruth Long asked.

"But what if you're leaving early? How would the magnet monitor know if you're up and out, or you never got up?" Sue retorted.

"Could we have two magnets? One that shows that we're alive and another to show if we're not home? Make them different colors." Ruth asked.

Sue looked offended. "Acton knows this is only standard protocol we're talking about here." Sue looked Acton's way. The group waited for an answer.

"Sue's system is standard operating procedure in facilities, to monitor who's on site," Acton said.

Sue beamed. "We should know who is coming and going. The clipboard gives us that information."

"So you're saying it's not enough to put on our door a magnet that says we're not home. We need to write, `going to the hardware store?'" Ray continued.

"And an estimate of what time you'd be returning. That way if you're not back, we can—" Sue started to say.

"And what if I decide while I'm out that I want to run into Annapolis, or I get a call and need to go somewhere? Or you, Sue, you get hung up in traffic coming back from the hospital? This is absurd. I'm not living in some kind of juvenile delinquency home," Ray snapped. He held up his beer can in a gesture to get others to agree.

"I agree," added Bryan. "We don't need this level of monitoring yet. I work at St. James and there's many a day when I don't know what time I'll get home. Jimmy knows that. We communicate when there's a problem."

"But there are those among us who don't have a spouse or partner to call. What about them?" Sue countered.

"I feel like there is some merit to Sue's proposal," Angelika Antwert chimed in. Angelika lived alone in her

A HORSE OF A DIFFERENT COLOR

cottage except for a blue-eyed, white-haired Angora cat that looked eerily like her owner. "If I were to die in the night, who would find me? And if I were to go out and not come back, who would miss me?" Angelika's German accent hung in the air.

"That's right," Sue said. "And let's not forget that a couple of weeks ago when John was gone and we had that tropical storm, we didn't know how to get a hold of him."

"We called him on his cell phone," Sandy remarked.

"But that doesn't change the fact that we didn't know if he was here or away," Sue snipped. No one had told John of the search they had made of his place.

"Could we consider these proposals separately?" John suggested. "It seems that we have three different ideas being presented. One is a method to indicate all is well by the morning magnet. Another is to indicate home or away by another magnet. And a third system is a sign-in/sign-out sheet. Could we look at them one by one?"

No one spoke.

"Let's start with the morning magnets," John offered. "Sue, you said that each person would be responsible for placing their magnet on their front door by 10:00 a.m. each day."

"What if I forget, or sleep in?" Ray countered.

"Then we check on you and all is well, but better to know that all is well, than not to know at all," Sue remarked.

Ray rolled his eyes.

"Who would be the monitor?" John asked, looking Sue's way.

"We would share the responsibility. We could create a calendar and each person takes a week at a time."

"But I'm often not here at 10 a.m.," Bryan said. "I'm often at the church."

"Working people could be excused," Sue said.

"Well, that's convenient," snorted Ray. "Sue, you work, so

you wouldn't have to do this."

"I only work three days," Sue said.

"Yeah, you propose something and then expect other people to get on board, but you don't." Ray smirked at Sue.

"I think we should at least try it," Angelika said. "I would be willing to take two weeks if it helped."

"There are enough of us that a rotation would mean each person would only be responsible once every eighteen weeks or so," Sue said.

"But not if you remove those who are still working," Ray said.

"We can figure this out. Sandy can cover my week. He can be the first monitor to iron out any glitches, if there are any."

"Sue, do you want to make a motion about this?" John asked.

"Yes. I believe a viability monitoring system is needed, as Acton also indicated," Sue said, including Acton to bolster her claim. "I move that Washington Spring enact a viability monitoring system with shared responsibility for tracking, beginning the first of next month."

"Is there a second?" John asked.

"I second," Angelika said.

"Discussion?" John asked.

"Who is going to get these magnets?" Jimmy asked.

"Acton can from the petty cash," Sue said, volunteering him. "And we can send around a sign-up sheet for monitors at our monthly meetings."

"This is ridiculous," Ray mumbled and took a swig of beer.

"Any further discussion?" John asked. "Okay. Then all in favor?"

Six hands went up.

"All opposed?"

Four hands went up.

"Abstentions?"

A HORSE OF A DIFFERENT COLOR

Three more hands went up.

"Who didn't vote?" John asked.

Three other hands shyly went up.

"If you're not voting, then it would be right to abstain. Would any of you three like to vote?"

"I'll vote for it," Ruth Long said.

"I'm voting against it," Larry Long said. Ruth looked sharply at her husband and crossed her legs in the other direction.

"I'll abstain," Tom Allgood said.

"That leaves our totals at seven for, five against and four abstentions. Mary Gray?"

"For," she said, although not being entirely for it.

"That makes eight for, five against, and four abstentions. The motion carries. Sue, we will look to you to create this system and get it in place for the first of the month. I propose that we table the other systems until we see how this one is working," John said.

At this remark Sue's victorious face froze.

"Will you agree to this?" John asked.

Sue merely nodded.

"Any other new business?" John asked. "Then let's adjourn." People began getting up, grateful to be released from their close quarters.

"Remember everyone, keep your eyes peeled for a pony," Jimmy shouted above the din.

"I thought these would adhere to the doors," Sue complained. She was holding one of Acton's new magnets against his front door. She had marched over to Acton's house the moment he phoned her to say that he was back from the store. He had spent the entire morning tracking down magnets, driving as far as Annapolis. They were birds, red, blue, and canary-yellow.

"I thought our doors were metal. We agreed to steel doors

A HORSE OF A DIFFERENT COLOR

to avoid warping and termites. They should hold these magnets," Sue declared as though ordering the birds to stick.

"Maybe the magnet isn't strong enough," Acton said, sad to think his hard-to-locate birds would not work.

"I know! Sandy can stick little magnetic strips on everyone's door. And then people can place their magnets on those strips."

"You might run that by John to see if we need to get approval. It means changing our cottages."

"Oh, this isn't a change. We are simply implementing the program we voted to carry out."

Acton remained still.

"I will send Sandy to the hardware store to get magnetic tape. In fact, I believe we may have some at home. We can try it at our place first. I'll take my magnet and see if I can get it to work."

Sue set off for home and within five minutes had confirmed her idea. She ordered Sandy to go to the store for more magnetic tape and by the day's end, Sandy had placed strips above each exterior dead bolt as the designated location for everyone's bird.

When he returned home after making his rounds, Sue met him at the door. "You did put a strip on the inside and the outside of the doors, didn't you?"

Sandy's face fell. He had not thought of that.

Sue, realizing his mistake said, "You needed to put a strip on the inside as well so people have a place to put it!"

Sandy said nothing, but turned and left.

The next week on Thursday at 10:00 in the morning Sandy made his round of the houses. By that hour, Sue had already left for work. The first two mornings she had been home and therefore took charge of the initial door checks. On Day One everyone had put out their birds, even Ray Miller, since Sue had called each person the night before to remind them the system was launching the next day. But on the second day, three birds were missing. Sue rapped on those doors and cheerfully extolled the virtues of her program. The third morning, two doors were missing their birds. Alone in his task, Sandy knocked. Those residents had also forgotten the system, apologizing that it would take some getting used to. Sandy returned home, glad to have that done. The moment he arrived the telephone rang. He answered it.

"Sandy?" a faint woman's voice sounded on the other end of the line.

"Mrs. Young?" Sandy still addressed his mother-in-law as Mrs. Young. Years earlier she had invited him to call her Barbara, and Dr. Young Bill, but Sandy could never bring himself to use their first names. "Is everything all right?"

"Bill died this morning. We were at the breakfast table and he slumped over. I tried to…" her voice trailed off until she could begin again. "I tried to wake him up, but he wouldn't come to. I called 911 and the rescue people came, but they couldn't revive him. I had to let him go."

"I'm so sorry," Sandy said.

Mrs. Young wept softly. After a few moments she collected herself. "Is Sue at work?"

"Yeah, she's at the hospital. Do you want me to call her?"

"Would you? Or, maybe wait until she comes home. She can't do anything from work."

"She will want to know as soon as possible," Sandy replied, knowing that Sue would be upset to think that Sandy had not notified her right away.

"Call her then, if you think it's best. I suppose she should know so we can make arrangements."

"Yes."

"Stacy and her daughter Dawn are going to be in custody hearings starting next week. Dawn is trying to keep her grandbaby away from her own daughter who is back to nonsense. It's not a pleasant situation. Stacy said the hearing may go on for several days, so we may not even be able to bury Bill next week. I don't know what we'll do."

"Let me call Sue and have her call you. I'm very sorry, Mrs. Young."

"Oh Sandy. It so frightened me. I can't tell you. One minute he was here. The next he was gone. I never thought he would go just like that."

The two ended their call. Sandy hesitated to telephone Sue. One thing he knew, he would not bring up the news of her sister setting the date of the funeral. Let Sue learn that from her mother and spare him the earful he knew was coming.

"Yeah?" Sue answered curtly. She had pulled her cell phone from her smock pocket, anxious to return to her patient who was coughing up blood in the next cubical.

"Your mother called."

Sue steadied herself. This could not be good news.

"I'm sorry but she said your father died this morning. He was at the breakfast table and apparently had a stroke or heart attack. She didn't say."

"Why do you assume it was a stroke or a heart attack? It could have been any number of cerebral or cardiac involvements, not to mention a variety of other things!" Sue snapped.

"Right. Sorry."

The news started to seep in.

"What did she say? Has she notified the funeral home? Did she call Stacy?"

"I don't know if she contacted the funeral home."

"Did she say if she called Stacy?"

"Yeah, she said she called Stacy."

"Of course. She would call Stacy first. Has she---You know what? Let me call her. I'll call you back."

Sue ended the call without another word.

Oddly, Sandy wondered how he would monitor the birds

A HORSE OF A DIFFERENT COLOR

the next eleven days if they were making a trip to Pennsylvania.

A HORSE OF A DIFFERENT COLOR

10

WASHINGTON SPRING

"John Martin." John answered the telephone in his real estate management office in Annapolis. He was waiting for several phone calls, hoping this one brought good news.

Four weeks earlier Ward, his son, who was also his business partner, had delivered some disappointing news.

"Dad, I think we're going to need to divest ourselves of Bay Haven Apartments. I know these were one of your first properties, but they've been losing money for some time and my projections show those losses worsening over the next five years. And even if the losses offset our other gains the buildings will need replacing and the land itself is not in a location worth continuing to take a long view. Plus, our exposure to liability could kill us. Insurance alone has doubled in the last three years."

Ward had learned the business from John, just as John had learned it from his father, each carrying forward the torch of commercial development. At that moment John wasn't hearing much of Ward's speech. His mind was elsewhere.

"I think that we should take a drive up there this Sunday," Ward continued. "The weather won't be great, but I think you need to see for yourself the condition of the buildings."

"If you say so," John offered.

"And while we're traveling, we can head west over to Ruston to take a look at Mill Crossing, a property that's going to be offered next week. I think we could make that work in our portfolio, but we have to act fast. If we can unload Bay Haven that will free up some capital. Right now I can get a margin in our favor so I want you to take a look at buying Mill Crossing."

"How many days do we need to be gone?"

"Just two. If we head to Bay Haven first, we can stay the night and then drive across the state to Ruston."

"Well, if we're going to Bay Haven, then we will stop in Baltimore at your Aunt Margaret's house," John declared.

"She'll want us to stay overnight," Ward said.

"No harm in that. She doesn't get many visitors."

"That will put us in Ruston on Monday at noon. I can set up a meeting."

"Fine. Make your arrangements. I'll call Margaret."

"Don't you know that a tropical storm is forming off the east coast? High winds and heavy rain are predicted for this weekend," Margaret announced.

"Margaret, you always were the optimist," John teased his sister as they talked on the telephone.

"You and Ward would be crazy to come up in such weather. Don't misunderstand. I would love to see you both. I just want to see you, not worry about you."

In spite of the forecast, that prior month John decided that he and Ward would make the trip. They started a day earlier with Ward picking up John on Saturday and the two

A HORSE OF A DIFFERENT COLOR

setting out toward Baltimore. The men were quiet, not needing excessive words to clutter the quiet car. Ward had handed his father a financial report on the first property outlining the reasons they should sell it. He also included his proposal on the property Ward thought they should buy, many pages of reading to occupy John as the miles clicked by.

The two-night visit with John's sister's taxed them all. Upon arriving, rain started pouring and the men had to dash from the car onto her front porch, getting drenched along the way. Margaret greeted them warmly, summoning them into her stately columned home. Yet, when they and their overnight bags dripped onto her fine Oriental rugs, she had a hard time masking her irritation and set off mumbling to fetch towels from a linen closet. After they finished drying themselves, she suddenly seemed not to know what to do, examining the two men like unwelcomed pests.

John's sister Margaret had always been easy company; however, on this visit she seemed agitated. Ward attributed it to his aunt growing older and alone—she was a widow determined to live out her days in her home of more than fifty years. During its inception, John had asked his sister to consider Washington Spring. Pauline had also urged her, but Margaret would not hear of tossing away the touchstones of her life, and if her 4,000 square feet were needed to keep her and her things, then so be it, regardless of the heating, cooling, and maintenance arguments that John leveled at her. Since she had made her decision, there had been no further discussion. Now seeing his sister easily bewildered and upset concerned John, but to open up the old dialog of her living situation seemed ill-fated.

The next morning, Sunday, the three had muffins and coffee at the dining room table before setting off for First Congregational Church. Margaret insisted on driving, even though it meant taking her clean Cadillac out of the garage.

A HORSE OF A DIFFERENT COLOR

She managed the car deftly, given that rain still came down. At church, Margaret glided through clusters of members to her spot by the stained-glass window that featured Jesus speaking to the woman at the well. After the worship service, John and Ward said that they would take her for the Sunday dinner buffet at a nearby inn. Once there, conversation seemed hard to sustain. Ward spoke of his wife and daughter. But soon the three ran dry of topics and mostly commented on the rain that continued to fall. Ward and John began to wonder if they would get out to Bay Haven to see their property. But after making it back to Margaret's house, and a break in the weather, they decided to keep their schedule. That afternoon the men set out and made their inspection of the property, John reluctantly agreeing with Ward's recommendation.

When they returned to the house, Margaret had cold ham and green salads waiting on the dining room table for their supper. John could not remember a time when the house seemed so void of life. When they were through eating, he and Ward insisted on helping with the dishes, practically rolling over Margaret and her protests, to carry their plates into the kitchen. Inside the kitchen for the first time this visit, John was shocked to see so much in disarray. Whereas the rest of the house was neat as a pin, each crisp doily perfectly in place, the kitchen showed not only the remains of breakfast, but dishes long left to mold. It was striking to see. Margaret followed them in, and realizing their shock said that her help had not come the past week. The men nodded as if this explained everything, but underlying her explanation seemed something untold. The men rolled up their sleeves and washed all the dishes, scraping off week-old food. John could see evidence of many weeks of lax housekeeping as he glanced at stray containers, open boxes, and smudged cabinets.

As he was drying dishes, John's cell phone rang. Sandy's

A HORSE OF A DIFFERENT COLOR

voice was on the other end. John asked how Washington Spring was faring with the weather. As they talked, John suddenly realized that he hadn't told anyone that he was going to be away. John's silent admonishment of his sister's behavior now seemed hypocritical, for he had slipped up, too, by forgetting to tell anyone he would be gone. Sandy was asking when would John be home? John told him tomorrow night. Ward was handing John a clean plate which required both hands, so John said little more on the phone before hanging up. He was unaware that four worried neighbors were standing in his living room.

The month after, inside his office, John replaced the telephone receiver. The call had come and it not been good news. He got up and paced.

Ward entered his father's office. "I have the papers for the Mill Crossing deal. Something wrong?" Ward asked, seeing his father now bent over peering into his office safe.

John was silent. He turned toward his son, enough to block Ward's view.

John's silence prompted Ward to continue his line of conversation. "I have the papers for Mill Crossing. Will you give them a look? They've been authorized by the attorney and everything's a go."

When John did not move to take them from Ward, Ward stepped forward toward his father.

"You can just leave them on my desk," John said.

Ward looked curiously at his father but decided he had other business to tend and no time for his father's idiosyncrasies.

11

WASHINGTON SPRING

"The horse!" Angelika cried, tucking her white hair under her fluffy blue hat.

Returning from a morning walk Angelika spied the horse in the field directly behind Waclaw's cottage. Her first thought was to knock on Waclaw's door and tell him, but overtaken by curiosity she began cutting across the lawn toward the horse. The animal stood munching on grass. As she neared, the horse's left eye darted her way registering her presence. Angelika slowed her pace. Her heart beat faster as she watched the animal who was watching her. She had grown up with horses in Texas, where her German ancestors had settled. Forty years had passed since she had been near a horse, and fifty since she had ridden one. Her Uncle Ernst and Aunt Mechtild had a farm that included horses, mules, and cows back when people were self-sustaining on their own land. Her German-speaking uncle was the one to introduce her to horses, starting first with the proper way to care for

A HORSE OF A DIFFERENT COLOR

them. Angelika loved animals, felt a direct bond with them. She suddenly longed to stroke the horse's long dark mane and to pat its neck and back. For many years she regretted not having an animal of her own and recently contented herself by obtaining a cat. Some people said that she and the cat looked alike, both having wavy white hair and long limbs. With twenty yards between them, the horse lifted and shook its head, relieving its black-tipped ears of pestering flies. Angelika stopped to see whether the horse would also send her a message to stay away, but it returned to the business of eating. Now Angelika was ten yards away, close enough to smell the animal. She slowed her steps to allow the horse to decide if it would welcome her into its space. It showed no sign of concern. In three paces she was near enough to hear its breathing. Now the horse raised its head and turned to look at her. Angelika froze. They eyed one another. She tried to register intense love. The horse appeared slightly skeptical, flicking its ears and swishing its tail.

"Mein schönes," Angelika said quietly, in German, as her Uncle Ernst would have. "Du bist ein Pony," she continued.

The animal trotted away from her. Angelika sighed, wishing the pony would acquiesce to her affection. Continuing to talk softly, Angelika slowly took six more steps and now she was close enough to touch the pony on its left flank. It watched her. Angelika stood still, saying sweet nothings. This arrangement went on for several long moments, Angelika waiting for any sign of being accepted. And then the pony dipped its head and resumed munching. Angelika took that as a message of consent. With an easy, flowing motion Angelika brought her right hand to the pony's haunch and, pausing within an inch let her hand remain suspended. To touch a horse was to connect with the animal, and if this were a truly wild pony, it would be foolhearted for her to try to stroke it, even dangerous. Her hand came down softly and connected. The horse jerked away

A HORSE OF A DIFFERENT COLOR

from Angelika's touch and began to trot farther out into the field. Angelika let out her breath. She felt both wonderful and sad, to see the animal up close and yet not to be able to stroke its body. She made a mental note of its features. It was light gray, with a dark mane, dark ear tips and striped legs.

Over the next minutes Angelika watched as the animal continued to walk away from her and disappear over a small rise and into the fields beyond where she stood.

"I saw the pony today," Angelika announced.

The group was gathered at the October meeting. "I would say it's an Assateague. A female. She showed up in the field. I can't tell if she's wild. Her feet looked as though she was being looked after, but her coat wasn't very clean as though she's been out in the weather. She wasn't interested in human contact, at least not when I tried approaching her."

"Did you by chance call the sheriff's department?" John asked.

"No, it didn't occur to me."

"I believe we need to contact the sheriff and raise our concern. Someone needs to take responsibility for the animal," John replied.

"I realize this will sound far-fetched, but could we include a stable in our community plan?" Angelika asked. "It wouldn't need to be very large or complicated. I used to live on my aunt and uncle's farm when I was young. Perhaps we could keep the animal, or at least provide some shelter. It's turning cool, and come winter, she's going to need protection from the elements. She seems to like our field, at least enough to return."

"Who's going to look after the horse?" Sue started to say.

"Pony," Jimmy interjected.

"I thought I could," Angelika answered, "and anyone else who feels inclined to."

"We don't have a license to keep animals. John, isn't there

A HORSE OF A DIFFERENT COLOR

an ordinance that prohibits us from keeping livestock on our property?" Sue asked.

"I would help," Jimmy answered, smiling disingenuously at Sue.

"Nothing that I'm aware of, Sue. But let's take this one step at a time." John said. "We need to find out if this animal in fact belongs to someone. Acton, what do you propose?"

"Contact the sheriff and let him tell us what we should do."

"Would you help us with that?" John asked Acton.

Acton nodded. Mary Gray noted their agreement in the meeting minutes.

"I'm ordering the pig this week," Jimmy announced to Acton as they met in their driveways. "You are going to have the most memorable and delicious culinary experience of your life. Have you ever had North Carolina pulled pork barbeque? It will knock your socks off. The ingredients I use for the sauce have been handed down in my family for four generations. Slow cooking is but one part. The other is the sauce."

"I look forward to it," Acton said. "How many are you preparing for?"

"About a hundred. The head count is due soon, but the committee thinks places for sixty will do it. People will circulate and not everyone will eat at the same time. We're picking up the tables and chairs from the church next Friday. How are the Phase II drawings coming along?"

"Good. I believe we will have the renderings ready to display."

"Personally, I love the Green House plan with the central kitchen and the bedrooms grouped off of the middle of the house. And the garden area looks spectacular. Pauline would have been so pleased."

"We want to finalize the plans and get bids by the end of

A HORSE OF A DIFFERENT COLOR

December. Weather-willing, we would like to break ground in the first two months of new year." Although he didn't say it, Acton thought of Waclaw's declining health and Christine's need for more help than Bill could give."

Waclaw Mulinski, at age 86, was the oldest member of Washington Spring. For more than thirty years he had run a dry cleaning business in Baltimore City. Before that he logged 20 years in the Army, rising to the rank of sergeant. He had served in both the Korean and Vietnam conflicts. His area was explosives and he had a particular penchant for chemicals.

The skill that Waclaw brought to the community would not have been obvious if reading his dossier only to that point. He was in fact a very good cook. His expertise with chemicals transferred to the kitchen. After leaving the dry cleaning business, Waclaw poured himself into developing culinary skills. And he was a natural. He watched cooking shows on the new cable networks, going so far as to write a complaint letter to the station when Martha Stewart was pulled from their offerings. At Washington Spring the plan was for him to be the lead food preparer in the Phase II home. Waclaw was so fit and vital, it came as a surprise to everyone when he had a massive heart attack a few months after moving into the Washington Spring Community, and although he survived it, Waclaw was required to have a defibrillator inserted in his heart and to use bottled oxygen. He had recently started to lose his stamina.

Christine Worthington had become more than a little forgetful. Her husband Bill ferried her to and from doctor's appointments and her care was wearing on him. Bill was a retired stock broker and Christine had been an insurance agent. They each understood money and numbers which suited them to guide the portfolio that was needed not only to build Phase I—the twelve millhouses—but also to handle

A HORSE OF A DIFFERENT COLOR

the expense of creating and running Phase II, the assisted living house, which was originally planned for five years after Phase I's completion. That time horizon was not playing out as projected. Bill had gone to John to confide that he was considering hiring someone to assist him with Christine so they could avoid leaning on the community before Phase II was ready. John had insisted that caring for Christine at home by Washington Spring members was precisely why they had formed the community, whether the person was still at home or in Phase II. All the same, the community did vote in favor of starting Phase II as soon as possible.

"Mary Gray? We need your help," Jimmy said into his cell phone. "Who do you know at St. James with a pickup truck? Sandy left me the keys to his truck when he and Sue left yesterday for her father's funeral, but I didn't know until right this minute that it's a dadburn stick shift. I don't drive stick shift. We need to get the tables and chairs from the church for Saturday." Jimmy could have been talking to Mary Gray through tin cans, her cottage being fifty yards away.

"That could be a tall order. An Episcopalian with a pickup truck," Mary Gray teased.

"Well, someone with a pickup truck, then. We're supposed to be over there in 25 minutes."

"Doesn't Acton know how to drive a standard shift?"

"No, he does not. I don't know what we're going to do on such short notice," Jimmy went on.

"I can drive it. What is it, a five-speed?"

"You can drive a standard shift, Mary Gray?" Jimmy said, wonder in his voice.

"She can drive a stick shift," Jimmy said to Acton.

"It's been a little while, but yes, I can." Metro traffic to her job at the National Archives caused her to make the shift to an automatic transmission. But once learned not easily

A HORSE OF A DIFFERENT COLOR

forgotten, or so she hoped.

"Well come on over then. Your country needs you," begged Jimmy.

"And so, on behalf of the Board of Commissioners of Parabar County I proudly present this Good Citizen award to Washington Spring," the woman commissioner said, handing a plaque to John. Applause went up from the gathered group.

"We thank you, Commissioner," John said, shaking the commissioner's hand. "Washington Spring has been a dream realized. As all of you may know, the Close where we are standing is Phase I of our development and we proclaim this to be a complete success. We have eighteen members each contributing to the life and livelihood of the community. Although we are not a co-op in the strictest sense, we share our resources and freely give our skills to keep the community running and our footprint minimal. Phase I is in full swing and today celebrates one year since opening.

"On this, our anniversary, we would like to announce the launching of Phase II. Phase II will be our care home." John pointed to a large drawing on an easel. It showed both exterior and interior sketches of the building.

"Willow Home will have a central shared living area that includes a kitchen, dining and living room along with six personal rooms each with private bath and work space. The idea is that our able members will provide rotating care shifts for Willow Home members. As needs progress for Willow Home residents, we will bring in skilled personnel, but our own members will continue to remain involved."

"Mama, a pony!" a little girl shouted over John's remarks. "There!"

Everyone turned to look where the four-year old was pointing.

The animal stood between two cottages, visible to the crowd.

A HORSE OF A DIFFERENT COLOR

John, not missing a beat went on, "And we have outdoor recreation here at Washington Spring."

Nervous laughter sounded.

"We thank you for coming today. We want you to enjoy our food and hospitality. Take a look at our Phase II drawings. Our community members can answer questions. They are the ones wearing WSC shirts."

"I want to see the pony," the child whined.

"Thank you all for coming," John quickly concluded. Everyone applauded. Bryan cued the music and people began mingling and talking.

The year before when no one had thought of a canopy it poured down rain. Today was a perfect blue-sky day with the tables and chairs set under a tent in case a storm unexpectedly blew in.

Bryan's idea of a string quartet was nixed by the planning committee when the subject of rain came up and where would the quartet and 100 people go. Instead, Bryan wired outdoor speakers and plugged in his playlist of 50 best-loved classical hits. This created a sophisticated atmosphere not entirely congruent with North Carolina barbeque. But then, he and Jimmy had made their life together work.

"Do you think we should do anything about the horse?" Mary Gray muttered to John as he finished speaking with the Commissioner.

"I guess none of us took the horse into consideration when we were making plans for today. We want to be careful of liability here."

"Do you have a copy of our insurance policy?" asked Mary Gray. "Would it say anything about people being hurt by a horse?"

"Have some barbeque, you two!" Jimmy exclaimed, breezing by on his way to the serving table.

"Mama! Let me see the pony!" The four-year old was ebullient.

A HORSE OF A DIFFERENT COLOR

Waclaw stood at his kitchen sink washing the mammoth communal canning pot. He was breathless as he scrubbed, even with bottled oxygen. But anyone would be, he said to himself. He had made Johnny beans, Polish lima beans with pork cracklings, just like his mother would make in late summer when beans were in season and his father butchered a hog. Outside the window he noticed something move. Squinting, he realized it was the horse heading into the distant wood. During the afternoon the horse had allowed the children to pet it, which was hard to believe if this were a wild pony. But Waclaw didn't know about these things. Most of his adult life after military service had been spent in Baltimore City.

Waclaw looked down at his bean pot. He decided it was clean enough. With some effort he hoisted it into the dish drain. It annoyed him to be so weak, nothing he could have imagined two years ago.

Angelika knocked on Jimmy's door. "Aussie's still here." The day after the anniversary event and every day thereafter the pony returned, always remaining through the afternoon before mysteriously wandering off. Sunday evening, however, the pony remained standing in the field, as though she had nowhere to go.

"She didn't leave?" Jimmy asked, incredulously.

"No. She's just standing out there. And it's predicted to get down to freezing tonight. It will be the first real cold weather for us this season."

"What do you think we should do?" Jimmy asked.

"I have an idea," Angelika answered.

A HORSE OF A DIFFERENT COLOR

12

WASHINGTON SPRING

Sue began pulling out items from dresser drawers to pack for Pennsylvania, the second trip north in a month. Her earlier trip had been to bury her father. She had managed stoically to get through the visitation and funeral, although deep down she knew her heart was on the brink of breaking. She could hardly imaging having Thanksgiving without her father. But she would go to be there for her mother and do her part for the class reunion. It was scheduled for Saturday evening at the Reading Sheraton hotel.

"Sandy, would you get me the large suitcase from Tom and Tracie's?" Sue shouted toward the living room. "I put it on the community calendar so they know I'll be coming for it."

Sue assumed he had heard her and continued laying out items on the bed.

When Sandy didn't answer she said again, "Sandy, did you hear me? Will you get the large suitcase from Tom and

A HORSE OF A DIFFERENT COLOR

Tracie's?" She began walking into the living room. "Where are you?" Sue huffed.

The front door opened and Sandy walked in, shaking off snowflakes.

"I believe we're getting a few flurries," he happily announced.

"Where were you?" Sue asked, annoyed.

"Just checked your oil and your tires. You should be good to go."

"Oh. Thanks. Would you—"

"But I need to look up the recommended maintenance schedule for your timing belt. I can't remember if it's 80,000 or 100,000 miles, not that we can do anything about it before you leave tomorrow. Just good to know."

Sandy made his way across the living room to their second bedroom, which Sue insisted become his office and for him to start his own business.

"Did you need something?" he asked.

"Oh never mind. I'll get the suitcase. Did you take the folding chairs back to the shed?" Sue queried. She started to pull on her coat to prepare to go to Tom and Tracie's.

Sandy didn't answer.

"Did you take the folding chairs back to the shed?" Sue asked, louder now.

"Uh, no. I'll do it later," Sandy mumbled distractedly from his office.

"It's not good for those chairs to be out in the weather, especially if it's snowing," Sue growled.

On her way out the door she picked up a key to the shed. Coming to four folding chairs she grabbed two per arm, awkwardly balancing them as she lumbered across the Close.

"His idea of later is never," Sue complained as she arrived at the shed.

She undid the lock of the double doors to open the right side. The left one swung open with it. A nose nearly touched

A HORSE OF A DIFFERENT COLOR

her face.

Sue screamed. Then backed up quickly, stumbling over the chairs still in her arms. She fell with a thud, all four chairs toppling with her. Her left arm caught in the tangle. Pain shot through. In a fog of fright and hurt she cried out. "Sandy!" Light from a nearby lamppost shone across the open doors, enough to spill into the shed. The pony stood mutely within.

"The horse is in the shed," Sandy spoke into his cell phone to John, "and I'm taking Sue to the hospital. No, I have no idea how it got there."

Sue left for Pennsylvania a day later than planned. Her left arm was in a sling to keep it immobilized.

In their earlier plan, she was to have gone solo for Thanksgiving weekend. Sandy had managed to extricate himself by pointing to his long maintenance checklist. He knew he was being a bit selfish to avoid the first holiday after Dr. Young's death, but Sandy also knew that the family was better off focusing on themselves, and he was a long way from belonging to that family. He could have visited his own mother who lived near Sue's parents, but she was slipping into a demented state and might not even know that he was there. He thought it was better simply to stay at the Close and spend time with paint brushes and ratchet sets, things that didn't have opinions or emotions.

Now he was behind the wheel and they were racing up the highway toward a world of grief he preferred not to know.

Sue tossed her cell phone into her purse.

"That is so like her! First a Sunday funeral. Now she says she won't come to Thanksgiving dinner at Mom's, that we're all supposed to crowd into her duplex in Reading."

They were approaching the Pennsylvania border.

"Stacy can't come to Mom's because of the baby. Dawn is living there in the duplex—again, I might add–keeping her

A HORSE OF A DIFFERENT COLOR

own daughter's baby. That will make how many generations squeezed into that place for the meal? Let me count, Mom, Stacy, Dawn, oh, we have to skip Dawn's daughter who's back to living on the street, and then her illegitimate daughter Tessa. I count that as five. You would think our family came from back woods degenerates. And don't be saying we need to take a picture for posterity. I don't want my picture taken with all of them."

"If Thanksgiving dinner is at Stacy's then you don't have to worry about preparing all the food. I should think that would be a relief," Sandy reasoned.

"Oh, you don't understand. She said it was fine for us to bring as much food as we wanted. She was only going to make a turkey. She said she would pick up some sides from the deli. The *deli!* This is Thanksgiving, not some Fourth of July picnic!" Sue steamed.

"Honey, I know you and your sister have had some words, but could you get along for my sake, for your father's sake, this one day?" Mrs. Young sheepishly asked her younger daughter.

Sue, Sandy, and Mrs. Young were on the road heading into downtown Reading with Sandy at the wheel.

"We know that Stacy's situation is far from agreeable, but we do want to be together and—"

"I'll be kind, Mother," Sue snapped.

When they arrived, the house teemed with tots and grownups in various stages of dress, some with very little covering. Most of the grownups displayed ink-decorated arms, ankles and bosoms. Sandy and Mrs. Young dodged a flying ball as they carried in covered casserole dishes and portable Pyrex pans.

"Yoo-hoo, we're here!" Sue shouted above the din.

"Hi!" a plump, sweatshirt-wearing Stacy greeted them, coming into the living room from the kitchen.

A HORSE OF A DIFFERENT COLOR

"Here, let me show you where to go with those," she said to Sandy and Mrs. Young. She led them into the kitchen. "You're probably wondering why you don't smell turkey."

The three arrivals now noticed the lack of cooking aromas.

"We only started thawing the turkey last night. Probably should have started it yesterday morning. It's still in the sink, but we've got it in warm water, so maybe we can still get it in the oven.

"Honey, it takes hours to cook a turkey. Did you get a whole bird or just a breast?" Mrs. Young asked.

"A whole 20-pound bird. The Rescue Mission was offering them last week and Dawn went down and got one. Well, maybe we'll have to eat side dishes instead. What did you bring?"

"We made your favorite whipped sweet potatoes and we brought green bean casserole with onion rings. That one will have to be broiled to crisp up those onion rings. And we cooked Cope's corn. Soaked it overnight and stewed it this morning. And we brought some potato rolls."

"Martin's potato rolls?"

"Sure. I know you and your clan like those."

"We love them. Thanks, Mom," Stacy leaned over and kissed her mother's cheek. Mrs. Young smiled.

Sue and Sandy stood in the kitchen watching the events unfold.

"Looks like you really have a doozey there, Sue," Stacy said, turning her attention to Sue's arm.

"Yeah," Sue replied.

Silence followed.

"Well, come on in and take a load off. Tom will be back shortly. He ran out to the convenience store. We forgot to get soda."

Indignation roiled in Sue's gut.

The four returned to the living room where the remaining sitting surfaces were cluttered with children's toys and

A HORSE OF A DIFFERENT COLOR

accessories. Stacy began removing the detritus, tossing things on the floor.

"Here, have a seat," Stacy waved like a casually-dressed game show hostess.

"You knew we were coming. Couldn't you at least have cleaned up?" Sue muttered under her breath.

"I would have cleaned things up a bit but Tessa got sick and we all had to take turns with her last night. "

"Hi!!" Shouted one of the children in the room. The three-year old's innocent pleasure took the adults by surprise.

"Well, hello there!" Mrs. Young replied sweetly. "What is your name?"

"Devon?" the child said, suddenly shy and unsure of himself.

"Well, Devon, do you know what day it is?" Mrs. Young continued.

"Thanksgiving!" the child answered, gleefully.

"And do you know what that means?" Mrs. Young asked.

"Turkey!!" the child boasted.

"We've been telling them that Thanksgiving is turkey day. I guess we should have told them that we might not have..." Stacy started to explain in perfect composure and by the end of the sentence was in tears. She retreated to the kitchen, starting to sob.

"Oh Honey!" Mrs. Young was on her feet, following her daughter into the kitchen. "It's going to be alright. Look, we will have plenty to eat...." Mrs. Young placed a tender hand on her daughter's cheek.

"Got the soda," Tom declared as he burst in through the door. "Oh, hi," he said, glancing at Sandy and Sue. "Welcome. I hope you're making yourselves at home. No Shangri-La, but it works."

Tom offered his left hand to Sandy since his right arm was occupied with two 12-pack boxes of Pepsi cans. "Sorry about the south paw," he said as Sandy rose and shook Tom's left

A HORSE OF A DIFFERENT COLOR

hand with his own left.

"Yeah, we forgot about thawing the bird. Sorry to say I don't think we'll be having turkey at two o'clock like we thought. Maybe by six or seven tonight though. Stick around and we'll have some. Hi Sue," Tom said and continued into the kitchen. "Mrs. Young, always good to see you," Tom said as he brushed by the two women.

"Happy Thanksgiving, Tom," Mrs. Young offered, trying to lift the mood.

"You ladies having a nice conversation?" he chirped as he leaned over an open refrigerator door to load in his soda cans.

"We are *not* staying until seven o'clock tonight," Sue quietly sneered to Sandy in the living room. "I should have figured Stacy would pull something like this."

"I don't think she did this to upset anyone. She just forgot," Sandy tried.

Sue shot him an indignant look.

"Oh, there's Tessa," Stacy chirped as she entered the living room and saw her daughter, Dawn come down the steps holding the baby. Dawn looked nearly young enough that this could have been her own child rather than grandchild.

"How are you doing, baby girl?" Stacy chirped toward the baby, meeting her grown daughter and great grandchild at the bottom of the stairs.

"She's better. Slept until a few minutes ago. She certainly didn't sleep last night. Had us all awake. But she's some better. No fever. And I think she might keep some formula down. I want to try," Dawn said, heading toward the kitchen to prepare a bottle.

"Is everything squared away with the custody hearing?" Sue asked.

"We have one final step, but the lawyer thinks it's just a formality," Dawn answered from the kitchen.

"That's as much as I want to know," Sue mumbled to

A HORSE OF A DIFFERENT COLOR

herself.

Over the next hour Mrs. Young, Sue and Sandy made polite conversation among the various people wandering about the duplex. The weather and road construction seemed safe subjects but quickly wore thin. Everyone seemed intent on focusing on the football game on the large flat screen television.

"So what about your arm, Aunt Sue?" Dawn asked.

"This is all because of a horse," Sue answered, patting her sling, disgust in her voice.

"A horse?" Dawn exclaimed.

"A horse got loose from some farm and started showing up at our Close a few months ago. One of the members took pity on it and put it in our community shed thinking the horse couldn't survive in the cold. But of course, nobody said anything, and Monday when I went to take some chairs back to the shed," Sue cut a look at Sandy, "when I opened the door, this horse stared back at me. Scared the tar out of me. I backed up and fell with the folding chairs, twisted my arm. A fracture in my mid clavicle radius. Hurt like a devil. Four weeks immobilized before I can get six weeks of therapy to strengthen and stabilize my shoulder."

"What are they doing about the horse?"

"That will be decided at our next community meeting," Sue stated flatly.

Isn't this the weekend of your high school reunion?" Stacy asked. "Where are you having it?"

"At the Sheraton." Sue answered.

"Bill Blankenship runs that now," Stacy said. "You remember him. He was in your class, I think."

"Yeah. You would think he might have retired, but I guess he wants to put in his time so he can collect a nice retirement check. Can't say as I blame him," Sue replied.

"Lucky you won the lottery," Stacy quipped.

Sue went stone cold. This was forbidden conversational

A HORSE OF A DIFFERENT COLOR

territory, even more than Stacy's teenage dramas, multiple husbands, or current unmarried status.

"You don't have those worries," Stacy continued, sucking down Pepsi from a can.

"Yes, we were lucky," Sue said, with a carefully calibrated tinge of sarcasm.

"So you two live in, what do you call it, an intentioned community?"

Mrs. Young jumped in. "Stacy, how about we see to the green bean casserole. I know your little ones must be hungry."

Mrs. Young rose and pulled her older daughter into the kitchen.

Tom, unfamiliar with family protocol on taboo subjects, took up the topic.

"Yeah, Stacy tells me you got lucky with the Powerball there in Maryland. A cool $6 million. That's more than I can fathom. More than I could spend," Tom laughed. "Sue, I understand that you didn't approve of Sandy's playing the lottery until he announced he'd won." Tom chuckled, freely.

"Sometimes life turns out in ways you can't predict," Sue replied to Tom. She rose to go to the bathroom.

Dinner turned out to be sliced deli turkey on potato rolls, casserole sides and canned cranberry sauce. The turkey sat mockingly in the kitchen sink. Sue, Sandy and Mrs. Young left at 5:00 p.m. shuttling their empty dishes out to the car.

"You get a pass," Tom said to Sue, indicating her injured arm as Sandy and Mrs. Young toted the empties. Sue smirked at his innocent remark.

Chilly hugs were offered and a moment later the three were sailing down the road in various states of relief to be done with Thanksgiving.

"Hello Winnie," Sue said, offering a pre-printed nametag to her classmate. Sue stood behind a table in front of the

A HORSE OF A DIFFERENT COLOR

hotel ballroom. A banner over the door read, *Welcome Wilson High Class of 1971!*

"Hi Sue. Thanks for being here. What happened to you?" Winnie asked, indicating Sue's arm.

"I fell in a horse accident."

"A horse accident? I didn't know that you rode," Winnie asked, curiously.

"Long story," Sue quipped.

"Oh. Well. How are your parents?" Winnie asked.

"I guess you didn't hear. My dad died last month. Cardiac arrest at the breakfast table. He went quickly. Shocked us all."

"I am so sorry, Sue. I didn't know. Your father led our school district through some tough storms. He knew how to survive school board politics. I know he retired years ago but he's still remembered fondly. I'm just sorry I missed his obituary. When was his funeral? I would have come."

"It was on November 3rd."

"Oh. Was that a Sunday?" Winnie asked, beginning to scowl. "People don't usually have funerals on Sundays. I guess that's another reason I missed it."

"My sister had appointments the entire week, so we had to hold his funeral on a Sunday." Sue explained, hostility in her voice.

"Oh, I see. How *is* Stacy?"

Sue looked up the corridor hoping for someone else's arrival so she could defer her answer. "Fine. She's fine."

"You know my brother dated her. It's a good thing they didn't get married. He's on his third marriage and she's on her third, or fourth?"

"I don't count anymore," Sue answered, mortified to be having this conversation. With all the events leading up to the reunion, Sue hadn't stopped to think that she would be fielding questions about her family.

Winnie continued. "Hey, I meant to ask you. Has Rowan Pope ever shown up at any of our reunions? Our exchange

A HORSE OF A DIFFERENT COLOR

student from Holland?"

"I don't think so," Sue answered.

"You should see what he wrote in my yearbook." Winnie pulled her yearbook from a large tote bag and slid it across the registration table and opened it. *To a lovely lady I would like to know more. You're in my dreams. Rowan.* Winnie giggled as the seventeen year-old she had once been.

Sue tried to disguise her rancor. "I don't think you'll be lucky enough to see him this time around, either. After all, he's probably got grandchildren somewhere back there."

"I heard he started a rock band back in Holland and toured throughout the U.S."

"I never heard that."

"He was really interested in me. I should have pursued him."

"How is your husband?" Sue asked.

"Oh he's fine. He had to take our grandson to hockey practice tonight. Hockey season's upon us. Oh look! There's Sharon!" Winnie announced, closing her yearbook and tucking it into her tote before disappearing into the ballroom.

Alone at the registration table Sue leafed through her own yearbook searching for one particular entry. *To Sue, a lovely lady I would like to know more. You're in my dreams. love, Rowan.* The pig, she thought. He wrote the same thing to Winnie, although he did sign mine *love,* she noted.

Sue looked up to see a man walking toward her. "Martin? I didn't know you were coming. I don't believe I have you on my list."

"Sue!" Martin boomed. Ignoring the table between them he reached across and pulled Sue into a generous hug.

"Yow," Sue winced, reflexively pulling away from the embrace and re-arranging her arm.

"What in the world did you do?" Martin chuckled, now seeing her sling.

"It's quite a story," Sue replied. "Has to do with a horse."

A HORSE OF A DIFFERENT COLOR

"A horse?"

A stream of classmates began to arrive, squeezing out Martin. Sue checked off names and distributed badges as groups flocked toward the ballroom, abuzz with school days stories.

At 6:30 p.m. Sue decided to abandon the registration table. Even though she had four unclaimed name tags, registration was supposed to have ended at 6:00 p.m. She started to leave, and then on impulse, grabbed a blank tag and magic marker and inscribed it with a name.

"How about the time the drum major brought the band onto the field before it was actually half time!" One of the female classmates roared. "Sue, over here!" Trixie Waffler yelled and motioned. Sue joined the music group from Wilson High. She had played the flute through her high school years, in marching band, concert band, and pit orchestra for the annual musicals.

"What'd you do to your arm?" Trixie asked.

"It's a long story." Sue waved off the question.

"Classmates! If I can have your attention. It's time to take your seats. Dinner is about to be served," Jack Kettering boomed into the podium microphone.

People milled about the banquet tables looking for places to sit, Indian corn bundles decorating each table. Suddenly the lights went dim.

"Oooh," people said.

"That's just to get your attention," Jack said. "We're going to have our blessing and then the meal will be served. After the meal we have two presentations and a game during which time the cash bar will remain open. I ask that you drink responsibly. We've lost three classmates since 1971 due to drunk drivers. Arthur, will you give the blessing?" Jack motioned to one of the men dressed in a suit and tie. The man stood and prayed.

A HORSE OF A DIFFERENT COLOR

"Mom?" Sandy called, letting himself in the back door. "It's me, Sandy." The place seemed quiet until he heard voices in another part of the house. He crossed the kitchen and into the den, the room his father had converted from a garage. The room had been a bone of contention between his mother and father, his father preferring to keep the garage. Even if it were a single-car affair, it provided him one place he could claim as his own. His wife had said that he could get one of those shelters she saw advertised in the mail circulars. That would keep the snow off the car, she said. True, but it wouldn't stop ice from forming, he replied. And more importantly, his father had no place to tinker and be alone.

"Mom?" Sandy called into the den. "I don't want to startle you."

"Sandy?" A crinkled old woman with shocks of white hair lay with an afghan draped across her body in a brown suede recliner. She didn't move.

"Mom." Sandy walked to her, leaned over and kissed her. "How are you doing?"

"Sandy."

"Right, Mom. What are you watching?" he asked, hating himself for such a lame question.

"Nothing," his mother smiled, keeping her eyes trained on her son.

"Looks like you've got Andy Griffith on," Sandy said.

"Um hm."

"Are the girls looking in on you?" Sandy knew that his sisters were shouldering the load of taking care of their 94-year old mother.

"Um hm."

"Have you had your dinner yet?"

"Um hm."

Sandy took a seat in his father's old recliner next to his mother and settled in for a long quiet evening.

A HORSE OF A DIFFERENT COLOR

"Oh!" Sue exclaimed, whirling around from a poster mounted on the ballroom wall and knocking into someone. Everyone at the reunion was up and playing a game, matching world events with the correct year. Sue had just placed "Robert Kennedy shot" on the 1968 page.

"Caught you," Martin said, helping her to rebalance.

Sue straightened up but then inexplicably wobbled into a tray of dinner dishes left on a stand, toppling it and herself.

Martin immediately reached for Sue's good arm. "My dear, you seem to have found the floor."

Her face flushed as she allowed Martin to help her back to her feet. "How embarrassing," Sue muttered.

"Not at all. Happens to the best of us. A drink or two and we—"

"I haven't had a drop to drink," Sue snapped. "Oh, look at my blouse." Sue looked down at her once white top to blotches of blueberry cobbler stains. "This has to be washed out," she declared and started for the nearest ballroom exit, dodging classmates enthralled in conversation and revelry. Martin followed.

A few minutes later Sue emerged from the Ladies Room.

"I see you've put yourself back together," Martin said, surveying her as she reappeared.

"I'm far from put back together. I'm afraid my blouse is ruined." Her blouse clung haphazardly to her body where she had splashed water in an attempt to address the stains.

"I look…" she paused, surveyed herself, and started to giggle. Her hair had come mostly undone from her headband, her blouse was a mess, and her left arm was in a sling. "I look…" Her giggle turned into a laugh, and then exploded into full side-splitting laughter. Martin began to laugh with her.

"I was going to say, 'Those were the days of our lives,' when I tacked up the Bobby Kennedy assassination date. It all seemed so sad. But now I see that *these* are the days of our

A HORSE OF A DIFFERENT COLOR

lives, when we can't walk straight, or keep ourselves upright." Sue continued to laugh. "Here I am, stone cold sober and I can't keep myself from falling down. You want to know how this happened?" She indicated her arm. "It was a horse. Someone put a horse in our garden shed. Scared the bejesus out of me. I was putting folding chairs back into the shed when this huge horse nose met me face to face. I was so startled I fell back and took the chairs with me. Hell of a thing. I nearly broke my arm." Sue wiped tears from her eyes.

"So that was your horse?" Martin asked.

"Not my horse. A stray that someone in our community thinks needs to be saved," Sue explained.

Martin began leading Sue along the corridor to a nest of seats away from the reunion gala.

"Here, let's sit down," he indicated.

Sue chose the sofa. Martin sat down with her.

"I just can't believe how we got here, I mean one minute we're eighteen and the next we're…" Sue began, then dropped off.

"I know. Time is a cruel mother. She'll tell you all is well, and then, BAM! You wake up and you're fifty years older," Martin said.

"And your hair has gone gray and your pants don't fit anymore," Sue added.

"No, not you, Sue. You look great. You look like time has truly stood still. I remember you as the adorable flute-playing, chess winning champion who made all the girls jealous because they wanted to be as pretty as you and as smart. No one had both beauty and brains. But you did."

Sue blushed. "You've got to be joking. Jealous of me?"

"You didn't know that?" Martin's eyes widened playfully. "You were the girl every girl wanted to emulate. You were the girl every boy wanted to date. And when you went to nursing school, I know that Bob Babbitt still thought that he could convince you to marry him."

A HORSE OF A DIFFERENT COLOR

"Oh Bob. Yeah, good old Bob. He really had a thing for me."

"A thing is right. You didn't have to hear him talk about you all the time. The entire brass section of the band knew every move you made because of the close tabs he kept on you. I know. I heard him."

"I can't say it didn't hurt me to learn that he was killed in Vietnam. You know he enlisted thinking that signing up would help his chances of being sent somewhere safe. I guess that didn't work."

"We lost fourteen of our classmates in the war."

"I know. I hear that every time we come to one of our reunions and they read the names and dates of the ones who have died. How come you decided to come this year?" Sue asked.

"I had the space on my calendar," Martin answered. "And I thought I might bump into you." He leaned into her shoulder with his own.

"Oh stop," Sue said, waving him off. "You and Mary Wetzel were always meant to be together. How is Mary?"

"She's fine. I mean, I guess she's fine. We divorced a few years ago."

"What? I hadn't heard that," Sue said.

"We needed to keep it on the q.t. Her work on City Council is pretty public. She didn't need extra drama the year she was running for re-election. We just quietly separated and then a couple of years ago made it official."

"I had no idea, Martin. I'm sorry."

"No need. We weren't really a couple for a long time. We raised the kids, got them through college, and then said what's the use of keeping up the charade. It's better this way. Feels more genuine. What about you? I heard you and your husband live in eastern Maryland in a fifty-five-plus community."

"It's a very small development. Eighteen of us sixty and

A HORSE OF A DIFFERENT COLOR

older. We have a cluster of cottages grouped around a central courtyard. We have a plan underway to build a small care center. We all had to bring a skill. I guess they wanted me for my medical training."

"And your brilliance," Martin said, taking her hand.

Sue looked down. Martin was holding her hand. She wasn't sure what to do. A cauldron of feelings swirled inside, caution and reason, guilt and pleasure, but mostly glee at finally being seen for her brains and beauty. Like Martin had said, she had both, but it had been a very long time since anyone paid attention to either, let alone both. Her heart ached more than she realized and Martin's hand felt warm and snug. Safe. She told herself, this is a lovely safe gesture.

They sat talking, both aware they were holding hands.

A HORSE OF A DIFFERENT COLOR

13

WASHINGTON SPRING

Mary Gray sat in an easy chair in her open floor plan living room, having decided that she could put off cleaning for another day. The Washington Spring Close in Parabar County was near the village of Parabar Shore. Apart from the founding sign at the start of the little hamlet with one stop light, a post office, a grocery and a locally-owned hardware store, she knew little about the area, which is why she was eager to begin her research. She opened a coffee table book given to her as a parting gift from a friend at The National Archives. *Parabar County, History and Legends.*

Parabar County acquired its name from two early British settlers, James Paramore and William Barclay. These men arrived to the New World in the mid 17th century, holding roughly the same ambition: to amass as much land as possible. The men helped each other as new immigrants frequently did, for weather and circumstances called for all hands to work in partnership more often than not. But as more men arrived and land grew less available, Barclay and Paramore forged a gentlemen's agreement to keep others from acquiring territory that the two viewed as

A HORSE OF A DIFFERENT COLOR

their own. And it was theirs in so far as they paid their taxes to Britain. Their larger concern was Indians, but their British muskets managed to convince a majority of the natives to clear out or face execution.

Mary Gray put down the book. She thought the settlers of Parabar County seemed no better or worse behaved than others who arrived on these shores. She wondered how many generations had passed from the original Barclays and Paramores in the mid-1600s. She made a mental note to check if any descendants still lived in the area.

"We can't have a horse living in our shed," Sue sneered. "Look at what happened to me," she lamely lifted her arm, still in a sling. "And it's against the rules."

The December meeting was underway.

"We can't leave the pony out in the elements during the winter weather. It will die of exposure," Angelika said.

"We're predicted to get a foot of snow in two days," Jimmy added.

Mary Gray wondered about that as she typed meeting minutes into her computer thinking that these weather things were always overblown.

"There is no regulation against keeping farm animals, not in our county and not in our community," John stated.

"Then we should have one," Sue countered. "That was a big oversight in our bylaws. I make a motion that Washington Spring prohibit the housing of horses and farm animals on our property, pets excluded, of course."

"Is there a second?" John asked.

"Wait a minute," Bryan spoke up. "I don't think we can make a motion until more of this horse business is cleared up. Has anyone done due diligence on where this animal came from? If it actually belongs to someone in Parabar Shore?"

"There's a motion on the floor," Sue reminded Bryan.

"Is there a second to the motion?" John asked.

A HORSE OF A DIFFERENT COLOR

No one spoke.

"Hearing none, the motion dies. Is there an answer to Bryan's question about ownership of this Assateague pony?"

Acton began. "The sheriff said he knew of no farm or stable other than Jackson's that might claim ownership. And since it's not Jackson's we should take the sheriff's suggestion to run an ad on the local AM station and in the Annapolis newspaper."

"I assume this has not yet been done," John said. Nobody answered. "May we have a group consensus to run this ad both on radio and in the newspaper?"

Heads nodded. "Daily for one week?" Heads continued to nod.

"I think we should run it for two weeks." Sue added.

"If we receive no response in one week, are we in agreement to run the ad for an additional week?"

Heads nodded once more. "We will take the money from petty cash. Meanwhile, is the pony safe in the shed?" John asked.

"Yes." Angelika answered. "I brought in wood shavings for bedding and I have a delivery of hay coming. You have my word I will clean the shed each day." She did not wish to say that the items in the shed were smelling like a barnyard. People's stored Christmas decorations were going to be aromatic, to say the least. It would be better to get them out as soon as possible.

As though reading Angelika's mind, Jimmy offered, "I will deliver everyone's Christmas items this week."

Jimmy had no experience with horses or farm animals but he liked the idea that this wild thing could be part of their community, and so he conspired with Angelika to keep the pony in the shed.

"Cleaning day," Mary Gray announced as she hoisted the vacuum cleaner from Larry Long's closet in WSC-12.

A HORSE OF A DIFFERENT COLOR

"Thanks for letting me borrow it."

"Sure, anytime," Larry replied. "Here, let me carry it over to your place for you. You don't need to lug that all the way across the Close."

Mary Gray smiled brightly. A man who volunteered to help. What a pleasant and refreshing response. She picked up the cleaning attachments and the two walked over to her cottage.

Mary Gray could never ask for help from her former husband. If she did, he either refused her request or did it with such disdain that it became easier to do things herself. He was a bright man, handsome, and occasionally funny which attracted her when they were young, but he had turned worse than surly. Getting a job proved difficult. With an anthropology degree he tried first to work for a historical foundation and then to teach high school, but these didn't pan out. He had then taken a job at Sears selling appliances and many an evening after work he would tell a funny story about a new wife naively inquiring about washing machine features. In 1965 Frigidaire introduced the first automatic ice maker which quickly became the gold standard, yet it took Kenmore, Sears' line of appliances, some time to catch up and produce the same. In the early 1970s this put her husband at a distinct disadvantage since shoppers were looking for modern gadgets to keep up with their neighbors. Some years into their marriage the late evening glass of wine they shared turned into a bottle and sometimes two, and his funny stories degenerated into gripe sessions. It took awhile for Mary Gray to catch on that she was not the one finishing the bottles and that these dark tales were fueling her husband's anger and justifications.

The divorce was not easy. He blamed her for their lack of children, which wasn't entirely false. Early in their marriage she prayed not to get pregnant. She was busy building her career. When she learned about the Pill she asked her family doctor if he could prescribe it for her. She didn't discuss it with her husband because he was never in a mood to have that kind of conversation. Her career was solid and moving forward while he languished and complained. In the end, they divided their possessions in equal parts, both moving from the place they had lived.

"Here you go," Larry said, setting down the vacuum cleaner. "Call me when you're through and I'll come back and get it."

Shutting the door behind him, Mary Gray burst into tears. All of her life she was the one to do the work, constantly having to justify that work to men who saw her only as an impediment to their advancement. She was eminently qualified to run research departments, to advise directors, and to lead esteemed causes, and here she was bawling over a man who cared enough to help her by shuttling the community vacuum cleaner. Behind her front door, she dropped to her knees and cried. Pulling a crumpled tissue from her pocket, she looked down at the floor and for once was glad for entryway carpeting.

At the Parabar Shore post office the next day, Mary Gray asked the postmaster if any Paramores or Barclays remained in the area.

"Richard Barclay lives out on Millbeam Road. No Paramores I can think of," he replied.

"Would Richard Barclay be related to the founder William Barclay?"

"I believe so. I've been here all my life and as far as I know, he has been, too. He'd be in his 80s. Lost his wife last year. Children long grown and gone. Why do you ask?"

"I'm starting to compile research on the county, its founding and history."

A HORSE OF A DIFFERENT COLOR

"Old Richard can tell you a story or two. He still has a sharp mind," the postmaster said. "It's a slow day. Let me make a call and see if he would let you pay him a visit. Is that what you had in mind?"

"Yes, exactly."

Twenty minutes later Mary Gray pulled up to a home that dated back to the 1700s. She had to drive along a lane of hard-packed dirt and ice that wound to-and-fro until the pine trees on both sides opened wide to reveal a two-story stone house. A beagle raced up to her car in greeting. About then, the front door swung open and a compact elderly man stepped out to call off the dog. The dog paid him no mind, baying at Mary Gray who remained in her car. The man came toward her and grabbed the dog by the collar, displaying unusual strength for a man of his size and age.

"It's safe," he yelled while he walked ahead of Mary Gray's car pulling the dog with him. "You head into the house. Be in there in two shakes. Should've put Nellie in her kennel before you came," he yelled over his shoulder.

After he disappeared behind the house, dog in tow, Mary Gray followed his directions and let herself in through the front door. Inside could hardly have been a greater contrast to the day. Outside a crisp wind blew in spite of brilliant sunshine. Inside was dark, warm, and silent. The house smelled of musty books and bacon grease. As she turned back toward the front door, she could see that the windows across the front of the house had wavy glass which distorted the view, causing her to wonder if the glass could be original. She noticed heavy draperies on both sides and then, straining to look out the windows, realized that the house faced inland which seemed odd since the house must be close to the Chesapeake Bay. She turned to look along a narrow central corridor which terminated at a closed door. She then looked up and saw above a simple antique fixture, probably converted from oil to electric. About then the interior

A HORSE OF A DIFFERENT COLOR

corridor door swung open. The man ambled toward her in the tiny vestibule. Age had compressed his frame so that he teetered side-to-side as he walked, his legs bowed. His head was bald but his salt & pepper brows had grown thick and wild over his piercing blue eyes.

"Nellie'll get you every time. Sorry not to take care of that. Now let me take your coat and you come sit down and tell me what it is you want to know," Richard began. He indicated the room on his right with an old sofa and a couple of chairs covered mostly in newspapers, magazines and old mail.

"Sorry for the mess. Didn't expect company, but that's alright. I'm glad you're here." He took her coat with one hand and with the other shoved some newspapers together and threw them into a rough stack on the floor by a stone fireplace.

"Here, have a seat," he said, indicating the sofa. He disappeared for a moment and when he reappeared he took one of the chairs that for all its worn spots appeared to be the one he used on a regular basis.

"How about start by telling me your name?"

"Mary Gray Walterson. Please call me Mary Gray. I live at Washington Spring outside of Parabar Shore. It's the new community of people who are--"

"Oh I know about you. Your story was in the paper. Been thinking that I should ride over to tell you hello. I've been in these parts all my life and while I hate to see change, I reckon we have to live with it, and why not at least welcome the kind of change that improves things. I hear your little community has been a model for people helping older people. I think that's right nice. And how did you become associated with this group? You don't look old to me, if I may say."

Mary Gray blushed slightly and pulled her skirt a bit more over her knees.

"I saw a notice in the newspaper about this experimental

A HORSE OF A DIFFERENT COLOR

community and since I had recently retired, I decided to join." She paused.

"What sort of work did you do?"

"I was an archivist for the National Archives and Records Administration."

"Oh, that sounds mighty interesting. How did someone such as yourself end up there?"

"The quick resume is Middlebury College as a history major, then Brown University for graduate school in public humanities, after which I received a post-doc appointment at the National Archives in Washington DC and later transferred to the College Park location."

"You're a little far from home out this way."

"I thought about where I would go when I retired. Like most people, I got tired of the traffic and the high cost of living. I was thinking of moving north to Vermont where I have some family, but when I saw the notice in the newspaper about this experimental community, I decided to apply."

"Apply...so you had to be assessed before you could join?"

"Something like that. You have to contribute a skill for the good of the community and be willing to downsize to 1,100 square feet of living, which means sharing items we hold in common," Mary Gray explained.

"Such as?"

"Well, large cookware, luggage, vacuum cleaners, ironing boards, that sort of thing. Each unit has a washer and dryer so we do have some personal conveniences. Were you thinking you wanted to join?"

"Me? Oh no! Just look at all I have." He indicated the abundant piles around the room. "I'm afraid I am here to stay." Then, with a fresh voice he began. "I should have introduced myself, for which I apologize. My name is Richard Barclay. And you are Mary Gray Walterson." He reached across and shook her hand. His was soft with age; hers was rough and chapped from the weather.

"With that name of yours, I would say you come from the South."

"My father was born and raised in Texas. He went to school at A&M for geology and then went to work for Simcorp Mining. After several years they sent him to Vermont where he met my mother who was from there, and the rest, as they say, is history."

"So you have blood of two kinds running in you, then."

"Yes, I suppose that's why Maryland seemed like a natural place for me to land, not exactly north, not exactly south." Mary Gray chuckled. "My mother's family could never accept that my father always wore metal-tipped boots. They saw him as rather unrefined. How about you tell me about your family, Mr. Barclay?"

"Oh, I believe that other people's families are much more interesting than my own," he began. And then he proceeded to talk for the next hour and a half about his ancestors.

From his litany of details, Mary Gray learned that Richard Barclay was a descendant of the original William Barclay.

"William Barclay homesteaded on the land where we are sitting. He was a pioneer of these parts. His very first shelter was more of a hut than a house, although it didn't last long. Indians set it ablaze. Nanticokes," Richard added, as if in confidence. "But the stern William Barclay would not be deterred and loading his munitions he and a group of others, probably including Paramore who had also been burned out, stalked the Nanticokes and fired on them. The pioneers killed all but one young brave, a boy about ten years old who had a birth mark like a mask over his right eye. The pioneers left him alive to return to his tribe and tell of the supremacy of the white men. Barclay and company's plan seemed to work and before long each of the settlers busied himself building a new shelter. The men helped one another and grouped their

A HORSE OF A DIFFERENT COLOR

huts together as a way of providing protection. One man always took sentry duty since Indian skirmishes were not uncommon," Richard Barclay explained.

"Within three years the men had tamed enough territory for each to claim his own land. Barclay and Paramore acquired as much coastal land as possible. They knew this would allow them to control supplies coming and going along the inlets. Both men eventually sent for their wives and children back in Britain. Barclay set out building a log cabin with three rooms, two sleeping rooms and one main room. The foundation of this house was built on the same site as that log cabin. And the reason his house, as well as the log cabin, faced inland was not to deny a pretty view, but entirely for safety from storms rolling up the Bay. That cabin lasted more than fifty years," he said, "until a storm ripped through and took it down."

Richard spoke fondly of the third generation Barclays who built the stone home where he lived, saying that they dwelled long and happily in that space, raising a brood of children, several of whom ennobled themselves by fighting for the Continental Army under George Washington.

When talk came to the War Between the States--as Richard called it--he further disclosed names of Barclays who went to their deaths in defense of the right for Southern states to govern themselves. The contemporary Barclay neither condoned nor opposed their position. He did mention that the original land holdings were far more considerable prior to *that War*. The family's debts which resulted from *that War* mounted during Reconstruction years and therefore required large portions of property be sold, and at shamefully low prices. What he said next surprised her.

"It was Northerners who swooped in to make some of these purchases. This did the situation no good seeing as how the Barclays understood the land and cared for it, and those others cared nothing for it, but that it would make them

A HORSE OF A DIFFERENT COLOR

money," Richard declared.

Mary Gray couldn't help but see the irony in his comment, since the original Barclay had wrested the land from the natives for his own lucrative purposes.

"The third generation Barclay built the stone house where we're sitting. This was my grandfather eight generations back. Edmund Barclay established a saw mill on the land. He milled lumber for every purpose including for ships. Edmund Barclay tried his hand at shipbuilding for a few years until he realized that other men understood better than he the engineering side of the business. Edmund Barclay decided to stick with what he knew, which was wood. Perhaps because he understood that the first basic property of wood was that it burned, he built his own home of stone. Others laughed at a saw mill operator building in stone, but when their own houses were blown down or burned to the ground, Edmund Barclay reaped the benefits as they built back, again with wood, something Edmund could never understand."

Richard spoke of his direct grandfather. "Why, my granddaddy was born in this house in 1866, just after *that War*. His father had survived *that War* whose homecoming produced this final child, the only boy, my granddaddy. My granddaddy grew up working in wood like the earlier generations, supplying lumber for the expanding economies in places like Baltimore and Washington.

"This house has been altered over the years. The original contained four rooms, two up and two down. Would you like to see the upstairs?" Not giving Mary Gray a chance to answer he withdrew the invitation. "Maybe next time," he explained. "My wife died last year and I haven't exactly kept an orderly house."

Mary Gray lightly asked, "Who will next inherit the house?"

Richard Barclay waved her off. "That remains to be seen."

While he was speaking, she noticed various family

A HORSE OF A DIFFERENT COLOR

photographs mounted on the walls and sitting on bookshelves. Some looked as though they dated back to the first use of cameras. In many of the photos people were clustered in front of the house, men in suits and hats, women in bonnets holding babies against their hips, and children of all sizes in various states of mood and pose.

"Ms. Walterson, you have kindly let me talk your ear off about my family. I hope that you will excuse my obvious lack of civility. My dear wife would have had my hide my not offering you a warm beverage or something to eat. May I do that now?"

"Oh, thank you, Mr. Barclay. Please call me Mary Gray. I'm afraid that I should not hold you any longer. I have taken your entire afternoon. And you have been the perfect gentleman," she assured him as she rose from the sofa.

"Next time you will tell me more about your family, I hope."

"That would be lovely," she answered. As she stood, she wondered if she should remind him of her coat. He seemed not to catch on. "My coat?" she suggested.

"Oh, my manners. Yes, of course, your coat." He disappeared for quite a while, during which time Mary Gray busied herself by examining the photographs. Mr. Barclay seemed to be the genuine article of history. He was lovely, if lonely, a feeling she deeply understood. About the time he emerged Mary Gray had spotted a photograph of a very old Indian chief standing by a tree.

He helped her into her coat.

"You promise you will return?" he asked.

"Of course, Mr. Barclay. You have so much to share and I have so much to learn."

That evening Mary Gray launched an online search of the local Indian tribes. She began reading about the Nanticoke Indians mentioned by Richard Barclay. She discovered that

A HORSE OF A DIFFERENT COLOR

the Nanticokes belonged to the Algonquian tribes, who were in alliance with the Powhatan Confederacy.

The Powhatan Confederacy constituted several Algonquian tribes united by Chief Powhatan, an early seventeenth-century ruler. Powhatan controlled tribes throughout most of eastern Virginia and portions of Maryland. Chief Powhatan's favorite daughter was Pocahontas. He allowed her to marry two different men. The second man was John Rolfe, a Jamestown settler. Their marriage was meant to ensure peace between the Powhatan and British Empires. Unfortunately, both she and her father died too soon. Pocahontas was 21. She had one son from John Rolfe named Thomas, through whom are numerous descendants.

Several years before Pocahontas married John Rolfe, she met the young man she married first, a brave named Kocoum. During her coming of age ceremony, she officially took the name Pocahontas. After the ceremony a powwow was held in celebration where she met Kocoum. After a courtship period, the two married. Pocahontas' father was happy with her choice, as Kocoum was the brother of a close friend, Chief Japazaw of the Potowomac tribe, and Kocoum was also one of his finest warriors. When rumors surfaced of the English wanting to kidnap Pocahontas she and Kocoum moved to his home village. While there, Pocahontas gave birth to a son. He was said to have been born with a birth mark like a mask around his right eye.

A HORSE OF A DIFFERENT COLOR

14

WASHINGTON SPRING

"John, you might want to see this," Curt Compton said, rising from the small hole he had made for his surveyor's stake. He held something in his hand. "Could just be kids stuff left lying here, or it could be something else," Curt said, hesitantly. He turned the object over in his hands, wearing away the loose dirt.

"What is it?" John asked.

Curt placed the object in John's hand. "Looks old. Looks Indian."

"Yeah, but you know what that means."

"You would have to have a full anthropological excavation. That wasn't my intention. As boys we used to come across stuff all the time, old arrowheads, bottle caps, even old medicine bottles. My brother once found a buffalo nickel. Didn't mean we had to do anything, like declare it," Curt said.

"Times have changed since we were kids," John said. "Seems like we might find something more or we might find nothing at all. You do surveying work all over this county.

A HORSE OF A DIFFERENT COLOR

Tell me, do you find a lot of this stuff?"

"Every now and then something turns up, sure."

John waited hoping for more explanation, but Curt didn't elaborate. "I thought you said when you excavated for your home sites that you found some things."

"We did, but I didn't want archeologists crawling all over creation and I needed to get the work done on schedule, ahead of schedule, if possible."

Now Curt fell silent.

John continued. "They didn't find much. Or, I guess not much. I told the head of the excavation crew not to concern himself with anything that might turn up."

"Did you have to pay him a little more?"

"No, I just paid him on time and with cash."

"That helped."

"What helped was that he was Mexican, or Latino, as that goes. He had his own set of worries."

"You going to use him to do this job here?"

"Probably, except his brother took over the business, or cousin, I can't keep it straight. I believe the boy's gone back to Mexico."

"Same outfit though?"

"Yeah, same outfit."

The men finished their conversation while walking back to the Close.

"Now look, John. What you're holding is kind of interesting, but I wouldn't worry too much. Looks like you can handle what little may be out there."

"That's right, Curt. I'll handle it."

Emptying his pockets that night, John removed the object that Curt Compton had found. Taking it to the kitchen sink he snapped on the overhead light. Thumbing off some of the remaining dirt, he could see the object still had a tight weave with a partially attached loop. The whole thing fit easily into

A HORSE OF A DIFFERENT COLOR

his palm, and the base looked like a big walnut. Gently, he shook it and thought he heard pebbles. The scene with Curt made him wonder yet again if he had made the right decision when the house in which he was standing was built. He remembered saying to Manuel, "Don't let anything stop you from getting the job done." Manuel didn't and the excavation work came in on time. John was proud of the fair-weather start to his project. Their project. He and Pauline had worked on the designs and pored over site plans, her cautioning, "If we don't have it right on paper, it will never be right standing up."

Often when he glanced her way over his evening newspaper in their two-story colonial he could see the wheels turning in her mind, assessing every nook, cranny, cupboard, and door swing of their proposed cottages. She was a big fan of useful space. Everything had a purpose, else why have it. Early in their marriage when he sent her flowers for no reason but to be romantic, she thanked him and said, "If it's no occasion, then let's not do this." It took the wind from his sails and so he never did it again unless it were an occasion, as she advised.

Pauline had wanted the project to be done right and, if possible, on time, but she also would have sided with John's mother, had Pauline known that there were artifacts under their feet. Like her mother-in-law, Pauline had called congressional representatives to strengthen conservation regulations. The scenes seemed like replays of the dynamics John had witnessed between his parents.

In the early excavation days for Washington Spring, John knew there was something amiss because he saw two of Manuel's boys passing something between them. John watched as they handled the object. He could hear them speaking in Spanish, but eventually one of them tossed it aside into the dirt pile Manuel was making with the bulldozer.

A HORSE OF A DIFFERENT COLOR

When the crew went home a couple of hours later, John casually went to that now larger mound, and looking around to be sure he was alone, took a shovel and started to dig. After nearly an hour and finding nothing, he wondered why he was being so crazy, and nearly stopped. But curiosity and concern spurred him on, past the point of wondering how he would explain his sweat-soaked shirt. And then 20 minutes later he found the object. It was a stick wrapped in heavy twine with a braided cord connected to one end. A metal shaft attached to the opposite end indicated it might have been a hand-crafted weapon. John handled it with wary curiosity. Now that he found it, he wondered what to do with it. To reveal it would mean at least a delay in construction and perhaps a complete derailment of the project. In the gloaming he decided to bury the piece back in the pile and pretend it had never been found.

"We're making steady progress," John announced to Pauline when he returned home, swiftly heading upstairs to their bedroom where he could change clothes. He hoped his news would distract her from his rumpled appearance.

"You look as though you were the one doing the digging," Pauline announced. He had not been able to draw her off his trail. She followed toward the stairs he had just mounted.

"Just had to do a little follow up work. You know they'll be laying the utility lines. I wanted to be sure they followed instruction," John said, as if this explained everything.

"Are you concerned they aren't doing it right?" Pauline called up to John's disappearing body.

John didn't answer.

"Well, dinner's ready," Pauline announced and turned toward the kitchen.

Over the next days the excavation crew found more items including some pottery pieces, but they tossed them aside leaving them for the scrap heap. John had no idea how many items were uncovered because he only visited the site an hour

A HORSE OF A DIFFERENT COLOR

or two each day to check that operations were on track. But each evening before dark, after the crews had gone, John returned and began to collect any artifacts that were readily seen. He did this to prevent building inspectors and anyone else from identifying them as relics in need of protecting. At first John shoved them into a plastic grocery bag he found fluttering on the site, and tucked the bag under the seat of his car. In time he had eight objects, then twelve, and finally eighteen plus some broken pottery as the excavation finished. He ended up using a second shopping bag, shoving it also under his car seat. Had he not been so busy advancing the project, he would have launched an internet search about the random items. But time was money and the project was gaining momentum each day. The construction schedule had them breaking ground April 15 with a projected completion date of October 15. Six months. John knew it was a tight turnaround to build twelve houses. But the beauty of it was that the twelve millhouses were neat, compact, and identical, and crews could work on all the houses at one time. It was a model of efficiency.

And then Pauline began to lose her balance. She rode with him one afternoon to inspect the property. Excavation was complete, foundations poured, and the beginning shells of the cottages were emerging. John knew this would thrill Pauline to see such progress. But the dream of her botanical garden in the center courtyard of the community is what occupied her mind. Nothing but dirt and scrap would be visible that day, although she would have the vision of what it could be. As they walked from their car to the construction site, John recounted the details of the work being done. She nodded, but he could tell that she was only half-listening, no doubt imagining the beauty she could create.

And then she fell. Her mind went blank, her knees buckled and she fell forward, landing face down in the dirt. In a split second John was calling her name. He knelt down and

A HORSE OF A DIFFERENT COLOR

put his hand on the small of her back. Almost immediately Pauline came to, swiveling her head to look at him, a glazed look in her eyes.

With a bit of dirt in her mouth she mumbled, "What happened? Am I on the ground?"

"You took a spill," John explained. He quickly surveyed the area for obstacles and her body for any injuries. He waited to let her mind absorb what happened.

"Did I trip? I think I blacked out," Pauline said. "Help me up," she said, a bit more coherently

"How about rolling over first. See if you're okay."

Pauline rolled onto her back and looked up at John and the sky beyond him. It was a clear blue-sky day. She squinted her eyes and furrowed her brow, puzzled as to how this could have happened. Then, glancing around she seemed worried about who had seen her fall.

"I think I'm okay," she announced, flexing her legs and arms. "I'll hurt tomorrow; you can count on that," she said, as she wiped away dirt from her face and hair. "I'm getting up," she announced.

"Go slowly," John advised, as she rolled onto her knees, then rose to her feet. They both stood together.

"Whoa," she said, wobbling. "Are you feeling that?" she asked.

"Feeling what?"

"The earth swaying. Maybe it's me," Pauline said. She grabbed onto John's arm and took a small step forward. "Must be some kind of inner ear thing. I've heard of people having that problem."

The two walked tentatively toward the group of houses being built, both concentrating on her steps.

When they returned home Pauline felt better, but not steady. She had a list of things to do. At first she perched on a kitchen stool and flipped through the day's mail, but her head felt swimmy and her body uncomfortable on such a tall

A HORSE OF A DIFFERENT COLOR

chair. So she carefully moved to the couch and lay there like it was a Sunday afternoon.

John found her on the sofa when he checked an hour later. He had been on the phone in his office at home. She seemed to be napping so he slid a blanket over her from the back of the couch and let her sleep.

It was all but dark when she woke, a disorienting feeling, because Pauline never took naps during the day. She had been dreaming of days at University of Maryland. In her dream she and John were there as students, but as adult students, and the requirements for passing had become more stringent for anyone over fifty years old. "Senior stars" they were called, with stricter standards and she was worried they wouldn't be able to pass.

She shook this dream away and stared into the dim, familiar family room. The day's events seemed far out of reach. Maybe if she sat up she would feel better. John came in as she was arranging herself in an upright position.

"Are you awake? I let you sleep to see if you might sleep off your wobbles."

"Wobbles?" Pauline asked. "Was I wobbling?"

"You fell at the construction site," John tendered. "How do you feel?"

Pauline's mind searched for answers both to what had happened at the site and how she felt. Her mind was a sieve.

"Sore. I feel sore. My nose hurts. Did I whack it on something?"

"You took quite a spill, said you were dizzy, like it was an inner ear problem."

"Oh. Maybe," Pauline offered. "Let me try to get up." She rose from the couch without help and walked into the kitchen. "I think I'm just woozy. I need to get dinner on," she announced.

John followed her into the kitchen. They ate quietly, their conversation subdued as Pauline searched for a memory of

A HORSE OF A DIFFERENT COLOR

having fallen, and for that matter, going out to the construction site. These seemed completely lost, while the image of her and John studying furiously at University of Maryland continued in living color.

The next day Pauline had another blackout. She was at the grocery store comparing product labels when she slumped onto the floor. She woke up as a rescue team was tending to her on the tile floor. She insisted she was fine, saying it must be an inner-ear issue. The young technician nodded and kept on with his assessment. He asked her orientation questions that sounded vaguely familiar, like questions she might have had to know for her pending University of Maryland exams. She thought she answered accurately. And then the three-person rescue team all helped her stand up, and she thought that would be that. Everyone could go on with their work and she could get back to her shopping, although she had no memory of why she was there or what she had come to buy.

But the team had other ideas. Apparently, her answers were not correct, and Pauline was taken to the local hospital for a more complete exam. Did she want them to call anyone? Yes, call John.

The workup took two days, which included an overnight stay at the hospital, not what Pauline expected. John had come immediately and stayed, sleeping in his clothes on a chair in her hospital room. Both he and Pauline expected news of inner ear fluid which they knew could upset a person's balance. And so they were not in any way prepared for the news delivered by Pauline's assigned neurologist.

"We conducted a CT-scan of the brain. We were able to rule out bleeding, but what we found were several areas of abnormal growth. These tell us that further imaging would be a good idea. Since Johns Hopkins Hospital is close by, I'm going to recommend you to be transported to them so they can do a full evaluation."

Pauline and John stared at the doctor in silent shock.

A HORSE OF A DIFFERENT COLOR

"What about an inner ear problem?" Pauline finally managed.

"We did a complete exam of both ears and nothing indicates any abnormality. As I say, the areas of growth warrant further investigation."

"So you're saying it's my brain?"

"Yes, that seems to be the area of interest."

"My brain," Pauline repeated, as if to let the news sink into the very brain in question.

Pauline was transferred to Johns Hopkins Hospital in Baltimore for two days of tests. She asked one of her doctors why they were looking at her abdomen when she thought the problem was in her brain. The attending physician said that they were following general orders. When all the labs and scans were completed, Dr. Graves, her newly assigned oncologist came to her room with his news.

"Your radiology reports confirmed several abnormal growths in the occipital lobe of the brain." From a folder he pulled out a pre-made sketch of a brain to show Pauline and John, using a pen to make his points. "We think these abnormalities are causing your black outs. It's not uncommon for this to happen when this area is weakened or affected." He paused.

"When we see multiple growths this makes us suspicious that they are originating from somewhere else in the body. When we looked further we found additional growths. These are in the pancreas. We believe those are the primary that led to the brain." Dr. Graves paused.

"Do you think I have cancer?"

"Yes, that seems to be the case."

"Is it treatable?"

"Yes, although we're dealing with an advanced stage, I'm sorry to say." Again he paused.

"What stage?"

A HORSE OF A DIFFERENT COLOR

"I would say we're looking at a quite advanced stage. Stage 4."

Pauline and John were silent.

"Two courses of action are possible. The first would be a resection of the growths in the brain. We have some success at slowing the metastasis with surgery; however, the drawback is that this only addresses the brain. The pancreas won't benefit, so even with surgery of the brain the prognosis remains about the same. The second approach would be more comprehensive and the one I recommend, which is high doses of radiation and concurrent chemotherapy. Think of it as a one-two punch."

Pauline looked at John. He took her hand to encourage her. The doctor explained the course of treatments, lining out the steps she would take.

Released to home Pauline confided her diagnosis to her friend Louise.

"Did they tell you what your life will be like during the treatments? And how much time these will actually buy you?" Louise was a fountain of clear thinking, exactly what Pauline needed. "I know this is not what you want to hear, but would palliative care be a more humane option for you?"

Armed with Louise's pointed questions, Pauline and John returned to Dr. Graves. There they felt the full weight of Pauline's situation descend. Until then, talk was all about moving forward and laying out the next steps. No one had actually asked her if she even wanted to follow this plan. Under the scrutiny of her quality of life questions if electing radiation and chemotherapy, the doctor listed fatigue, vomiting, diarrhea, hair loss, neuropathy, and more. He named these side effects like a list of small unpleasantries, dealt with by adding a variety of medications. He hardly knew what to say when Pauline inquired into palliative care rather than following the course he had laid out for her. He said that

A HORSE OF A DIFFERENT COLOR

her cancer was aggressive. When pressed, he admitted that even his one-two punch might only buy her another six months, more if she were lucky. And if left untreated? The doctor frowned and said she may have two-to-three months during which time she could expect further black outs, mental confusion and diminishing coordination.

Pauline and John left the oncologist's office in silence. The drive home to Annapolis took an hour. After thirty minutes Pauline spoke.

"John, I don't want to do it. I don't want to go through radiation and chemotherapy only to be sick for the remainder of my life. I would rather die a natural and quick death, than unnatural and long. Do you understand?"

John said nothing, keeping his eyes on the road.

"Do you understand?" Pauline repeated, now with an edge in her voice.

"I hear you," he said.

"I cannot believe the timing of this. Here we are about to launch the community of our dreams. Next week the framing should be done. This is all just a bad dream. Tell me this is just a bad dream and I will wake up soon and everything will be fine. We will be picking out plumbing fixtures and worrying about timelines. John, tell me that!" Pauline was nearly screaming.

John pulled the car to the shoulder and turned off the engine. Traffic whizzed by. How many times had he passed cars pulled off on the side of the road, with only mild curiosity at what might be the cause of their trouble. And now it was his turn, their turn. They were talking about a few months of life left for Pauline. Months. Not years, and maybe not even months. Maybe weeks. It was too much to take in.

"I think we should take this one step at a time," John offered, as much for his own welfare as for Pauline's. How could one absorb news that altered every single thing in life, her life or his?

A HORSE OF A DIFFERENT COLOR

Pauline simply stared at John, her mouth open.

He knew not to say another word. A torrent of rage appeared behind Pauline's eyes.

"You have not one single solitary idea of what this means right now. Not one. You are such a self-absorbed son-of-a-bitch to tell me to take this one step at a time. You heard the doctor. These are my choices: I make myself miserable and die anyway, or I take what little time I have and live. I know that I will become more incapacitated, but at least I will still be me. I am taking that door, John. I elect Door Number 2. Door Number 2!" She announced this as though she were on Let's Make a Deal. "There is no Door Number 3, which is the one I want, where this is all a dream and I get to wake up fine and with everything on schedule for our move in. I want Door Number 3!"

John hung his head with a slight nod.

Pauline crossed her arms over her chest and declared, "I will call the boys when we get home."

John stared at his hands in his lap.

"Did you hear me? I will call the boys when we get home!" Her voice started to catch and then tears came. "I will tell them they need to know that I have a few months to live and that I will be planning...I will be planning...a party. Yes, a party. In fact, I will plan the sort of party I have always wanted that no one has ever seen fit to throw for me, a party with '60s music and dancing, and festivities like nobody's business. That's what I will do, John. I will have a party." She would take back control of her life if it killed her.

Pauline threw herself into party planning as though an avalanche of lists would distract her from the reality of her condition. Their sons, Ward and Sam had been summoned to get the news in person after the second visit to Dr. Graves. They were shocked, and left the house stating promises of keeping in close contact.

A HORSE OF A DIFFERENT COLOR

Pauline notified the doctor that she was not moving forward with his one-two punch and instead would be planning a different kind of punch, Whiskey Sour punch to be exact, a recipe she hadn't tasted since 1963. As to her health, she requested a referral to a local palliative care team. When she met with them she was relieved when they did not try to talk her out of her decision for a natural death, but she was also secretly disappointed. She wanted a fight. She wanted to tell someone why she did not want to die doubled over with her head in a toilet. When no one disputed her, she was sad. So she turned her frenetic energy toward her party planning. She knew it was selfish, but if this were her last hoorah, then why not go in style?

For several days their meals were a riot of nervous conversation. Pauline provided updates on her party plans and John on the community's construction. November 15 had been secured from the mayor's office for the official Washington Spring ribbon cutting. Pauline's party was planned for October 12th a month away, the Saturday of Columbus Day weekend. She wondered aloud who should be on the invitation list. And should they be told of the reason for the party? Pauline's last hoorah, she started to call it, but then with the date being close to Columbus Day, she began to think of it as her own voyage into places unknown, and shifted to calling it Pauline's Final Frontier. She relished the ring, but it did mean explaining to the guests the reason for the occasion.

After telling Ward and Sam, who in turn told their families, she and John discussed how to tell their Washington Spring consort of soon-to-be residents. The group had been meeting every other Tuesday evening at John's Annapolis office until the land was cleared. Then the group happily met on the first Tuesdays out at the site on lawn chairs. John, Pauline and Acton had been working most closely so it would be impossible for them not to tell Acton, but for the sake of

A HORSE OF A DIFFERENT COLOR

the entire community, she decided that all the investor residents should be told. With Final Frontier invitations set to go out on October 1, she would have to break the news before their site visit in October. Just as well, Pauline reasoned. They don't need to mix my sad news with the joy of seeing their own homes going up. But that meant telling the community the next evening.

They met in the board room of John's downtown office, each taking a familiar chair. Attendance had been perfect with their occupancy date nearing. Acton began with an update on the home sites, projecting photos onto the wall from his laptop to illustrate the project's advancement. He announced a certificate of occupancy target date of November 8, one week prior to the ribbon cutting. Landscape crews were set to start work in another two weeks, a good time for sod, seeding and planting. Pauline's plant orders had been confirmed. Mary Gray Walterson confirmed the Parabar Shore mayor's agreement to attend on November 15 and said that press releases were going out. Talk turned to the likelihood of actually being moved in by that date. Most said they could do so, which would give the press photo opportunities to shoot interior as well as exterior images. With John's connections to the local newspaper, he knew that Washington Spring would get full spread coverage. Emotions ran high now that the project was coming to completion.

"We have one fly in the ointment, however," John began.

"Don't tell me it's our mailboxes again, Sue ventured. "We just can't seem to get--"

"Nothing about mailboxes," John interrupted. "In fact, I wish it were mailboxes. That could be solved." Sensing gravity in John's voice, all eyes turned to him.

"Pauline and I have some unsettling news we need to share." John indicated for Pauline to continue.

Remaining in her seat, Pauline looked along the expansive table at the people she had grown to know and with whom

A HORSE OF A DIFFERENT COLOR

she had expected to live, and she found herself suddenly unable to speak. At her hesitation, John's first thought was that she was having a brain episode. She had recently had a few small interruptions but nothing that knocked her unconscious again. When Pauline said nothing, panic began to rise in John's chest, which Pauline sensed.

To relieve him, she waved her arm toward him and said through rasps, "I'm fine, John, just a little emotional." Then, turning back to the group she began. "I've had some episodes lately where I've blacked out. At first I thought these were inner-ear related, but after a workup here and at Johns Hopkins the scans turned up a problem with my brain and my pancreas. My oncologist recommended immediate treatments, radiation and chemotherapy together. After talking it over with John, I decided that I am just going to let this thing play out naturally and skip the treatments." Pauline paused. The group gaped at Pauline, unable to take in the news. John and Pauline had briefed Acton before the meeting. It hadn't given him much time to absorb her diagnosis, but at least he knew the facts.

"Did they provide you with a diagnosis?" Sue piped up.

"It's stage four pancreatic cancer that spread to my brain." Pauline answered.

"And the recommended course is radiation and chemotherapy, but you're electing to forgo these?" Sue asked.

"That's right. When I considered how horrible treatment would make me feel, and only extend my life by a few months, I think it's better to let nature have her way with me. I have the will to live, believe me. I want to see our landscape installed and our houses finished. I hope to be well enough for us to move in on November ninth and at least enjoy what we've built. We will see what nature has in store. But meanwhile, I wanted you to know that I have planned a party. I'm calling it `Pauline's Final Frontier.'" As she said this, she realized how absurd the party seemed, and completely self-

A HORSE OF A DIFFERENT COLOR

absorbed. Here were these new friends, each with issues of their own and a thousand details to attend in being ready for moving. As she said Pauline's Final Frontier the idea suddenly sounded like the title of a junior high dance. In that moment, the weight of her condition caught up with her, the rush to be busy to ward off the thought that she was going to die. Now it all seemed real, and she knew that no party would be big enough to eclipse the stark truth. She would soon be gone.

"I... I, *was* going to have a party, but as I'm saying this, I realize that my timing could not be worse." Pauline redirected her speech. "You all have things to do, business to wrap up and movers to arrange. Let me get back to you on this party idea. It may not have been such a good idea, after all." Pauline turned to John, who looked at her with a mix of consternation and affection.

The next day Pauline phoned her friend, Louise.

"I think I'm canceling the party. As I was telling everyone about my situation and throwing this big Pauline's Final Frontier party, it just seemed so trite and misplaced. They are all focused on their own lives. A few are still waiting for their houses to sell, and I know one is planning to head to Ohio to help her daughter give birth. People have far bigger concerns than coming to a party for me. It's ludicrous. Just ludicrous."

"Well, would it help to say what you wanted to happen at the party? That may tell you what you're really after," Louise offered.

"I wanted a chance to see the people I know and love in one place, not have them linger by my bedside at some last vigil. I wanted to have fun. I feel as though my whole life has been waiting to let loose, like I've been a wound up spring that never got released. I feel as though I've led my entire life in John's shadow, always trying to live up to his standards, his family, always considering his reputation, how to protect it, better it, keep up appearances. We had our own version of that in my house growing up, but it wasn't like this. We were

A HORSE OF A DIFFERENT COLOR

vocal and loud and people said what they thought. In John's family, everyone was quiet, contained, people thought before they spoke. I feel as though I have been silent my whole married life and now, here I am at the end of my life, asking for a way to be me, the true me."

"Which is...?"

"Which is loud and vocal and outspoken and knows her own mind. She doesn't have to weigh everyone else's opinions before speaking her own. The party represented that, an expression of me, you know, the music I love, with the people I love, doing the things I love. But now it seems so self-centered and I don't know. I'm just scared, I think."

"Of?"

"Dying. Dying and having never really been me."

Louise let silence fill the phone line.

"I don't want to die, Louise. I don't want to die. Not now. Not ever," Pauline said. She began to cry.

"I know, Honey. I don't want you to die, either. You are way too young to die and you have so many dreams still to fill."

"John has loved me the best he could, but it was never enough. Why is the love we get never enough?"

"I don't know. Maybe it is enough, but we can't feel it, so it doesn't seem like it's enough."

"The times I have truly felt love were when my boys were young and I would just look at them, you know, just look at them. I could spend my whole life just looking at them, watching them laugh or giggle or discovering the world. That is when I felt love. My whole body felt that love, sweet and thick like molasses. I could have fed off that love forever. I still feel it when I see them, and when I think of them, which is all the time, but it's not the same. I want to feel that thick, sweet love once more before I die. I think that's what the party was for, to try to have that deep river of love flow in and through me once more."

A HORSE OF A DIFFERENT COLOR

Pauline canceled the party. The invitations had already gone out and everyone had to be called, mostly by John to say that Pauline's condition had worsened and a large group event wasn't advised. These were very difficult conversations because he had to repeat to each person the story of Pauline's falls, diagnosis and prognosis, as well as the state of Washington Spring being nearly ready to occupy. John tired of this quickly, resenting that he was now the one shouldering a hundred extra things. His way of coping with Pauline's impending death was not to be busy at all, but to linger over each day for its own riches. He didn't need to manufacture things to do. His goal was to rid himself of activities, certainly not take more on. After a point, he told Pauline that he was sending an email to the remaining guests rather than make more phone calls. She had urged him to call because that was the better way, but in fact it was her way, not his way. His way was to carve out space and time for what little life they had left.

John had his own grief to sort through. He loved his wife, and ached for the life they were creating at Washington Spring. It would be their best days yet. He had retired from banking and his son Ward was running their small development company. After forty years in the same house, they had to sort out what they would keep and what they would let go. They had not faced such questions in their marriage, for when they moved into their current home, it was much larger than their first home, and the challenge then was how to fill this seemingly cavernous space of two floors and four bedrooms. Of course it didn't take long before each room took on its purpose and was furnished appropriately. But now the challenge was disposing their possessions. It seemed an insurmountable task until the news of Pauline's cancer. John only wished that their problem was one of dividing up household furnishings. He had rushed along the construction

A HORSE OF A DIFFERENT COLOR

crews on the slim hope that Pauline would actually live long enough for them to get settled into their new home, but she was having more brain episodes. Since her collapse at the grocery store she had ceased driving. John didn't like to leave her alone in the house for very long. She tired easily and slept long hours. She joked that she would be able to sleep as long as she wished once she were dead, she hated to miss so much while she was still alive. However, her body began its predicted slide into dysfunction. Twice a week a hospice team came to check her vital signs. John felt that he should attend Pauline as much as anyone. Sam came by almost daily after work, staying long enough to see his mother smile. He could make her smile even when John and Ward couldn't.

Friends dropped by with casseroles and words of consolation. A few people asked if they could pray with them, which Pauline gladly welcomed. When their minister came, he sat with Pauline and asked whether she wanted to talk about her funeral service. She said now was as good a time as any, and they planned the service from start to finish. With that done, Pauline felt like things were falling into place for her to leave the earthly plane. When John reported that the landscaping was installed and that the cabinets were going in their cottage, Pauline insisted on a tour. When she wasn't sleeping or seeing the construction site, she sorted her things looking for items to give to Sam and Ward for safe keeping. The problem was that there was so much worth preserving. Yet, after a while she simply began tossing out things that two years ago she could not have let go, pen pal letters from her childhood, grade school report cards, a Raggedy Ann doll, and her first Communion certificate. Other items she placed in boxes for charity. Soon, the house was turned upside down, with rooms in upheaval. She tired so easily that jobs were left half-finished. John would come behind to remove trash bags and carry charity boxes to the car, but Pauline complained that she had more to put in them, and so after

A HORSE OF A DIFFERENT COLOR

while he let the clutter remain.

On October 17 Pauline didn't wake up from her nap. John saw that she was sleeping deeply on the family room sofa where she often lay in the afternoons. He let her sleep into the evening believing that she would wake for dinner, even though she had lost most of her appetite. They still had meals together, always praying before eating. John had taken over preparing their food mostly at Pauline's instruction. He was happy to heat up the dishes others had brought. That evening would have been beef stew, which Pauline loved, but she never woke up. When John tried to rouse her, she didn't respond. Her breathing came in a slow deliberate rhythm so he knew she was still alive, but now a world away. The hospice nurse said that coma was a probable late stage event for brain cancer patients. John could expect that Pauline would simply not wake up one day, having slipped away in the night. John didn't know what to want, should he even dare to want anything at all, except for his wife to wake up and be her old self.

Now, he sat on the sofa with her and lay his hand on her stomach looking at the woman who had been with him through his entire adult life. He so missed his mother and father, and now there was only Pauline who knew him head to toe. She had been so good to him, to carry the load of their domestic lives, to raise two sons, to play hostess to his banking friends, and do everything she could to further his career and livelihood. And now to fall asleep on a sofa and never wake up. It wasn't her. And yet, she looked so serene, so peaceful. Her chest rose and fell slowly, deeply, like she was having a good dream. Maybe she'll wake up before bedtime, he consoled himself, and went into the kitchen for a lonely bowl of stew.

Pauline did not wake up. John let her lie on the sofa. The minister came, as did others, who asked after Washington Spring, all the while knowing that even this small talk was a

A HORSE OF A DIFFERENT COLOR

deep pain to John as it appeared he would never experience it with Pauline.

On October 25 Pauline died. The hospice team had moved Pauline to a hospital bed which they set up in the family room, stating that Pauline would need to be turned and repositioned to prevent bed sores. Hospice personnel were now at the house daily, with John remaining around the clock. He slept little, lying on the couch in the family room near Pauline's bed where he could track her breathing patterns. At night he started to read to her as his mother had read to his father. One evening he picked up a Hardy Boys novel from a nearby charity box and began to read. Once, he thought he heard Pauline's breathing quicken, as though she were waking, but then she settled down into the same rhythmic pattern as before. When he finished the first novel, he went on to another, and the nights progressed, one after another. In the daytime John tended to the community's final details with a mixture of satisfaction and dread. Acton assumed the role of chief communicator and kept up with the inspections needed for the much anticipated certificates of occupancy. At home John pretended to make progress on sorting and packing. He mainly fiddled with things at the house and made frequent checks on Pauline. Sam and Ward and their families came in the evenings. They took turns holding Pauline's hand and recalling memories of their family times.

No matter how ready one ever is for death, it always comes as a shock when the person ceases to breathe and the body lets go of its soul. John dozed on the couch, *The Hardy Boys Secret of the Old Mill* open on his chest when Pauline took her final breath. He did not know it would be her last or he would have stayed awake. He only remembered coming to, with a quiet he didn't quite recognize, and though the table lamp still shone and everything was in place, something was different. With a bolt of revelation he knew that the missing

A HORSE OF A DIFFERENT COLOR

element was the sound of Pauline's breath. He swung off the sofa and sped to her side, intuitively knowing she was gone. Her head had rocked toward the sofa, toward him, which was unusual because he had not seen her move her head for two weeks. Maybe her head had been that way and he had forgotten. But inside, he knew that the last he saw her she was facing upward, as though surveying the ceiling for its soundness.

She had an expression of solace, although her mouth drooped in a slack way. John called her name, as if this would summon her return. He shook her once, barely, softly. She was cool. Her body had lost its heat in that short time. What time was it? He spun around to the mantle clock. 4:16 a.m. He didn't know how long he had been asleep. Maybe an hour? Perhaps longer, if she were so cold. "God rest your soul," he said aloud. And then his tears began to flow.

Pauline's funeral and burial was on a day of complete sunshine and autumn brilliance. Three weeks later the Washington Spring inauguration was held under umbrellas. The press wore plastic ponchos and had protective covers for their cameras. Mary Gray offered remarks and then introduced the mayor, who had his own speech for the huddled crowd. In all the ceremony took sixteen minutes for the forty-three attendees. Everyone gladly made their way toward John's cottage, WSC-1 for refreshments and cover from the rain. John's house was bare but for borrowed tables and chairs from St. James-in-the-Wood that held catered food and drink. Acton had spread paper over the fresh carpet to prevent soiling from the well-wishers and press. The lack of a central community house now seemed an obvious flaw, and it rankled certain Washington Spring members who had lobbied for just such a building. Outside, fall flowers bloomed in earnest.

A HORSE OF A DIFFERENT COLOR

15

WASHINGTON SPRING

"**H**ave you ever read *Misty of Chincoteague*?" Mary Gray asked Angelika. They were at the shed. Jimmy and Mary Gray were returning people's Christmas decorations. Angelika was cleaning the horse's overnight accommodation.

"No, I haven't," answered Angelika.

"It's a charming story of two children acquiring a Chincoteague pony and her foal. The wild horses from Assateague Island are called Chincoteague ponies after they swim over to Chincoteague Island in Virginia. Some say they descended from Spanish horses that survived a shipwreck back in the 1500s. You would enjoy *Misty of Chincoteague*," Mary Gray said. "I'll look for a copy for you when I'm at the library. At some point soon I need to get over to Halifax County to see what local lore I can dig up."

"I know that we can't keep Aussie permanently," Angelika said, "but I believe it would be best to get her to a horse farm that will look after her properly." Dejection lingered in her voice.

A HORSE OF A DIFFERENT COLOR

"I think we should sell the horse," Ray announced at a specially called January community meeting. "We're not set up to be a stable." He fiddled with his Miller beer can.

"I agree," Sue said, smiling at Ray. Sue hoped to build a bridge with Ray since he had initially opposed her on the sign-out sheet plan to monitor people's presence at the Close. She needed his vote when the matter came up again.

"We ran the ad for two weeks in the newspaper and on the radio," Ray continued. "Acton says that no one responded except a man who said he would buy the horse. I say sell it."

"She is not ours to sell," Angelika interjected.

"We need to have her removed from our land," Sue said. "I agree with Ray. We are not set up for keeping horses. I don't care how much you clean our shed, my Christmas decorations smelled like horse manure. I couldn't even have them inside my house. I told Jimmy just to throw them away."

"We do have the liability issue to consider. We were fortunate that no one was hurt at the anniversary event," John said.

"The horse was a hit with the children," Jimmy said.

"It was a chance thing that it allowed people near it. Angelika, would you say that it has remained tame?" John asked.

"The pony has allowed me to work with her quite a bit. I believe she is safe."

"But you can never tell when something has been wild," Sue rejoined.

"Acton?" John asked.

He shook his head, indicating he had nothing to contribute. The others were silent.

"I move that we contact Jackson's Stables and ask if they will take the horse," Sue announced.

A HORSE OF A DIFFERENT COLOR

"For free?" Ray asked.

"If that's the only way. They'll have to come down here and transport her to their farm. They have been kind enough to supply us with hay," Sue answered.

"I have paid for those deliveries," Angelika retorted.

"Well, they know the situation," Sue parried.

"Is there a second to the motion?" John asked.

"I say that we ask Jackson's to pay for the horse," Ray continued.

"We need a second to Sue's motion before we can change it," John offered.

Jimmy rolled his eyes at the procedural rigmarole of living in an intentional community. Their earliest efforts of deciding by general consensus had not proven successful, requiring that they operate by Roberts Rule of Order.

"I'll second," Tom Allgood said, nodding his mop of dyed red hair.

"Is there discussion?" John asked.

"I believe we should ask for some amount of payment. According to the reading I've been doing, these ponies when they're sold at auction bring as much as $5,000. That would go a long way in our petty cash fund," Ray said.

"She is not ours to sell!" Angelika snapped.

"We can't keep this animal in our shed!" Sue exclaimed.

Bryan spoke up. "If this pony is an Assateague, why can't we ask them to come for her and reunite her with the rest of the herd? She probably would do well with her own kind. We have no idea how she got here, other than speculation that someone bought her at an auction on Chincoteague and she somehow wound up on our land."

"That's reasonable," Sue said.

"I could live with that," Ray answered. Heads began nodding in agreement.

"Is there an amendment to Sue's motion?"

"I ask for the motion to say that we contact the Maryland

A HORSE OF A DIFFERENT COLOR

National Park Service and request them to come for the pony," Bryan spelled out.

"For free?" Ray asked.

"Without payment," Bryan added.

Ray huffed, then took a swig from his beer.

"Sue, will you accept this as a friendly amendment to your motion?" John asked.

"Yes," Sue answered.

"Tom, you seconded the original motion. Do you accept the friendly amendment?"

"Yeah, sure," he said.

"Is there any discussion on this new motion?" asked John.

"Who will make the call?" Bryan asked. People's eyes went to Acton.

"I'll make the call," Acton answered.

"Anything further?" John asked. "Hearing no further discussion, let's vote. All those in favor of our contacting the Maryland National Park Service to request them to come for the horse without payment, say Ay."

"Ay," sounded voices around the table.

"Those opposed?" John asked.

"Nay," sounded a few voices, Angelika and Jimmy's being prominent.

"Do we need to put it to a paper vote?" John asked.

"No, the Ay's were greater in number," Mary Gray announced.

Heads nodded. John looked to Angelika for ascent.

"Fine," she said, relenting.

"National Park Service," a man answered.

"To whom would I speak about a wild Assateague pony turning up on the main shore of Maryland?" Acton asked.

"Let me put you through to the wildlife ranger." The extension rang. The ranger's voicemail answered. Acton left his phone number and hung up.

A HORSE OF A DIFFERENT COLOR

Almost immediately Acton's phone rang. A woman was on the other end of the line.

"Acton?"

"Hello Grace," Acton answered.

"It's the new year and time for our annual lunch and gallery tour, weather-willing, of course."

Acton had been underwriting a portrait gallery in Baltimore. During his time at the VA Hospital he had developed an interest in African American artists. While climbing the ranks at the medical center he took only a passing notice of the art displays throughout the hospital. Memos announcing the coming and going of art pieces were a mere backdrop to the important work of serving veterans as he saw it. That sentiment changed the day a man stopped Acton in a hospital corridor. Acton was on his way to a meeting across the campus, his thoughts focused on his plan—to convince the Secretary of Veterans Affairs to approve changing the mission of that particular VA Medical Center so his facility could become a continuing care retirement center for veterans. This would involve shifting ongoing patient care to other Maryland VA facilities. The morning's meeting would solidify the final draft proposal to the VA Secretary. His mind was occupied with these thoughts when a man stopped him in the hallway.

"Are you responsible for this being here?" The man caught Acton off guard.

"Pardon me?" Acton replied, bringing his attention to the inquirer. Acton saw that the man was missing his right leg.

"This here." The man pointed at an enormous, colorful portrait on the wall. "I wanted to know who decided to show this?"

Acton had no idea. A public relations announcement had gone out to the staff, but he had paid it no mind.

"I want to thank whoever hung this here," the man

A HORSE OF A DIFFERENT COLOR

continued. Acton followed the man's gaze. The piece was a disjointed collage of images of men with missing limbs. At the center of the canvas the figures were multiple, painted tightly and small; then moving outward from the middle the images expanded until at the edges one could see in large scale only the torsos of these same men, without indication of missing arms or legs.

"I have been coming here for eighteen years. I lost my leg in the Gulf War and grieved over myself for many of those years. I got to drinking and drugging to take my mind off of my misery. I couldn't see anything other than what was missing. My life was so small. Thanks to a friend I got clean and sober, and for the last few years I've been trying to put my life back together. Life is about what I have, not what I'm missing. And what I have is two good arms, and one good leg, and I have my heart. I've got to use what I do have, which is so much bigger than what I don't have. That's the message in this piece of art here. See how the painter makes the middle so small and wrapped up in itself. And here at the edges it's not about the missing arm or leg; it's about the heart and soul. I've never seen anything so right in all my life. I think I see now why people fall in love with art. It says so much more than words."

Now Acton could see it, too. What were words when one could use line and color to communicate a perspective far greater? The focus needed to be on what was good and possible, not what was missing. Acton nodded his head in agreement. At the hospital he had been lobbying for change by expounding the details of what the hospital could no longer be, rather than focusing on the vision of what it could be. He left the man and went to his meeting, shifting his talk from avoiding negative outcomes to a positive perspective of what could be created. The laggards around the table now embraced the plan, with everyone agreeing to reframe their proposal.

A HORSE OF A DIFFERENT COLOR

In the days following, Acton made a point of noticing the art around the complex. Now that he was looking, art was everywhere. Acton even stopped and asked people what they thought of this piece or that, always amazed at their insights.

When memos came across about new art displays, Acton began seeking these out. During a trip to Philadelphia he visited several art museums. He mentioned to his brother, Arlen his new interest. Arlen chuckled and told Acton to let his daughter, Clarisha, show him around. She knew all about her native Philadelphia. She was aghast that her uncle had not visited the Richard Allen Museum at Mother Bethel AME church on South Sixth Street. She explained that Bishop Allen had founded the first African American church in America in 1794 as minister, artist and an early leader of equal rights. In her college class on art of the African diaspora, her first assignment was to tour the Mother Bethel church and Bishop Allen Museum. She remembered that seminal day and exploded with enthusiasm to share all this with her Uncle Acton.

Clarisha was Arlen's youngest child. Acton saw her as a determined young woman with a head for dates, events and especially for figures. She acquired her MBA in finance after which she had been hired at one of the large brokerage houses. It was a hard start. She was given a quota of new investor dollars she was required to bring in. Scrambling to meet this demand or risk losing her job, she had telephoned her Uncle Acton in Baltimore to ask if he would bring some of his money to that investment firm. She would manage it with the utmost care. It was true that Acton had considerable wealth, having inherited a hefty estate from his parents, as had his brother, Arlen. Arlen was perhaps less prudent with his reserves, but that was Arlen's business. Arlen's daughter had been a crackerjack in school and he wanted to see his niece succeed in this first initiative. He agreed to bring a $250,000 to her, which allowed her to meet that quarter's

A HORSE OF A DIFFERENT COLOR

quota. Her investment choices performed well and so when she called at a later point and revealed that her job was again in jeopardy for not making her quota, Uncle Acton brought her another $250,000 to manage. This happened several more times until the majority of Acton's wealth was being handled by his niece. In four years she kept pace with the market.

When Acton retired from VA hospital administration, he had a tidy sum. He used this to help open an art gallery in Baltimore and also to draw the $1 million needed to become a member of Washington Spring. Enough remained to see him through his retirement years during which time he planned to travel, native African art now being his central focus.

"I have so much to share with you and I have an idea for promoting this year's award winners. Your sponsorship means the world to us here at the G.W. Hobbs Gallery. Can we get our calendars together to see when you can come up to Baltimore?" Grace asked.

A gnawing feeling grew in Acton's gut. He had not told anyone, nor could he face it himself. Two months earlier Clarisha had bungled his portfolio. She had placed the majority of his money in an initial public offering of a company she felt sure would soar. Instead, the new stock tanked and there was no rebounding. She had telephoned him with the horrific news. Acton was utterly speechless. For the first few hours he walked about his cottage in complete disbelief. He had managed multi-million dollar budgets for the federal government. He was skilled at reading and executing complex contracts. And here he was undone by a junior member of his family by failing to follow Rule Number One: Know where your money is invested, and Rule Number Two: Do not put all your eggs in one basket. Pacing inside his house, he shook his head as though trying to dislodge this horrid dream.

Two days after her call he was still shuffling through his

A HORSE OF A DIFFERENT COLOR

house, a man without a connection to reality. Only when Sue called to remind him that Monday began his week to be the magnet monitor did Acton muster enough strength to leave his house. It helped that no one knew the ruin of his finances. Everyone treated him normally, with the usual greetings around the Close. He wondered if any of them had such secrets. He would certainly have to cancel his trip to Ghana, where he had planned to visit a bronze-casting community. He wasn't sure he could get his plane fare back, but canceling was the only way to avert further capital outlays. And his obligation to the G.W. Hobbs Gallery. How would he continue providing the $100,000 per year infusion of cash they needed to operate? Or even to fund the spring competition, which required $10,000 in prize money? The gallery director's call had come early and he was ill-prepared to answer. He tried to breathe. His lungs seemed compressed and his mouth had gone dry.

"Yes, Grace, I think that we should get together. Do you have any time next month," he heard himself say.

"I have Monday, February the twentieth open. Since we're closed on Mondays that would allow us to meet in the gallery without interruption."

"I'll make that work," Acton replied. He would have to figure out how he would break the news of withdrawing his support. If he was anything, he was a man of his word. Respect and honor were ingrained both by his father and his military training. But how could he raise that kind of cash? His heart continued to race when his telephone rang again.

"Is this Mr. Alexander?" a man inquired.

"Yes, Acton Alexander."

"Officer Kramer here. I'm a law enforcement officer for the Maryland National Park Service. I'm returning your call. You believe you have an Assateague pony over there on Parabar Shore?"

"Right. A pony on our property."

A HORSE OF A DIFFERENT COLOR

"What can you tell me?"

"About three months ago it showed up in a field beyond our cluster community."

"Can you describe the animal?"

"Light gray with dark ears, mane and tail. It's kind of stout, not tall and sleek like a race horse. We think it's a feral female. Oh, and its legs are mottled, sort of striped."

"Is it shorter than a standard horse?"

"Yes, I would say so."

"And you haven't been able to establish ownership?"

"No. We ran an ad for two weeks in the local newspaper and on the area radio station. No one has claimed they've lost a horse."

"Are you interested in keeping it?"

"No. We have a woman in our group who has been looking after it, stabling it at night in a shed. She's making sure it has hay."

"If there's no interest in keeping the pony, I would suggest that you call Animal Control in your county. They should come and pick it up."

"We had hoped that your office would transport it to the Eastern Shore where it must have originated."

"Sorry. We can't do that. Taxpayer dollars. Next thing you know people will be calling us with buyer's remorse after the summer pony sales asking us to remove them."

"I see," Acton answered.

"Has it been giving you any trouble?"

"No, it's actually been rather tame, even let some children pet it."

"You say it's light-colored with striped legs, a dark mane and tail?"

"Yes, I would say so."

"You could have a Konik pony. That would be a head-scratcher. Koniks are short Polish horses, mild-mannered, usually white or gray. We don't see them because they're

A HORSE OF A DIFFERENT COLOR

mainly in Europe. Poland, Germany. Not the U.S. If you had a Konik that could be worth exploring."

"In what way?"

"Well, they're so rare here. You might find a buyer."

"How would we do that? Are there brokerage houses that sell horses?"

"All the time. Just be careful you're not working with a slaughterhouse buyer."

"How will I know the difference?"

"Ask. If you call Animal Control and they don't place the horse with a rescue group or sanctuary, it's probably going to end up with a slaughterhouse buyer because there are so many of them."

"I see."

"You might contact a horse buyer or two and see if they have an interest in a Konik. Chances are you will find someone."

"Okay. Thanks." They hung up. Acton went to his desk and began looking up photos of Konik horses.

Mary Gray sat in her cottage reading a book on the Powhatan Indians.

Children of the tribe did many of the things children do today, play, go to school, and help at home. They had toys such as rattles, miniature bows and arrows, ball games and dolls. However, the idea of keeping a child's toy as a lasting memento was not known. For example, dolls were usually made of perishable materials like cornhusk, palmetto fiber, or bundles of pine needles; even dolls that were made of wood or leather were not often built to last as adult crafts were. In many tribes it was considered inappropriate to discipline a very young child, so they simply weren't given toys they weren't allowed to chew or toss into the river. And in some tribes, the impermanence of children's toys was a meaningful sign, for as these fell apart with time, it showed that the child was growing up. Even though Native American dolls were not traditionally

A HORSE OF A DIFFERENT COLOR

made to last, they were often beautifully adorned with miniature doll clothing and jewelry, beadwork or painting, animal fur or even hair from the mother's head. To find an intact toy would be highly unusual.

"I'm going to need the property tax receipt for Bay Haven Apartments to give to the lawyer tomorrow," Ward said to his father. "Could you put that on my desk before you go? I'm heading out to be with Melinda. She has a callback from her mammogram. Probably nothing, but we want to be sure everything checks out. I won't be back before you go."

"Sure," John replied.

At 5:00 p.m. the office administrator poked her head in John's office.

"Heading out," she said.

"Have a good night, Sheila," John replied. A few minutes later John went to the safe in his office and pulled out two plastic grocery bags. His safe contained property deeds, vehicle titles, and critical contracts. Setting aside the bags, he sorted through paper documents not finding the Bay Haven property tax receipt. A look of consternation crossed John's face. He left his office and went to the file cabinet in the administrator's office. He pulled open the drawer of "B" files and rifled through it to the Bay Haven folder. It was full of documents, but no tax receipt appeared. Worry began to well inside John. Closing was at week's end. They needed to show proof of payment so the sale could go through.

Leaving the file open on Sheila's desk, John returned to his office. He played back in his mind the documents he had already taken to the lawyer's office. Hadn't he in fact handed them the receipt? He thought he had taken it when he was last there. Thinking it was true John returned to Sheila's desk, reassembled the Bay Haven file and put it back in the "B" drawer.

He was about to return to his office when Sheila reappeared.

A HORSE OF A DIFFERENT COLOR

"My car won't start. Would you be able to give me a jump?"

"Sure," replied John. He returned to his office for his overcoat and cap. Seeing the safe door standing open he quickly shut it, spun the dial, slipped on his cap and coat and set out to help.

"It was supposed to be a sure thing," Clarisha had told him. Acton's anger festered as he reviewed his latest brokerage statement online. He felt nauseous. He left that page and went to his email. A new message appeared from *locohorse*. "We would like to confirm your Tarpan," it read.

"Dad, I won't be coming into the office. I need to stay with Melinda. Can you call the lawyer to see if he needs any other documents for closing?" Ward sounded anxious. He was calling his father at home in Washington Spring the next morning.

"Sure. I'll take care of it," John said. "Is everything okay?"

"We're not sure. I'll have to get back to you when we know more."

John sensed that Ward did not want to stay on the phone. "Okay. I'll handle this end." John rearranged his day so he could spend time at the Annapolis office. He had originally planned a conversation with the Smithsonian National American Indian Museum. Weeks earlier he had placed a call to inquire about their interest in the relics he had found. They asked John to send photographs and a list of the excavation locations and dates. Initially John hesitated. He was at war within himself between his own interests and the greater good. To reveal his findings could expose him to liability. And yet, to pretend he never found two bags of historically significant items was to live a lie. Capitulating to what he believed was right, he forged ahead to fulfill their request. After photographing the items, all of which he had kept at his

A HORSE OF A DIFFERENT COLOR

cottage, he placed them back in the plastic grocery bags, except for the one item Curt Compton had found. Its design especially intrigued him. He wanted to do more research. The rest he took to his office in Annapolis and placed in his safe until he knew if they were of any value to the museum.

The larger concern was his daughter-in-law. With Ward's troubling news of Melinda's situation, John wished once more for Pauline's presence. She would have shared his worry which would not have halved it, but at least been a place to contain it. He tried calling Acton to say that he was heading into town for the day. Acton didn't answer. Then John remembered that Acton was on bird duty. He quickly sped to his own door and placed the magnetic bird outside.

When John arrived at his office in Annapolis the door was closed and locked. Sheila wasn't there. John used his key and let himself in. He wondered if she was having more car trouble. He telephoned her to check. Sheila answered, although the voice did not sound like her.

"I just finished at the dentist. I probably sound stupid. I feel a little stupid. They gave me something for pain."

"So your car is okay?" John asked.

"It's fine. I guess I just needed a jump yesterday. Are you in the office?"

"Yes. Ward isn't here and I wondered if you needed help getting in."

"He didn't tell you that I would be out this morning?"

"It probably didn't cross his mind," John answered.

"I plan to be there at one o'clock if that's okay," Sheila said.

"Only if you think you can come in. I can hold down the fort if you need to take the day off."

"No, I think I'll be okay."

They said goodbye. John replaced the phone and then picked it back up to call the lawyer. He was surprised when they told him that the Bay Haven property tax receipt was not

A HORSE OF A DIFFERENT COLOR

among the documents that Ward and he had dropped off earlier. That meant it had to be somewhere in his office.

When John hung up he went to his safe. Opening the door, he once more removed the stack of papers inside. He decided he must have overlooked the receipt when he searched yesterday. He placed the folders on his desk and started going through each one. He was midway when a thought bolted through him. He glanced over to the safe. The door was open, the safe empty. He looked back to his desk to the papers at hand, then back to the safe. Where were the grocery bags? Panic rose in his chest. His heart raced. Think, he told himself. They were here yesterday. I was going through the safe for the Bay Haven paperwork. I took out the bags. I must have returned them when I closed the safe. Who would have taken the bags?

And then he remembered. He was searching the papers when Sheila came back in the office and asked for help with her car. He had put on his coat and closed the safe. Had he neglected to return the two grocery bags? Could they have been left out and taken by the cleaning crew overnight?

His eyes darted from side to side across his office floor. Leaving the stacks of paper on his desk he quickly began a search through his office, Ward's office, the administrator's desk and file area. No bags. How could they vanish? There must be an explanation. The cleaning crew, if they disposed of the bags, where would they have put the trash?

He spent the next hour tracking down the cleaning service. When he finally got someone on the phone, the man spoke Spanish. John tried his best to communicate in Spanish and the man in English. In the end John learned that his trash would have been added to the trash of other offices and then disposed of across town. It was not likely that anything could be salvaged at this point.

John hung up, feeling sick. He kept glancing in the corners of his office praying for the bags to reappear, but they did

A HORSE OF A DIFFERENT COLOR

not.

"What do you mean she's gone?" Angelika exclaimed. The week had flown by, her last week with the pony and now Jimmy stood at her front door in the early light. Angelika's hands absently went to her robe sash and tightened it.

"I don't know what to tell you. When I went into the shed this morning it was empty."

"Did it look like someone had pried open the lock?" Angelika's voice sharpened as she grabbed her keys, shoved on shoes and a coat and began to push past Jimmy. She fled toward the shed with Jimmy following her.

Arriving at the scene she quickly undid the lock, flung open one door and then the other. The inside was dark and vacant. Only the familiar smell of the barn met her. "She's gone!" Angelika cried. "Did you check the field?" Angelika barked. Fleeing the scene she took off toward the field beyond their community. "Maybe she's out here," Angelika called backward toward Jimmy who trailed behind. The sound of their rapid feet crunched across the frozen ground. Breathing heavily, Jimmy reached Angelika where she stopped by the field's edge.

The field stood bare. No birds. No deer. No sounds. No horse.

"Maybe she wandered off into the woods," Jimmy stammered, his cheeks puffing.

"I put her in the shed last night. I locked up like usual. I *thought* I locked up like usual." Angelika shifted her thoughts to the earlier evening's events, wondering if she could have forgotten to close the padlock. The doors had not appeared to have been breached. From the pockets of her overcoat she pulled out gloves and slid them on. "Did the people come early?" She turned on her heel and headed to Acton's cottage. Jimmy trailed behind. When she arrived she knocked loudly.

Waiting for the door to open she said to Jimmy, "Did you

see anyone with a horse trailer?"

"No," Jimmy managed.

"Aussie couldn't have broken out of the shed." When no one answered the door she began to walk toward John's cottage. Jimmy tried to keep up. Their breath made steam in the brisk morning air.

"I don't understand. It's seven-thirty," Angelika said as she tromped across the Close. "Acton said nine o'clock. Did you hear him tell me nine o'clock?" They reached John's door. Angelika knocked.

John answered, surprised to see them. "Good morning, you two."

"Do you know if the people came to pick up Aussie?" Angelika began, anxiety in her voice.

"No, why?"

"The horse isn't in the shed," Jimmy answered.

"I didn't put her out to pasture. I was planning to see her before nine o'clock when Acton said the people were coming."

"Did you check with Acton?"

"We just came from his house. Nobody's home," Jimmy said.

"I wish I knew."

"Thank you for providing us with our competition funding this year, Acton. I'm just sorry that your situation has caused you to have to face such drastic cutbacks in your budget," Grace said. "Without you the Gallery would never have opened and remained so vital. We can't thank you enough for all you have done, year in and year out." Her eyes showed warmth and pity. He preferred her warmth.

They were seated at a table for two in a café not far from the Gallery, after-lunch cups of coffee on the table in front of them. "Please tell me that you will present this year's awards for us," Grace said, sounding hopeful.

A HORSE OF A DIFFERENT COLOR

"I appreciate your understanding, Grace. I will be happy to be on hand for the awards," Acton replied, saying nothing more about the grave situation he had just created. To his relief, she shifted to talking about the rise of black artists across the United States and her optimistic outlook for the gallery. Preparing to leave the café, they retrieved their standard-issue black wool coats from the common coat rack.

The two said goodbye on the slushy sidewalk outside the café with a customary brief hug and assurances of keeping in touch. When Acton departed he glanced behind him toward a disappearing Grace and Gallery. It had gone as well as it could have, but resentment and fear lodged in the base of his belly. He was aggravated that he had not been able to bring himself simply to tell Grace that he couldn't spare even $10,000 for the award. Her admiration that held him in high esteem played him for the fool his was. To keep up appearances, he had seen to selling the horse.

On the National Park Service ranger's tip, Acton did some digging. His research revealed that their horse was not an Assateague or Chincateague pony. Neither was it a Konik. It was far more rare and valuable. What they had was a Tarpan, an ancient forerunner to the Koniks. He read that Tarpans had once been the predominant wild horses of Eurasia, now all but extinct, and that Berlin breeders tried to restore the earlier line of Tarpans by creating a small herd through back-breeding. Unfortunately, during World War II Germans facing starvation ate whatever they could, including the iconic horses.

Acton looked up the characteristics of Tarpans: a small horse of up to 13 hands, known to have had a mouse-colored coat lighter than the mane and tail, a dark mask on its face, cobwebbing around the eyes, dark tips of the ears, and zebra-like stripes along its back legs. This described their horse to a T. If theirs was a Tarpan pony, it would be worth real money. Acton had rested his head in his hands at this thought.

A HORSE OF A DIFFERENT COLOR

With sad resolve he pressed on. He discovered a vigorous market in horse trading, and after a number of exchanges with *locohorse* he was able to broker a deal. That he was not able to produce ownership papers and wasn't pressed about this, gave him the sick feeling that he was engaging with an underground market, he prayed not for horsemeat. He comforted himself with the thought that anyone paying $50,000 for a horse was not about to send it to the slaughterhouse. He had started at $100,000, but then learned there was high controversy over whether Tarpans could still exist. When *locohorse* demanded photos, Acton sent snapshots. When *locohorse* then asked for a Coggins test and health certificate, Acton, afraid that he might lose the sale, agreed to $50,000. He requested payment in two forms, a check for $5,000 and the remaining $45,000 in cash. *Locohorse* put up no resistance.

Acton had gone to the Community meeting having practiced his speech, most of which was true—the National Park Service would not transport the horse to the Assateague nature preserve, and short of going back to square one, he had located a buyer for the horse that would allow Washington Spring to reap the benefit of a $5,000 cash infusion. Angelika hung her head, as he knew she would, but the vote around the table had been in favor. He said the pick up date would be the following week. After the meeting Angelika pressed him on the exact time. He told her it would be Thursday morning, around nine a.m. What he didn't say was that he had actually arranged for the horse to be picked up before dawn. He wanted the transfer to be as private and unencumbered as possible.

In the end it had been very easy. At five a.m. he simply undid the padlock, unlatched the shed door and walked the pony out to the main road to a waiting horse trailer. The driver handed him a thick 9x12 envelope that had been folded in half and ringed with a couple of rubber bands. Fearing that opening the envelope to count the money would

A HORSE OF A DIFFERENT COLOR

expose him as a novice, he simply took it and shoved it inside his jacket. After the driver secured the horse he gave Acton a tip of his hat and disappeared into the cab of his Ram Charger. It had been that simple. Even his explanation to Angelika, Jimmy and John when they cornered him later that day was plausible and therefore unquestioned. He said that his phone had rung at four a.m. from the buyer saying that he had to move the pick up time to five a.m. to avoid rush hour traffic. Acton apologized profusely to Angelika, saying that he didn't know what to do, but that given the hour, he hoped she would forgive him. He looked away when tears spilled from her eyes.

Acton had never before committed a crime. The closest he had come was rearranging paperwork at the VA so that dates would correspond within a contract's timeframe. But that was a mere formality with no victims or sleepless nights. Now, he could hardly live with himself. He fidgeted and lost track of conversations. He could not remember a full night of sleep. He justified *the transaction* as he came to think of it, as his helping to secure a better home for the horse. It was clear that the Washington Spring community was not going to go for the construction of a stable. Emotions ran high on all sides especially for Angelika, but she also accepted that the horse was destined to be removed. He tried to tell himself that he had, in fact, helped everyone. As he drove home to Parabar Shore from Baltimore after his meeting with Grace he wished for full lanes of traffic to saturate his mind with driving. The relatively empty road left him with too much time to think.

A HORSE OF A DIFFERENT COLOR

16

HALIFAX

"I see you have one of my favorite books."

"Is it? This is one of my favorites, too. I used to read it over and over. I think it may be why I came to the area to retire." Mary Gray put out her hand and introduced herself. "Mary Gray Walterson. I live at Washington Spring near Parabar Shore."

"Alice Barclay Croft. Pleased to meet you." The two women shook hands.

They were standing in the bright vestibule of the Halifax County public library during a dull winter morning. Alice Barclay Croft wore heavy boots and jacket along with a red knit cap that exposed none of her gray hair. She stood half a head taller than Mary Gray who was dressed less well for the cold. Alice had noticed the book *Misty of Chincoteague* that Mary Gray was holding.

"Did you say Barclay?" Mary Gray asked. "Are you by any chance descended from the original Barclays of Parabar County?"

"Yes, yes I am. My late grandfather, back ten generations, was William Barclay."

A HORSE OF A DIFFERENT COLOR

"I'm new to this part of the state and would appreciate knowing more about the area and about your family."

"Well, in a nutshell, William Barclay and James Paramore established the first settlement in this part of Maryland. One of the Barclay homes still stands, dating back to the 18th century. It's owned by Richard Barclay, a distant cousin."

"I met him last week. He let me come out and hear his family tales."

"Well, then you must know at least the basics. The two men came to create a settlement much like Jamestown Virginia in 1607, only Mr. Barclay and Mr. Paramore arrived fifty years later, in the mid-1600s. They were establishing another outpost for the English crown. They and those who came after them built the small communities in this part of Maryland. Halifax was founded in 1701. Of course the first buildings no longer stand. They were either razed or burned, several times over." Alice looked around indicating the trees beyond the library. "Wood was certainly available for construction, if you could fell trees and cement logs together. But wood doesn't last and it's easy fuel for fires. And, too, the furious storms we get here take down dwellings. That hasn't changed. We experienced that several months ago with that tropical storm. My barn burned when lightning struck it. Destroyed it completely. Thank God I got my horses out before they burned, too."

"I'm sorry to hear about your fire. That storm really walloped us in Washington Spring. At least for us it was just a few hours without power. What are you doing about your barn? It's been a very cold winter."

"At first I set up a temporary structure for my six horses, well, five, because one went missing--"

"Your horse went missing? Did it come home?"

"No, it's still on the lam, so to speak. It's a very special horse because it's descended from Tarpan genes. Those are horses from ancient days, ponies, actually. But more than

A HORSE OF A DIFFERENT COLOR

that, it's my grandson's favorite. He's been heartsick about her. She fled during the fire and we've had no sign of her."

"I can't believe this. I think we have your pony. Or, did. It ended up in the fields by our property. We have been in such turmoil over what to do. We've been caring for your horse, keeping it fed and housed in our garden shed for a few months now. One of our residents could tell it had been taken care of, but we couldn't find the owner. You must be the one we've been looking for. We put out notices through the sheriff's office and Jackson Stables. We even ran newspaper and radio ads for a few weeks, but we never found you."

"What good luck!" Alice exclaimed.

"Yes! Well, no. One of our residents sold it last week. As a community we voted to sell it. Our vice-president, Acton Alexander handled the transfer. I believe it was with an out-of-state horse buyer. Let me call Acton right now and see if he can give me the contact information."

"Sally May is the pony's name."

Mary Gray pulled her cell phone from her purse and dialed.

"Acton, this is Mary Gray. You won't believe it, but I just located the pony's owner, Alice Barclay, from..." Mary Gray paused.

"Barclay Croft, from Halifax, near Halifax," Alice answered.

"Alice Barclay Croft from Halifax. The horse is hers," Mary Gray said. "It got out during that bad storm back in September which is about the time the horse showed up at our place. Do you have the contact information for the man who bought it?" Mary Gray listened. "Sure, I'll hold on."

Turning to Alice she indicated for her to get a piece of paper and pen. "Okay. Ready." Mary Gray called out the numbers for Alice to write. "And the name? Fortune Farms?" Mary Gray repeated.

A HORSE OF A DIFFERENT COLOR

Worry crossed Alice's face. Mary Gray continued dictating and repeating. "Jerry Wagner, buyer. We will see if we can track him down." Mary Gray said goodbye and hung up. She saw the grave look on Alice's face.

"Jerry Wagner is notorious for selling horses to meat packers," Alice said. "He works out of Richmond, where there's a processing plant, handy for shipping meat to Asia where they are happy to consume it."

"What should we do?" asked Mary Gray, concern rising in her voice.

"First we call. If he knows it's me, he may not respond. He and I have had run-ins in the past. You call and ask him if he still has the mare. Say that you found the pony's owner and want to buy her back. Do you know how much he paid? I wonder if he even knows she's a Tarpan descendant," Alice said, exasperation in her voice.

"I believe we got five thousand dollars for it."

"I am able to pay that. Tell him the owner can come with a trailer tomorrow to pick her up."

Mary Gray dialed the number.

"Wagner," a man answered in a clipped manner.

"Mr. Wagner? This is Mary Gray Walterson of Washington Spring, Maryland. Last week you picked up a pony from us that we sold to you. I am happy to say that we located the horse's true owner. Can you tell me, is the mare still with you?"

Mary Gray held out the phone so both women could hear.

"Which horse?" Wagner asked.

"The gray mare, a pony from Washington Spring," Mary Gray repeated.

"I seem to think that mare may have been taken to one of our other farms," he said.

"Where would that be?" Mary Gray asked.

"I would have to check. We have a number of horse farms in neighboring counties." The man sounded purposely evasive.

"Mr. Wagner, we want to restore this pony to its rightful owner. We would like to return your money and pick up the pony," Mary Gray came to the point.

"I don't know if that's possible."

"What do you mean, not possible?"

"I would have to check our records—"

Alice looked stricken. Mary Gray let the silence hang to see if he would be forthcoming.

"We transact many deals. There's a fair amount of activity between our properties. It would take me some time to—"

"Mr. Wagner, with all due respect, we are prepared to return the full value of your money, and more if you require it," Mary Gray said, taking a chance.

"I am just saying that we have many locations and I would have to check. We do have holding fees that would have to be considered in such a transaction."

"How much?"

"I will have to get back to you on that, Mrs. --- what did you say your name is again?"

"Mary Gray Walterson, and sir, time is of the essence. The owner is prepared to send a horse trailer your way to reach you tomorrow, and I believe would be prepared to pay the amount you paid to Washington Spring plus your fee."

"If memory serves, and as I say, I would have to look all this up, that would be fifty thousand dollars plus our holding fee."

"Fifty thousand dollars," Mary Gray repeated, trying not to gasp. She was certain that Washington Spring was given five thousand. "I believe it would be important to check your records. That figure sounds substantially inflated to me."

"No ma'am. I believe that is correct. Fifty thousand, although as I say, I would need to pull your paperwork." Now he waited.

Mary Gray looked frantically at Alice. Alice grimaced, and

A HORSE OF A DIFFERENT COLOR

nodded to indicate she would pay the amount.

"We would welcome seeing that paperwork and yes, we still would like to proceed. The owner will bring a horse trailer but will need to know where to send it," Mary Gray plowed on so as not to lose critical momentum to close the deal.

"I will need time to locate your answers, Mrs. Walterson. Let me see what I can do and call you back."

"Thank you, Mr. Wagner. We will be awaiting your call."

And with that, the line went dead. The two women stood staring at each other, trying to comprehend the conversation. Ten minutes earlier they were strangers. Now they were on a common quest to save a horse.

"Convenient for him that he won't say where your horse is. Does he in fact have several horse farms?" Mary Gray asked.

"Oh, he has horse farms, or more like holding pens. He does keep some horses, but as I say, he buys horses so he can sell them for meat. There's no knowing if he's kept Sally May. He may not know what he has."

"Or he may," Mary Gray said. "Fifty thousand dollars is a lot of money. But we only received five thousand. I'm fairly sure of it."

"Fifty thousand would be about right if he knew what he had. So this could be little more than a man trading for fair market value."

"Can you come up with that amount of money?"

"It would be hard on short notice, but yes, I will do what I have to."

"And then there's his holding fee. Is that typical in the horse world?"

"Yes, if it's reasonable. He's had to transport Sally May. Richmond isn't far from Halifax, all things considered, but then if he's turned around and sent her elsewhere, he's had costs for that, and of course her feed and care."

A HORSE OF A DIFFERENT COLOR

"What would be reasonable?"

"A thousand dollars, at most."

Mary Gray's cell phone rang.

"Hello?" She held the phone out from her ear for the Alice to hear.

"Mrs. Walterson? I located your mare in my Richmond stable." Both women looked at each other, relief on their faces. "The transaction will be fifty-five thousand dollars. I must add a five thousand dollar holding fee to the purchase price, and that is if the pony is picked up today by 5:00 p.m." The women looked alarmed. "And it's one thousand dollars per day beyond today. Plus, I can't guarantee that the mare will be there after today. We move our stable horses around as needed."

Panic rose in Alice. Was he saying that Sally May could be given up for horse meat in another day? Implausible since he was asking for such a sum of money. But he was also known for his cruelty. She wondered if he might be trying to sell her to someone else. Alice tried to hold her tongue.

"And the paperwork from the earlier transaction with Washington Spring?" Mary Gray asked, not comprehending the full message being sent.

"I'll have a copy of that waiting for you. And the new bill of sale."

Mary Gray looked at Alice, who appeared quite anxious. Mary Gray covered the phone's mouthpiece and asked, "Do you want me to say yes?" wondering how Alice would locate fifty-five thousand dollars on the spot and get her truck and horse trailer down to Richmond by 5:00 p.m.

"Can you help me?" Alice whispered to Mary Gray. "I mean, go with me. I could use your help."

Mary Gray had never been a farmhand, or around large animals. She had not even tried to see the pony while it was residing in Washington Spring, but, her impulse was to say yes. She was, after all, called as a Christian to help a neighbor

A HORSE OF A DIFFERENT COLOR

in need.

"Sure," Mary Gray replied.

"Then tell him yes, we'll be there today, and get the address," Alice said.

At 2:00 p.m. Mary Gray hoisted herself into Alice's truck. Having no time to go home and change clothes, she put on Dickies and extra socks that Alice pulled from her dresser drawer, a brown barn jacket taken from a hook in the kitchen and large paddock boots that had been stationed by the barn door. Mary Gray felt like an aging cowgirl and she sort of liked it.

Alice had done the majority of the work of preparing the horse trailer and hitching it to her Ford F-250. The trailer was large enough for a single horse. Alice had also been to the bank and extracted a check in the proper amount.

The February sky seemed to close in as the women set out. Mary Gray didn't want to speak ill of the weather in case she spoke a winter storm into being. She had heard on the previous evening's weather report that heavy snow was predicted, but these weather things were always overblown, she reminded herself.

17

RICHMOND

Snowflakes began to appear. In another few miles the flurries gathered momentum and wisps of white began swirling along the roadway. Alice gripped the steering wheel. Managing the empty trailer in snow was difficult. It would be even harder with a horse in tow. Flurries flew in a more determined direction until they became snow falling in earnest. Alice's heart began to race.

Ten miles remained to Wagner's stable. It was on the northeast side of Richmond. Alice exited the interstate and followed the first of six roads. Mary Gray looked at her watch. It read 4:00 p.m. She thought they should arrive with time to spare.

Turning onto the first road, the two followed a line of cars many of which had also come from the interstate. The volume of traffic and dim visibility made the forty-five miles per hour speed limit sign unnecessary since no one was going more than twenty.

"About six miles to the next turn," Mary Gray announced, reading her phone's GPS. The cars snaked slowly along, headlights beaming into a whitening world. They reached

A HORSE OF A DIFFERENT COLOR

their turn at 4:20. Mary Gray tried not to look, but the clock on the truck dashboard made it impossible not to know the time.

On the second road, they came up behind a school bus driving less than fifteen mph.

"We're on this for two miles. Then it will be a left," Mary Gray said.

Driving apace behind the bus, Alice maintained ample distance. At their turn, the bus turned right, while they turned left. Both women sighed with relief. 4:30.

"Take this about a mile to Luck Road where you'll turn right."

No one appeared to be on this road. Neither were there houses or barns. Fields stretched in every direction. Alice steadied herself for the mile drive. With no tail lights to mark the way, the road and land began to merge. The tires suddenly bumped along as Alice realized they were off-road. But where was the road? She slowed to a stop.

"There!" Mary Gray pointed. Through the snow they could just make out a speed limit sign on their left. They had missed a curve. Alice pushed on the accelerator, gradually moving in the direction of the sign and the road that must be near. The tires caught something like a surface.

Alice inched the truck along. The women strained to see more signs, trusting that the road remained beneath them.

4:43

"Here's a road," Mary Gray called, pointing to the right. "It's not labeled, though."

Alice paused their already slow progress and brought the vehicle to a stop. "Do you think that's Luck Road?"

"Have we gone a mile?"

"I don't know. I didn't look at the odometer. It's so hard to tell. What does your GPS say?"

"It's not cooperating. We're supposed to take Luck Road for .3 miles to Canter Lane. That's a right. And then we turn

A HORSE OF A DIFFERENT COLOR

right on Fortune Farm Lane, and we're there, or supposed to be there."

"Let's try this right. If we don't come to Canter Lane, then we know it wasn't right. I sure hope it is, because I would rather not turn this truck and trailer around." Alice lifted her foot from the brake and applied pressure to the accelerator. The truck followed her lead and they crept along the unnamed road. Suddenly they heard a rumble from behind. Alice looked in her rear view mirror in time to see the twin headlights of a Heavy Duty Ram Charger roaring up behind her. In a moment the truck boomed by on their right, scaring them so mightily that Alice drew up her hands and lifted her foot entirely from the accelerator.

"Am I off the road again?" Alice cried. "Why would he pass me on the right?"

"Follow him," Mary Gray ordered, hoping the idiot knew where he was going.

Alice obeyed, pressing the accelerator vigorously, but as she did the truck and trailer swayed on the slippery surface, unable to gain traction. She let off the gas and slowed to a stop. The red taillights faded in the distance ahead.

"He gave us an idea of direction. Just keep moving that way," Mary Gray said.

Alice shifted into low gear and tried again, more carefully, this time gently pressing the pedal. Her truck obeyed.

They moved ahead but without any idea of roadway. The wipers gave no help, nor their headlights, because the world was completely white.

"We've got to be within a mile of this place," Mary Gray said, trying to hold her voice steady. She had never before been so disoriented. Her palms were sweating and her heart pounded.

The tires again began bumping. The snow was deepening and soon nothing would remain to differentiate field from road. Alice tried veering toward the left and the bumping soon ceased, but whether that meant she was on the road, she could not know. Snow pelted the truck and everything around. A mile from safety and Sally May, they were in a white-out. Alice brought the truck to a halt.

"I can't see," she said. "I simply cannot see."

"I know," Mary Gray replied.

"I don't know what we can do," Alice said.

"Let me get out and see if I can tell anything from outside," Mary Gray offered.

"Here, put this hat on," Alice said, reaching into the back seat. "You'll need it. And take these gloves." Alice pulled gloves from her coat pocket and handed them to Mary Gray.

Mary Gray popped the hat on to her head and pulled the gloves onto her hands.

"Don't go far. Not more than ten feet or I won't see you."

"Agreed," Mary Gray said, then opened the door to exit. Snow immediately began falling into the truck. Mary Gray quickly shut the door after herself.

Outside a fantasy of white met her. The world was silent except for the truck's engine and the crystalline sound of falling snow. She couldn't even see a foot ahead. The snow was impossibly heavy, like skeins of cotton pelting down. She guided herself by touching the hood of the truck. Venturing beyond the vehicle she walked five more paces, counting each one so she would know how far she had gone. She squinted to improve her vision. The only difference was the quality of white where the truck lights illumined. Mary Gray inched her way back to the truck. Opening the door, she slid onto a now damp seat and slammed the door shut.

4:58

"I can't see a thing. It's a blizzard." Mary Gray said.

"Let's call. I shouldn't have waited until now. I thought we would make it. Can you use your cell phone? Jerry's number should be in your phone."

Mary Gray pulled out her cell phone and scrolled to his

A HORSE OF A DIFFERENT COLOR

earlier call. She wondered if Wagner's would already be closed. Could they have closed early due to the weather? Certainly they wouldn't have left if they knew the women were coming. Or would they?

She dialed.

Nothing.

She tried again and got a connection.

Voicemail answered but said that the mailbox was too full to leave a message. She held out the phone for Alice to hear.

Silence landed between the women.

"Now what?" Mary Gray finally asked.

Staring ahead in numb disbelief, Alice answered, "We wait. We wait out the storm until it lightens. It can't snow like this forever. We'll keep running the truck at intervals to keep ourselves warm." Alice then began taking a verbal inventory of the truck's contents. The trailer included two blankets, an empty water bucket, rope, hay, sawdust, trailering boots for the horse, a few tools and a shovel. They had no food other than hay for the horse.

"I'm going to retrieve some things from the trailer that we might need," Alice said. "May I have the hat and gloves?"

"Sure." Mary Gray handed these to Alice who put them on and left.

In a few moments she heard Alice shout, "Here," as Alice opened the truck's backdoor. She thrust the handle of a shovel toward the back seat. Mary Gray wheeled around and guided the shovel to the floor.

"And these," Alice said, throwing blankets toward her seat.

In another moment Alice was in the front seat of the truck, snow cascading down her hat and coat. The truck engine still ran.

"I should have thought to bring granola bars and water bottles for the road. I just thought we would be home in time for a late dinner," Alice said. She looked at her gas gauge: half

A HORSE OF A DIFFERENT COLOR

full. "I'm a Girl Scout, but I'm not sure I am prepared for this," Alice admitted.

"I should have been a Girl Scout," Mary Gray said. "Or watched some of those survival shows. I don't pay attention to the Weather Channel because they're always dramatizing storms."

"They didn't over dramatize the storm that hit us last fall," Alice said.

Mary Gray immediately felt guilty for her remark. "I'm sorry. I should have thought about that before I opened my mouth," she said.

"No apology necessary. I don't usually watch the weather reports myself because I can generally tell from the ache in my bones what's coming. I should have known this blizzard was headed our way, but then, maybe it's not headed to Halifax. It sure seems like it wants to be everywhere. We'll wait this out and see how far we are when the snow slows down. No one's going to move Sally May in this weather, I can tell you that," Alice said with more confidence than she felt.

8:23

Mary Gray awoke from a long nap. She was dreaming she was inside a castle of white crystal. Men in tuxedos were rushing around holding serving trays. She was hungry and was trying to get their attention but they kept whizzing by without seeing her. When her eyes focused on reality she remembered she was in a Ford F-250 in Virginia waiting out a snow storm. The truck was cold. She was wrapped in a blanket that smelled of horse. Her ears and head felt cold. It was dark in the truck, almost completely dark. Could the snow entomb them? What if they lost oxygen? Is this how people die, Mary Gray wondered. Her heart began to pound. She shot a look to her left. Alice was dozing under her own blanket, her head resting on the door. Should she wake her?

A HORSE OF A DIFFERENT COLOR

Ask her to start the engine? Mary Gray then wondered if maybe she should just open her own door and see if the weather had cleared. She tried opening her door. It wouldn't budge. She pushed harder. The door would not move. Bile began rising from her empty stomach.

"Alice, I think we're stuck," Mary Gray cried.

"Hmm?" Alice roused. "Stuck?"

"I'm trying my door and it won't open."

"It may be frozen shut. Here, let me try mine." Alice pulled on her handle. The door gave way about an inch. Alice leaned on the door. Very reluctantly it gave another inch.

"It's the snow," Alice said. "The snow is up to the bottom of the door. Hand me the shovel," she ordered. Snow sliced into the cabin of the truck from the small opening. It had not slowed in the three and a half hours they had been there. Alice slid her seat back to allow room for using the shovel. Awkwardly she stabbed at the snow but that was all she could do. She couldn't get a proper angle to shovel it away.

"I'm afraid we're really stuck," Alice declared.

"If this doesn't stop we'll be buried alive," Mary Gray said, trying to quell her rising panic.

"Let me start the truck again. We can try to move."

Alice turned the key and the motor engaged. Both women silently praised God. This one normal sound gave them hope.

While the motor ran, Alice turned on the interior lights so she could activate the defrost buttons for both front and back. Illuminated, the cabin became a friendly place.

"What do you think we should do?" Mary Gray asked.

"I have a couple of road flairs. I can light those and mount them to the truck. They won't burn the truck, there's too much snow. But to tell you the truth, I don't know who would be out there to see them. Only someone who's crazy, or who's also stuck. I think we should wait and use them when the weather's broken a bit."

"That could be morning," Mary Gray said.

A HORSE OF A DIFFERENT COLOR

"That could be morning," Alice echoed.
Alice put the truck in gear. It would not move.

11:47
The women took turns sleeping, hour by hour, until both fell into deep, dream-filled sleep.

3:16
Mary Gray awoke. The cabin was a mask of eerie dark gray. The atmosphere was stuffy. She wondered if the oxygen was low inside the vehicle. They would need fresh air to breathe. It was like they were being drowned in snow. She immediately wanted to open her window. What made car companies think that electronic windows were superior to crank ones? She would give anything for her 1972 Chevy Vega. She shot a look toward Alice who was asleep. She thought about turning the ignition key just to the first setting but she knew it would cause the bell to ring and startle Alice. But air was important. Necessary! Mary Gray reached over and turned the key. With her right hand, Mary Gray immediately pressed her window button. A wall of snow appeared midway up the glass. Her heart raced. She grabbed the shovel from behind her seat and, as Alice had done at the door, Mary Gray began stabbing at the snow. It fell in clumps onto her and into the cab. There was nowhere to go with it. How high was it? Were they completely buried? Would anyone know they were there?

She lowered the shovel onto the backseat, raised her window and shut off the key. She told herself to think. Next, she whipped out her cell phone and dialed 911. Why didn't she call 911 hours ago? What was she thinking? What was this other woman thinking, suggesting that they just wait out the storm? Who was this woman, Mary Gray thought, noticing Alice now rousing.

Mary Gray began knocking her phone like a dim flashlight.

A HORSE OF A DIFFERENT COLOR

"What? Why won't this work!?"

"I couldn't get a signal either. It's either because we're too far out or because the snow is too deep to let the phone signal reach a tower. I tried calling a few hours ago."

"Why didn't you call before all this started happening? Why did you wait!?" Civility began to vanish from Mary Gray's tone.

"I didn't think this could last. Storms like this drop their load and head on. An hour or two. This is pretty serious."

"Pretty serious?! We are completely blocked in. We can't get out the doors or the windows. One of us should have gone for help while we still could!!"

"And which way would we have gone? That person could be outside wandering in circles, now dead from the freezing cold."

"Or maybe finding the farm and getting help. We can't be that far away. The truck that roared by us tells me that we can't be that far!"

"I know. But we have to wait this out."

"And do what?!! We're going to lose air pretty soon."

"Snow carries some oxygen. Look, if you panic, you take in more air, which depletes our supply. It's best if we can both reduce our stress and try to breathe normally. Or even a little bit shallow."

"You have got to be kidding me. We really are going to run out of oxygen?!"

"We might," Alice said.

6:04

Since 3:20 in the morning they had not started the engine for fear of carbon monoxide poisoning. There was no using the interior light because that would drain the battery. Mary Gray began considering the hymns she knew, hearing in her mind the words and melodies that kept her sane during her difficult days. She tried not to think of stories she read of

A HORSE OF A DIFFERENT COLOR

climbers stuck on Mount Everest, unable to move up or down, and found frozen to death. The temperature was cold inside the truck. "There's nothing warm about it." She quoted the words of her camp counselor who was referring to the water in the showers when the boiler had broken. Everyone had to take cold showers for three weeks. The leaders rationalized that this actually added to their experience. That year she and Mary Kissling became best friends at camp, the two Marys. It was the summer they both turned twelve, Mary Kissling's birthday being in June and Mary Gray Walterson's birthday being in July. Mary Kissling told Mary Gray that she would have to prove herself worthy of becoming twelve by jumping off the high rock into the lake. The lake had several natural ledges that allowed brave souls to canon ball off them into the water. The day of Mary Gray's birthday Mary Kissling led her up onto the high rock which was large enough for the two to stand. Peering down, the lake appeared farther away than Mary Gray expected. Whereas on shore she had been all confidence, now her knees went soft and her breath short.

"You can do it," Mary Kissling said. "I did it, so you can do it."

"When did you do it?" Mary Gray suddenly demanded.

"The first day I was here. You didn't know me then. One of the boys told me that if I was turning twelve, then I had to jump off the high rock. You don't get to be twelve, unless you do it. That's what he said. So I did it."

"Were you alone?"

"I didn't have anyone up here with me, if that's what you mean. A bunch of boys were waiting on the trail to come up after I jumped."

"And did you jump?"

"Of course! And so can you, Mary Gray. Just close your eyes and do it."

"Do I have to aim somewhere, or try to jump out from

A HORSE OF A DIFFERENT COLOR

the rock?"

"That would be good. If you want, you can hold your knees when you jump. That might make it easier."

"I just want to do it...I guess."

Mary Kissling waited.

"So, do I take a few steps and then jump or do I just jump?" Mary Gray asked.

"You can do it either way."

"I think I will take a few steps and then jump."

Mary Gray backed up to where the trail was and started to walk toward the ledge, as though testing the number of steps it would take.

Mary Kissling watched.

"I just don't know if I can do it," Mary Gray admitted. "I don't want to be a coward, but, what if I hit my head or something? I could really hurt myself."

"You won't hurt yourself. Trust me, will you?"

Mary Gray stood still, trying to imagine it all unfolding, and going well.

"Okay. Here goes." She backed up to the trail line and taking four quick steps she hurled herself off the ledge, screaming as she leapt. A moment later she was underwater.

She remembered the water feeling very cold, and that it was completely cloudy when she opened her eyes and tried to see. She felt disoriented as to which way was up. Instinct carried her in that direction. Mary Gray was grateful that her body knew what her mind could not comprehend.

Inside the truck, she realized she felt a similar disorientation. She fought that emotion, making herself take stock of her limbs, looking at the dark dashboard in front of her. She was right-side up. Not in water. She could breathe, she told herself. She wondered if this was her right-of-passage to becoming seventy. She tried thinking of her truck companion as Mary Kissling.

A HORSE OF A DIFFERENT COLOR

7:40

Mary Gray perked her ears, wondering if she heard a noise. Yes. It was a noise. A rumble. How could she let whoever was out there know that they were trapped inside. Involuntarily, she began to yell for help.

"We're in here!" she shouted. "We're in here!"

Alice awoke.

"Someone is out there," Mary Gray exclaimed. I heard them. A rumbling. Listen!"

An engine was nearing them. Both women started shouting, one shouting for help, the other shouting directions.

"Let's shout the same thing," Alice said. "Let's both shout 'Help us!'

"No. We should use hard consonants. What can we say that has hard consonants?"

"What are you talking about?" Alice asked.

"Cs, Ds, Ks, Ts. They'll carry better. What words begin with Cs, Ds, Ks, and Ts?"

"We're wasting time."

"Ts are best. TRACK, TRACK, TRACK, TRACK." Mary Gray started shouting. Alice lowered the windows a crack and joined in.

"TRACK! TRACK! TRACK! TRACK!" the women shouted, hurling their words as far as they could, into a deep, stifling snow.

The motor was nearer now. And then it suddenly quit.

"They've gone!" Mary Gray raged.

"No, listen! Their engine is idling. Keep shouting."

"TRACK! TRACK! TRACK! TRACK!" the women continued. Both began feeling light-headed. Oxygen was scarce and they had used it without thinking.

They continued shouting, although their enthusiasm began to falter. Mary Gray held her head. "I think I'm going to pass out."

A HORSE OF A DIFFERENT COLOR

"Breathe slowly," Alice softly commanded. She didn't know whether to continue the SOS cries. It wouldn't be good for them both to be unconscious. If these were in fact rescuers, someone had to give them vocal guidance. She stopped the chant and listened. She thought she heard muffled speaking.

She pressed the truck's horn and then cried out, "We need help! Is anyone there?!"

"We hear you," she thought she heard in return.

"What do you want us to do?" She shouted at the top of her voice. She listened intently. No one responded.

"What do you want us to do?" she repeated, louder.

"Keep calm. We're digging you out," the voice returned.

That was reason not to use any further unnecessary oxygen. Whoever they were, they knew about the truck and were working to get them out.

The women could hear a plow begin hauling snow from the area. After an hour its engine stopped. The women looked at one another in question. Before long they heard hand digging until a shovel appeared scraping the glass of Alice's window. It knocked snow into the cabin. Alice quickly brushed it aside as though it were flaming ashes.

"We're here!" Mary Gray shouted.

"We're almost to you," a male voice called in return.

Blue-gray sky started opening up from the driver's side window. Two men appeared wearing coveralls, heavy duty barn gloves, and ski hats—one blue and one brown. They worked in earnest having to heave the heavy wet snow higher and higher to dispose it. The men's gloves were crusted with snow.

In time they created enough space to open the truck door. The amount of snow was so enormous a wall surrounded the area they had dug.

"Try to open the door," said the man in the blue hat.

Alice tried the handle and pushed. It wouldn't budge. "It's

A HORSE OF A DIFFERENT COLOR

frozen stuck," Alice answered.

"Jack. Get me my thermos," the blue hat man said. "I'm gonna to try pouring hot coffee on the door jamb and see if that helps."

In few minutes, brown-hat Jack was back. He handed an old green metal thermos to the blue hat man.

Mr. Blue Hat removed his wet gloves and having no place to put them, temporarily stuffed them in his mouth. He carefully unscrewed the thermos lid. Steam vapors curled up from the spout.

"This might do the trick. Roll up your window," he said. Alice turned the ignition key enough to activate the window. Once shut, he slowly poured coffee along the door seam.

"Give it another try," he said through the glass.

Alice pulled on the handle and leaned into the door. It started to move. She threw her shoulder into the process, shoving the door to knock it open.

"It's opening!" shouted Mary Gray.

"Uhh," grunted Alice as she gave the door another whack with her left shoulder. "There!" she exclaimed as the door opened wide enough to let the women escape.

"Get everything you can bring," Alice ordered, unwrapping herself from her blanket and handing it to Mr. Blue Hat, who handed it to Jack.

Mary Gray also shed her blanket, handed it to Alice who handed it on to one of the men. She then grabbed the shovel, carefully threading it from the back to the front and into Alice's hands. They each grabbed their purses and whatever else they could. Alice squeezed through the opening, taking the hand of the man in the blue hat who still had his gloves stowed in his mouth. Mary Gray ungracefully wiggled across the drive shaft, into the driver's seat, and then out the truck door. She wobbled on the snowy surface, pulling hard on Mr. Blue Hat's hand to steady herself. Alice was holding onto Jack who was ushering her up to the surface.

A HORSE OF A DIFFERENT COLOR

"Should I shut the door?" Mary Gray asked.

"Just pull it close without actually shutting it. It's liable to freeze again," Alice called behind her.

Even with a plowed place, traversing the snow was like walking in very thick sand, each step giving way and channeling snow down into the crater the men created. From the hand-hewn hole they climbed to a path about the width of the tractor. A plow was affixed to its front. Apparently, the men had plowed their way to the pickup truck. A small path led through what Mary Gray and Alice assumed was the road. The women gaped at the scene. They were in a channel with snow walls higher than their heads. A weak sun provided general light to the sky. Alice looked behind at her. Her truck was, in fact, buried in snow. Only a few feet of the windshield and top were visible.

"Do you have a horse in your trailer?" Jack asked.

"No. I was coming to pick up a horse," Alice answered. "I'm Alice Barclay Croft, Halifax, Maryland," Alice said. "How did you men know that we were out here?" she asked.

"We passed by you last evening when we were headed to the farm with a load of feed and hay," answered Mr. Blue Hat. "We knew this storm was going to be a doozy. We just didn't know how much of one. We figured you was trying to get to the stable but when you didn't make it I said to Jack, we better go looking for whoever that was that was out there last night. We brought the tractor thinking we might find you. Good thing we did."

"I'm Mary Gray Walterson," Mary Gray said, starting to reach out and shake hands, then realizing it was awkward since Mr. Blue Hat had on his gloves again. Mary Gray was happy to keep her hands buried in her pockets for warmth.

"Brown Howard," Mr. Blue Hat said. "Pleased to meet you both. Let's get you to someplace warm and dry."

"I'm Jack Wagner," the other man said. The women could now see that Jack was younger than Brown Howard by at

A HORSE OF A DIFFERENT COLOR

least thirty years.

"Are you related to Jerry Wagner?" Mary Gray asked.

"I'm his son," Jack answered. The four started toward the tractor.

"Looks like there's only going to be room for one passenger at a time," Brown said. "Jack, you drive," the older man ordered.

"Alice, you should go first," Mary Gray offered. Alice handed her gloves to Mary Gray and followed Jack.

Alice stepped up and onto the tractor with ease. She must be familiar with this sort of equipment, thought Mary Gray, and then wondered if she could mount a tractor as easily. In a moment Jack fired up the machine, put it in gear and started for the farm.

"How much snow fell?" Mary Gray asked.

"Six feet in places. Never seen anything like it in all my livin' days. Came down so hard and fast, why, we didn't get a lick of sleep. We had to get in that load of hay and grain and then do barn chores. It was 1 a.m. until we got through and then we couldn't hardly get the barn door open to leave. We bedded down with the horses for warmth, but couldn't sleep much. We could hear the snow falling, light and heavy all at one time. We was afraid the lights was gonna go out. God only knows why they didn't. We got to talking about the truck we saw coming in, and that if you didn't make it to the farm, then you was probably stuck outside, and that wasn't gonna be any good. I imagine others are stuck. We'll go back out after we get you two in."

"We were coming to pick up Sally May, a horse that belongs to Alice. Her horse had shown up where I live in Parabar Shore, in Maryland. We didn't know where it belonged. And then I just happened to run into Alice. I never met her before yesterday and something she said helped me put two and two together, and I realized that she was the owner of the horse. I was able to get Mr. Wagner's phone

A HORSE OF A DIFFERENT COLOR

number and call him to make an arrangement for picking it up. He demanded that we come the same day. Why would he do that? We didn't know about the storm. Did he think that we wouldn't set out because of it? Or that we would?"

"'Tween you and me, ma'am, Mr. Wagner's been having some financial difficulties. Could be that he was up against it, and needed the money," answered Brown. "I wouldn't say it in front of the boy," Brown added.

"Did he know this storm was in the forecast?"

"We all knew the storm was coming, but we had no idea it would be of this magnitude. That's why we set out to get more hay and grain. Had to ride into Richmond to Southern States Supply. And we didn't have a tarp to cover the load." Brown spat in the snow. "Told the boy to check the truck before we set out. He didn't. 'Course, we was in a rush. We needed to get there and back before it started to come down. We didn't make it, but at least the load wasn't ruined. The real snow started just about the time we pulled in."

"We heard you whiz by us. We wondered who would be in such a hurry," said Mary Gray.

"Three of our crew left early, sayin' they needed to make it home before the weather got too bad. I live on property, and 'course so does Jack, so it was him and me to take the truck to town. His dad's not one to roll up his sleeves too much. But as I say, that's between you and me."

"You sound like you're not from Virginia. Texas?"

"Yes, ma'am. Brownsville, Texas. That's why they call me Brown. My real name is Wilford, but I go by Brown."

"My father was from Texas. Near Galveston. We used to go to see his side of the family about every year or two. It was always so hot."

"That's where people misjudge Texas. They think that since Texas is so far south that it never gets cold. Couldn't be further from the truth. You try sleeping outside on a January night? You freeze quicker than water in a freezer. You just

A HORSE OF A DIFFERENT COLOR

visited at the wrong time, that is, if you wanted somethin' other than hot. 'Course, it's just two types of weather in Brownsville, hot and freezing. Seems like little else, and the hot does outweigh the freezing. It's good you two women kept yourselves from freezing."

"After a while, I was more worried about breathing than freezing. I thought we might run out of oxygen. We opened our windows but we could only get so much air because the snow was so far up the windows. If it had snowed another foot, I think we would have…well, let's just say your efforts to rescue us would have turned out differently."

The tractor was on its way back, coming toward the pair who were stomping their feet to keep their circulation going.

"You're going to go back out looking for stranded people?" Mary Gray asked.

"It's the only right thing to do," Brown answered.

"Do you know the horse we've come for, Sally May?"

"Don't know that name."

"Right. You wouldn't. Only Alice knew her name. It's a gray mare.

"Yeah, I know that one. A pony."

"Is she here, I mean, at the stable?"

"Yeah. I never seen a pony exactly like that. Got me thinkin' about some of them ponies I've seen at Chincoteague."

"Mr. Wagner wants fifty-five thousand dollars for it," Mary Gray blurted. If this was her one shot with this man who might know the difference, then she wanted to ask what she could.

"Well, I'd say that's a pretty penny for a pretty pony," he answered.

Jack pulled up on the tractor.

"Next?" he shouted.

"Looks like I'm the one," Mary Gray said. She approached the tractor warily. It didn't help to be in boots that were too

A HORSE OF A DIFFERENT COLOR

long for her feet.

"Here, let me assist," Brown said from behind. With only two feet of space between the snow wall and the tractor she had to maneuver to get a leg up and hope that her body would follow.

"If you'll allow me," Brown said. He waited for her approval and once given, removed his gloves, shoved them into his mouth and then, using the palms of his hands, gently supported her bottom to provide more lift so she could gain the seat. Once in place, she looked down at Brown. She noticed that he had a mustache. How had she missed that while they were talking? She was fond of men with mustaches since her father had worn one until the day he died.

She blushed at Brown. "Thank you. You're a true gentleman."

Jack put the tractor in reverse and started back toward a small turnaround space he had made. And then they were off, Mary Gray feeling as though Moses had lifted his arms and God had pulled back the sides of the sea.

The tractor was loud and conversation difficult while they made their way through the snow channel. Apparently, the land was mostly fields, although she wondered if it was fence posts making divots in the snow every so many feet. They came in sight of a building that Mary Gray took to be the stables. A path went toward it, but Jack followed a different lane, which soon led to a small one-story farm house.

He stopped the tractor by a side porch. The snow reached the porch which Mary Gray estimated was four feet from the ground. A rough patch had been cleared so she could mount the stairs, which she did, mouthing 'Thank you' to Jack, who nodded and then turned around for his journey back to Brown.

Mary Gray took a look at the place, a white frame house, a porch with a swing at one end, a central door and one closer by. She chose that door and was about to knock when it

A HORSE OF A DIFFERENT COLOR

swung open. Alice appeared.

"Come on in," she said, backing up for Mary Gray to enter. "We're alone, or at least I think we are. Jack dropped me off without a word. He turned the tractor around so fast, I couldn't ask him what to do, so I stood out there knocking. No one answered. I tried the door handle and it was unlocked. I don't know if this is where Jack lives and that's why no one's home?"

"Brown told me he lives on the property. Maybe he lives here, too," Mary Gray said.

"It's warm and dry and it's got a bathroom and a shower. And food, one can hope."

Mary Gray stripped off her boots and coat by the door and left them by Alice's. Alice led Mary Gray into the kitchen.

"Should we just help ourselves?" Mary Gray asked.

"We nearly died out there. Yes, I think we should." A kettle was steaming on the stove. "I found that in the cabinet. I thought I would make us some tea."

"The electricity is on," Mary Gray realized. "That's a miracle!"

A large wooden table took up the center of the kitchen around which were six chairs, only a few of them completely pushed in. Random crumbs littered the table top. Yes, probably the realm of men, Mary Gray thought.

"Do you want to shower first?" Alice asked.

"No, you go ahead."

Alice poured boiling water into a ceramic mug that had the word *Howdy* written on it, and handed it to Mary Gray.

"I found some tea in a jar, way back in one of the cupboards."

"You must have checked things out," Mary Gray said.

"One thing's for sure, I can tell a lot about people by the state of their cupboards and refrigerator. Oh, there's a ham hock in the fridge that I suggest we break into. And some eggs. We can make something to eat. In fact, why don't you

A HORSE OF A DIFFERENT COLOR

figure out something while I'm in the shower and I'll pick up where you leave off when it's your turn in the bathroom," Alice said, pouring her own mug of tea. This mug had the word *Rodeo* on it.

Mary Gray felt this to be a little forward, but then she was very hungry. She opened the refrigerator while Alice trotted off to the bathroom. Mustard and ketchup, some unwrapped vegetables looking a little wilted, a huge ham hock, a couple dozen eggs—she wondered if they had laying hens on the property, some assorted hard cheese in various states of decay, and a half-empty salsa jar. A loaf of Sunbeam bread rested on top of the refrigerator. This could provide something of a meal. She looked again and saw a stick of butter in the butter compartment.

After some investigating she found a frying pan, a toaster, a cutting board, knives, utensils, oil, and salt and pepper. They could make this work.

Re-dressed in their same clothes, but bathed and warm, the women set out a feast. When they sat to eat, Alice took Mary Gray's hand and said, "We must give thanks, and pray for those men." Mary Gray nodded and the two bowed their heads.

"Lord, we thank you for rescuing us from our plight. You have given us a second chance. Show us how to live that we may show our thanks to you. Grant safety and courage to the men who brought us here as they look for others who are stranded. Bless them and all who are in need of help. We thank you for this food, and every provision from your hand, for you are our strength. In your name we pray. Amen."

The women lifted their heads, nodded, and began their mid-morning meal.

They talked very little as they ate.

When their plates were empty Alice said, "That area of Parabar Shore where you're living, legend is that George Barclay was friends with George Washington and when

A HORSE OF A DIFFERENT COLOR

George Barclay was the state's governor he often had Washington to his home. He used the old Barclay house as a hunting lodge. Barclay had Washington and other men there and in the fall of the year, they would stay for two or three weeks at a time, sometimes venturing out several nights to camp under the stars. One fall when there was a severe drought and the men were on one of their overnights, the hunting party realized they didn't have enough water. They were a day's ride from the Barclay estate, far enough away that it would overtax the horses to ride them without slaking their thirst. Washington said he recalled a natural spring he had run across on an earlier expedition, and he led the men with their horses to it. Although it wasn't much more than a large puddle being fed by a freshwater trickle, it gave enough of a drink so that everyone could continue. I believe from then on, that little brook became known as Washington's Spring."

Mary Gray gasped. "That must be the spring that kept your horse alive! We wondered how the horse kept going when there wasn't a water source that we could see."

"Horses can smell water and will stay within easy distance of it. As long as they have food, shelter and water, a horse can be pretty content."

"Astounding! To think that Washington's Spring allowed their horses to survive back then, and your horse all these years later. Our developer, John Martin said he and his wife liked the name Washington Spring for our development, but I don't believe they knew of its significance. I'm the community archivist, so knowing this story makes all the difference."

They heard the tractor approaching. It paused and idled nearby. Footsteps approached the door. Mary Gray reached for the knob and opening it saw a mother standing on the porch holding a toddler. She summoned them inside and bid them to warm themselves. In a little while they were able to shed their coats. Like Alice and Mary Gray, they were

A HORSE OF A DIFFERENT COLOR

bedraggled refugees from the storm.

More people came, a man in his twenties named Marquon, a couple in their fifties, and a family of three. By dusk twelve people occupied the house, all in similar states of need. Mary Gray located a second refrigerator and a separate freezer with many more provisions than the one in the kitchen. She wondered why so few things were kept in the kitchen where they could be close at hand. Several of the women set to work preparing food. Around the table and living room, conversation centered on each person's blizzard ordeal and rescue. No one could fathom the fantastic and paralyzing amount of snow that had fallen so swiftly, except that they had been in it and had survived to tell the tale. People had propped their wet boots and shoes against the radiators, and one by one took hot showers.

Alice had been thinking about the horses in Wagner's stable. She pulled on her damp boots and overcoat and walked out to the porch. All was silent but for a soft wind that seemed to touch the snow with gentle kisses. A channel had been plowed to the porch, which was where everyone was being deposited. As she looked, she could see the branch veering off she assumed to the stables. Deciding she shouldn't go without notifying someone, Alice returned indoors momentarily to say that she was heading to the stable.

A frosting of snow glazed the porch steps, and Alice stepped down carefully, having no visible railing to grasp. Once on the frozen ground, she made her way through the tunnel. Darkness had not yet fallen and the white snow offered its own illumination. She reached the place she viewed from the porch and followed it. After five minutes she came to the stable. A wide area had been plowed to allow access to the barn. When she came to the barn doors she slid open the door to her right. Immediately the smell of horses, hay, and stable hit her and she relaxed into its familiarity. She

A HORSE OF A DIFFERENT COLOR

quickly slide the door shut behind her to retain the heat inside. The barn was huge. Except for being a space much larger than her own, everything felt like home: the smells, the equipment, the horses. Even the dirt under her boots was a welcome happiness. She started down the center aisle, scanning for signs of Sally May. As she walked, she noted that the horses were in contented states. They had bedding and their buckets still had water, unfrozen, she noticed. Although the stables needed to be cleaned, every-thing was in decent order. She kept walking. The variety of breeds interested her. A third of the way along the left side, she found her pony.

"Sally May!" Alice exclaimed. "You are here and safe!" she cried in joy. Alice entered the stall and reached for the pony's head and neck. She brought her face to the pony's face. Sally May whinnied and tossed her head in affirmation. The two nuzzled each other affectionately.

"I thought I might never see you again," Alice said, tears in her eyes. She looked at her long lost pony and stroked her head with both hands. They remained like this for some time, each enjoying the sight, scent and feel of the other. As the newness of their reunion faded to comfort, this brought Alice around to practical thoughts. Sally May had water, although she could use some hay. Alice set to work finding food for her and then for all the horses.

Brown and Jack did not appear by the time the new twelve occupants needed to decide who would sleep where. The house had two bedrooms and a small office. It seemed to the group that no one should occupy the bedrooms in the event that the rescuers came home needing beds. People helped themselves to blankets and sheets from the linen closet as they had helped themselves to towels for their showers. And as with the towels, some people had to share. Although the floor was not especially comfortable, wall-to-wall carpet softened the surface. Some people balled up their coats and

A HORSE OF A DIFFERENT COLOR

clothes into makeshift pillows and covers. People separated themselves into small areas with their own families. To everyone's surprise, the toddler was amazingly quiet. It was as though she knew the plight she had escaped and was simply happy to be warm and safe again. That was an emo-tion everyone shared. Their stomachs were full, their bodies were clean, and they had a warm place to sleep.

Alice returned just as the group was bedding down.

"Here, let me fix you a plate," Mary Gray offered." I lost track of the time. I probably should have sent out a search party."

"All's well. Sally May is here and she's fine. Healthy as a horse.

Both women laughed.

The night passed quietly with the small sounds of sleeping and people adjusting their bodies to their various surfaces. Mary Gray and Alice took a carpeted corner of the living room nearest the kitchen. As they had been the first guests to occupy the house, Mary Gray felt herself to be the primary organizer. She went to sleep telling herself that she would try to rise early enough to put on coffee before others awoke.

In fact, she slept the sleep of the dead. When the toddler woke up in the wee hours and began to cry, Mary Gray never heard her. At dawn, Mary Gray continued sleeping while others tip-toed around and in muffled voices began the day's order of more showers and food preparation. At seven fifteen when the chatter reached audible levels, Mary Gray finally awoke. Her first thoughts were a confusion about where she was. Her right shoulder hurt where she had been lying on it. Why was she on the floor? Who was speaking? As conscious-ness took over, she recalled the storm, the horse, the house. She had been away from home two nights. She decided she should get word to Washington Spring. Sue's edict of tracking everyone's whereabouts suddenly seemed like a prudent idea.

A HORSE OF A DIFFERENT COLOR

People were eating in shifts around the kitchen table while others elected the living room to eat from plates on their laps. The morning's menu was bacon and eggs--a mountain of each. The smell of a roast in the oven mingled with the breakfast aromas. Around eight o'clock someone said, "Shhh," and everyone quieted down to listen. The tractor was coming closer. Would more people be coming, everyone wondered.

The engine shut off and the snow crunched as footsteps approached and stomped outside. The door swung open and to everyone's delight Brown and Jack appeared. The occupants applauded. The men awkwardly smiled and began stripping off their outer clothes that were entirely frozen. The men were not in good shape. Their hands and noses were of various shades of blue gray. Alice could see that frostbite had set in. Getting the men gradually warmed was the first order of business. Alice feared that the house would be too hot, and as much as she hated to do it, she knew the men must go into the barn for its marginal heat. She softly explained this to them, and hurried them out of their wet garments and into dry ones. Alice summoned Mary Gray and asked for blankets and warm water in a thermos. As the men exited, Mary Gray explained to the group that Alice was worried that the men had been in the elements far too long and risked losing fingertips, toes or noses if they didn't warm up slowly.

Everyone listened as the tractor started up and faded into the distance while the men drove to the barn. Alice followed on foot. When the men reached the barn, Jack jumped down and swung open both doors. Brown steered the tractor inside the wide barn, and Jack shut the cold white world out closing the door. The men were glad beyond speaking to be in their own safe place. Brown shut off the engine and, overcome with exhaustion, collapsed onto the steering wheel. Jack said nothing. He slid down against a stall, using the post as a backrest. His head slipped toward his shoulder as he fell fast

A HORSE OF A DIFFERENT COLOR

asleep.

When Alice reached the barn she undid the outer latch and let herself in. First she saw Jack who appeared to be deeply asleep. She then searched for Brown. Noticing him perched in the tractor's seat she grew alarmed that he was slumped over.

"Brown?" she called. He did not respond. She hoisted herself up to the driver's seat. "Brown?" she said, softer now, but into his ear.

"Hmm?" he mumbled, not moving.

"Are you okay?" Alice asked.

"Hmm," he mumbled again.

"You must be exhausted," Alice said. She climbed down to the barn floor to retrieve one of the blankets, then mounted the tractor again and maneuvered the cover around his body. She reasoned that his own heat and the mild interior temperature would warm him at the right speed. She did the same for Jack, who sleepily cooperated. She prayed they would be okay. She took care of some chores, then sat down across from Jack to keep watch. In a moment, Alice was also deeply asleep.

Back at the house as one hour stretched into two, Mary Gray began to grow concerned. She knew that Alice had said that the men needed a gradual warm-up, but how gradual? What amount of time?

At the beginning of the third hour, Mary Gray told the others that she would check on Alice and the men. The young man named Marquon offered to go along. Mary Gray started to wave him off, and then agreed, seeing the benefit of two versus one in case of an emergency. They bundled into their winter clothes and set out into a sparkling sun. The glint off the snow was so powerful that they had to shield their eyes. It made for hard going. Mary Gray and Marquon walked side by side, marveling at the deep walls of snow. They came to the fork and took the way to the left.

A HORSE OF A DIFFERENT COLOR

In a few minutes they could see the barn. When the two approached the doors, Mary Gray lifted the latch and let the doors swing open. The barn smell hit them full on. Mary Gray's eyes tingled. Marquon blinked as if to disperse actual particles.

The pair entered a completely black world, wondering if they would ever see. As their eyes adjusted from the extreme light to relative dark, they both took in the scene: an enormous wooden cavern of stalls and equipment. Neither had ever been in a working barn, and the sheer size and smell overwhelmed them. Mary Gray's eyes snagged on the sight of Alice lying outside a horse stall. She went toward her, thanking God when she saw Alice's chest rising and falling.

"Here's Jack," Marquon said, seeing Jack across the wide aisle. "I think he's asleep."

"Where's Brown?" Mary Gray wondered aloud, keeping her voice low.

They both peered deeper into the barn. They could hear horses smacking their lips, shaking their heads. One snorted.

The two walked side by side pacing the entire length of the interior. Mary Gray noted the variety of horse breeds and wondered if she would be able to identify Sally May. In the dim light she walked right by the Washington Spring squatter not seeing her for who she was. At the end of the barn the pair turned and strolled back, wondering where Brown might be. As they returned to the entry doors Marquon happened to look up at the tractor to see a man seated with his head slumped to one side.

"Is that Brown?" Marquon asked.

Mary Gray nodded. "Can you check on him?" Both were suddenly worried.

Marquon gripped the side of the tractor and hoisted himself into the passenger's seat.

"I can tell he's breathing," Marquon softly called down to Mary Gray. "He's probably just asleep."

A HORSE OF A DIFFERENT COLOR

Marquon jumped down and stood next to Mary Gray rubbing his gloved hands together as if for warmth. "Now what?" he asked.

"I suppose we wait for them to wake up," she answered.

Alice began to rouse. "Mary?" she asked, in a sleepy voice.

Marquon and Mary Gray walked toward her.

"Are you okay?" Mary Gray inquired.

"Yeah, I think I just fell asleep. I was doing barn chores and then sat down to rest and watch the men. Are they okay? Is proper color coming back to their faces?"

"As far as we can tell. They're out like lights, exhausted." Marquon nodded.

Taking a deep sighing breath, Alice got to her feet. "I think I'm exhausted, too. How long have I been out?"

"You left three hours ago," Mary Gray answered.

"Oh geez, that long?" Alice replied.

"Is it safe for them to come to the house?" Mary Gray asked, indicating the men.

"They should be fine, now," Alice answered. "What they really need is hydration and nourishment. Here, see if this water is still warm." She held out the thermos. Marquon took it and opened it. No steam rose so he raised it to his nose to detect any heat.

"Still warm," he announced.

"Then get them to drink it," Alice softly ordered.

Mary Gray looked at Marquon in affirmation. He climbed up on the tractor, gently nudging Brown, and speaking his name. Brown didn't budge. Marquon shook the man's arm with more intention. He began to come to.

"Here, take a sip of water," Marquon offered, holding the thermos close to Brown's lips.

Brown took a small sip, and then drank more deeply. He reached out to take the thermos from Marquon to help himself. Marquon wondered if he should limit Brown's intake to be sure there would be enough for Jack, but just then

A HORSE OF A DIFFERENT COLOR

Brown dropped the thermos from his lips, wiped it off with his cuff and held it out to Marquon.

"Here, give some to Jack," Brown said.

"Sure," Marquon agreed and scrambled down the tractor and over to Jack. After waking Jack, he gave him a drink. Jack drained the thermos.

Alice announced that they needed to get to the house. The men nodded.

Brown fired up the tractor's engine and offered to take one of the women. Both declined, saying that Jack should go. Awkwardly agreeing, Jack took the passenger's seat and the two men set out from the barn, with the three others following on foot. Alice called after them ordering the men to get food and more water as soon as they arrived.

The men were applauded once more when they entered the house. Several of the women dished up some of the roast and poured tall glasses of water. The men ate like starved bears and drank a gallon of water between them. Once fed, they fought fatigue. Jack nudged Brown telling him to take a shower. While Brown left for the bathroom, Jack tried to answer questions from the gathered crowd, including Alice, Mary Gray and Marquon who had returned from the barn. Jack explained that they had gone seven miles out to the interstate. They couldn't tell if the interstate was being plowed, but he thought so. He said that the school near the highway had power and was serving as a makeshift community shelter. They had cleared passages into several farms and houses so people could get out, if necessary. Jack said they were the only ones plowing along the country roads. He said it was good they had taken extra fuel because they had needed it.

Brown emerged from his bath, wearing Jerry Wagner's britches.

A HORSE OF A DIFFERENT COLOR

"I don't believe he and I are quite the same size," Brown said, adding emphasis by lifting his feet to show the short hem of his pants.

Mary Gray presented Brown with a mug of coffee. "Do you take anything in your coffee?" she asked.

"Black as night and thick as mud suits me," he replied. "And preferably over an open fire," he added. "That's how I learned to drink it on the trail."

Brown held up his mug with the word *Rodeo*, and began to talk about his cowboy days on the range. "I ran cattle drives from Texas to Oklahoma and one time to Colorado, the prettiest country God ever made."

As Brown talked, Jack appeared and leaned on the door jamb near the kitchen. Alice approached him and asked about Sally May.

"She came in a week ago. My dad told me that she's a special one," Jack said.

"She's a Tarpan descendant," Alice replied.

"I didn't know that."

"I want to pay for her and start back home as soon as the road's clear."

"That could be two or three days," Jack said.

"Can I give you the check and we do the paperwork?" Alice asked.

"My dad left me your forms. He normally handles the business end, but he went to Richmond before the storm. We also have a house in town," he explained. "Come in." He indicated the room serving as an office.

Jack handed her the new bill of sale.

"Did he also leave a copy of the original purchase?"

"Let me see. Is this it?" He handed her another document.

Alice took it and read. It showed $50,000 for the purchase. So he did know Sally May's value after all, she thought. She also wondered about Mary Gray's assertion that Washington Spring received $5,000 for the horse. That didn't square with

A HORSE OF A DIFFERENT COLOR

this document.

"Huh," Alice said, affirming her confusion.

"Something wrong?" Jack asked.

"No, this is the right document. It's just that the numbers are different from what I thought they were."

Worry crept into Jack's face. Had he shown this woman something he shouldn't have?

"I thought your father was telling me a story when he said he paid $50,000 for Sally May, but it appears that, in fact, he did." Alice considered whether to share the discrepancy with Mary Gray.

The opportunity to tell Mary Gray came the next day. After Brown and Jack had a full night's sleep they began taking some of the people to their vehicles. Marquon had remained behind, as had the mother and her toddler. Alice went to the stable several times for barn chores, taking Marquon with her. Mary Gray busied herself in the kitchen, content to oversee the efforts toward meals while the mother chattered away.

When Marquon and Alice returned for lunch, Mary Gray laid out a spread of food. The conversation centered on the day's weather. Warm air had blown in and was starting the melting effect. The staggering drifts and walls of snow were hardly touched. Everyone agreed that this snow would still be around for Easter, which was more than a month away.

After the meal, the mother ushered her toddler to the living room for a nap. Marquon left to scout for the returning tractor. Mary Gray assumed her station at the kitchen sink, washing the lunch dishes. Alice took a dishtowel to dry the plates and glasses coming her way. She decided to broach the subject of payment.

"I squared up with Jack yesterday so Sally May can come home." Alice began.

Mary Gray nodded.

A HORSE OF A DIFFERENT COLOR

"Jack showed me the bill of sale from a week ago. It was for $50,000," Alice said.

Mary Gray turned to Alice, her hands in suds. "You mean he really did pay $50,000?" she asked.

"Yes, he did," Alice answered.

Mary Gray looked incredulous. "I know Acton told us he got $5,000 for the horse."

"I have a copy of the paperwork if you want to see it."

"I wonder what that means. And what became of $45,000?" Mary Gray began turning over possibilities in her mind.

"I don't know, but I can ask Jack if he will make a copy for you," Alice answered.

Brown and Jack returned late in the afternoon. Marquon asked if it wasn't too much trouble, that he be their final run of the day. Brown and Jack had taken turns all morning dropping off their temporary residents, plowing out each of their vehicles and making sure their engines turned over. Brown had smartly tossed into the tractor a portable jump starter which was needed in each case. During the afternoon the men went out together, plowing and shoveling more places and widening lanes so cars could pass on the main road. People were beginning to creep out into the world again, and one of the convenience stores had re-opened. After Marquon's departure and Brown's return, Mary Gray, suggested to Brown that groceries were needed, even if it meant shopping at a quick mart. He offered to take her in the morning, but Mary Gray asked if, after he had his dinner, he could take her then. She explained that provisions were running very low and she didn't know what she could possibly make for the next day's meals.

Brown looked at Jack. "I'll take her," Brown said.

"You might use the truck," Jack said.

"I don't want to chance it. Drifts may have set in," Brown

explained.

After dinner Mary Gray and Brown donned coats and boots, hats and gloves and walked out into the dusk of the day.

"What an incredible sight," she said, indicating a deep pink streak of color crossing the sky. "I'm glad the days are getting longer," she added.

"By a margin," Brown said. "We used to call this the sweet spot. February gave us a little more light to see by so we could move the cows into their pens a little later, which meant we could get our dinner early enough not to be starved, but not so early that we had too much time to get into trouble before sack time."

"Trouble?" Mary Gray asked.

"You know, the usual ways men get into trouble, wine, women and song, mainly wine, I suppose," Brown said.

Mary Gray's chest tightened. Since her divorce she did not drink wine or alcohol in any form, except for Holy Communion. She suddenly wondered about this man.

"And the more the wine, the louder the songs," Brown laughed.

"And you?" she cautiously asked.

"Me? I got sober years ago. I knew I was destined for disaster if I kept on drinking. A young man can drink, or not, and I learned early that I could not. Caused me too much trouble."

"You don't drink?"

"Can't touch the stuff. Other men, that's their deal. I know mine."

Mary Gray breathed a small sigh of relief as though maybe he were someone she could perhaps trust.

They boarded the tractor. This time Mary Gray hoisted herself into the seat without help. The two were silent as Brown took off. They puttered along the path under a magical sky with glistening white walls guiding them. The

A HORSE OF A DIFFERENT COLOR

breath from their bodies met and joined in puffs ahead of their faces. Mary Gray blushed. She would never forget the unlikely beauty of this tiny slice in time.

On the way to the convenience store the tractor began to sputter.

"What's this?" Brown said, his face cross with concern.

The tractor slowed and stopped.

"Hmph," Brown uttered, then dropped to the ground and sticking a glove in his mouth, used his free hand to raise the hood. After examining the inside, he slammed down the cover and reached behind the tractor seat into the stowage pen. He pulled out the fuel jug and jiggled it. It was empty.

"I should have thought to fill this before we left," he said, a chuckle rising as he shook his head. "I believe I have fallen under your spell, Little Lady."

Fallen under your spell? Mary Gray repeated to herself. She looked at him. His eyes were on her. Crisp night air trickled into the cab. Was this man making a pass at her? Her head suddenly held a million crazy thoughts. She had no idea what to say.

"I could have told you when I saw you that I would do some idiotic thing. And now looky here, I have. I was so over the moon about taking you to the store that I let my guard down. Didn't even think about carrying extra fuel. Mistake number one."

Which was the mistake, she wondered, his taking her, or forgetting to fill the fuel container? She wanted to ask but didn't dare.

"I believe we will have to make the best of it, hunker down for the night, or walk," he announced.

"How far is it?" she asked, glad to have something tangible to hook her thoughts to.

"About seven miles," he said.

"No. It can't be. It's seven miles to the interstate from the farm."

A HORSE OF A DIFFERENT COLOR

"Sorry. It's ten miles from the farm to the interstate. We've gone about three of those ten. And the convenience store is right off the exit."

She remembered now. She looked at him as he spoke to her. His eyes remained on her.

"If we walk, how long will it take?" she asked.

"On these roads? It's slow going. Have to watch each step, especially with the ground freezing again."

"We could walk back to the house instead. It's closer than the store," she reasoned, and then wondered if she might actually want to be stranded with this man under the twinkle of stars.

"That we could," he said. She sensed that he was waiting for her to decide which direction they were headed, more than which way they would be walking.

"What would you like it to be?" He lifted his eyebrows in question.

"What are the chances that someone will come along and give us a ride?" she asked, aware that she was stalling. Her mind whirled with emotions. Her heart pumped adrenaline.

"Not likely. People won't be out on these roads, not tonight."

"I believe we will have to hike back to the house," she said, trying to sound logical and put together, which she suddenly was not. How had this man unhinged her so easily?

He came around and helped her down from her seat. As she stood on the earth's hard surface, he lingered, facing her. She dared to scan his face for intention. A slight smile turned up the corners of his mustached mouth. He was all play. She thought he might kiss her when he turned away and started down the road.

After a few paces he turned around. "Ah! There I go again. I need the jug," he said, returning to fetch the container.

They set out together walking back toward the farm. Light

A HORSE OF A DIFFERENT COLOR

was gone from the sky and now stars started to peek through a thin veil of clouds.

The shushling of their coats sounded loud in an otherwise silent world. Mary Gray was lost for words.

They had crossed some sort of line and were in a suspended space of possibilities. This was the most uncomfortable she had ever been. As they walked her mind see-sawed between the incredible beauty around them, and replays of earlier scenes with this man. Had she missed something that would have given her a clue of his affection?

One mile passed. Then two. Neither spoke. During the last mile the moon began to rise in front of them, first, a glow above the snow, and then a huge orange ball. Mary Gray gasped but did not utter a word. Even this glorious sight did not seem worthy of breaking the spell of magical silence surrounding them.

Their steps continued along the path, icy now as Brown had predicted. Almost on cue with her thoughts he started to slip.

"Whoa Nellie," he cried, and then fell onto his backside.

Mary Gray dropped beside him to check on his condition. He was laughing.

"Are you okay?" she asked, peering into his face.

"Never better. I have you to look at," he answered.

She leaned over, smiled, and kissed him lightly. His lips were warm in spite of the cold. She raised her head and looked at him. He smiled more broadly. Caution be damned, she thought, and kissed him once more.

At the house, Alice and Jack worked on a plan for getting her truck and trailer to the barn and loaded. Jack said that Sally May was welcome to remain at Fortune Farms as long as necessary. He wouldn't require additional stabling charges, although inwardly he knew that his father would disagree. Jack had ignored most of his father's phone calls. During the

A HORSE OF A DIFFERENT COLOR

calls he did take, he assured his father that the horses were being taken care of. He mentioned that the owner of the new horse had arrived and had paid the purchase price and transfer fee. He didn't explain that the owner was staying at the house and would need time to get the horse home. His father ordered that the check be deposited immediately. The city of Richmond was a mere fourteen miles from the farm, yet the storm had not been quite as bad there, dropping only two and a half feet of snow. The worst had fallen in a very narrow band exactly across the area where Fortune Farms lay. His father did not indicate that he was returning to the farm, which relieved Jack as he also had not bothered to mention that the house had become a makeshift camp for stranded travelers.

On the first full day at the house, Alice had been able to call one of her neighbors in Halifax who said that the snowfall there had been about two feet. They were digging out and thankfully had not lost power. Alice asked if anyone could look in on her horses, explaining her predicament. The neighbor said to consider it done.

Now, Alice called the same neighbor and inquired if the roads were passable. He thought they were. Alice said she wanted to set out the next day with the hope of reaching home by late afternoon. Her neighbor said that he had already plowed her lane.

Alice and Jack were so involved in their conversation that they both jumped when the kitchen door opened. Mary Gray and Brown appeared, both red-faced.

"We didn't hear the tractor," Alice said.

"Didn't have it to hear it," Brown replied. "Ran out of gas. It's about three miles on. Had to walk back. We'll take the truck tomorrow and gas her up."

Mary Gray removed her gloves and boots and unzipped her coat. Brown did the same. He turned her toward him and stealthily plucked a piece of hay from her hair.

A HORSE OF A DIFFERENT COLOR

"We think we can move Sally May tomorrow," Alice announced.

"Really?" Mary Gray stated quizzically as she joined Alice and Jack at the kitchen table. Brown went to the kitchen counter and poured two mugs of coffee.

"Jack thinks the roads in Richmond aren't as bad as back here," Alice said. "The interstate should be open and the way clear. I just spoke with my neighbor who says that we should be able to make it to Halifax and home."

Brown set down a mug in front of Mary Gray and pulled up a chair beside her.

Quiet fell.

Brown spoke to fill the awkwardness. "I was just sayin' to Mary Gray here that the time will come for you all to shove off. Can't say as I look forward to it. We was just coming to know one another."

Mary Gray blushed.

Alice and Jack looked from Brown to Mary Gray and then to each other. They arched their eyebrows in curiosity.

"Well, if it isn't obvious," Brown began. "This beautiful lady and I might want to spend a little more time gettin' to know one another. We think this snow storm was God-sent. Brought us together in an unlikely way. How else could we have run into one another?"

After their long walk back to the farm, Mary Gray and Brown went first to the barn on the presumption of filling the gas can. In the stable's warmth, he had told her that geese choose one partner for life. She knew that already but found it a quaint reference. And then he said, "Even black holes exist in pairs," which she did not know. Neither did she know how to hear such a random comment.

She had taken this man to be a kindly soul, near her in age, yet someone who probably had not been educated as she had, nor holding to the same political party, religious beliefs, or life

A HORSE OF A DIFFERENT COLOR

outlook. In the barn she learned otherwise. Yes, he had been to college, yes, he followed the same politics, wondered about the state of his soul, and he felt that history explained everything, especially about current world affairs. He simply loved the outdoors and could not exist without being in it. He referred to his talk as trail slang, something he couldn't seem to shake, although he indicated that he would like to have a reason to.

Brown explained that he had been married once, early in his life. His wife had died of cancer, and he felt ashamed for not being more attentive. He said that his guilt over her death drove him from a desk job at the local Agriculture Extension office to the open field. He said he had to work out his offense after she died. And here he was in the last third of his life wondering if he would ever have a mate again. He had prayed on it, he said, and then Mary Gray appeared.

For her, this Texas man reminded her of her father with his gentle swagger and self-assurance. Brown's disclosures endeared him to her all the more, as one who thought deeply about the world and his place in it. As they talked, she learned that they had read some of the same books. How unlikely to find a literary cowboy, she thought.

"I am thanking God for this chance," he had said. She could not believe anything other than what he was telling her, putting it as he had, that God must have invented the snowstorm for this particular purpose, and for that matter, that God had seen to the entire horse escapade to ensure their meeting.

"I have asked Mary Gray to marry me," Brown announced. "She hasn't given me her answer yet, but I expect she will and soon," he added, taking her hand into his.

"Mary Gray?" Alice said, blindsided.

"I need to think this through, of course," Mary Gray replied. "Do you help with housework?" she turned to Brown

A HORSE OF A DIFFERENT COLOR

and asked playfully.

"Housework," he considered the word. "Such as painting and plumbing?"

"Well, no, I mean vacuuming and dusting and mopping, those sorts of things." She chuckled a little.

"For you, Little Lady, I would do it all," Brown declared.

Mary Gray smiled, although she felt a kernel of caution inside. Was he being truthful? She also didn't know how the charter of Washington Spring treated new members. She remembered a provision in the paperwork, but at the time she signed, it wasn't relevant to her. Would he want to live with her? Could he do that, not simply by charter; it was a question of his spirit being so contained. Washington Spring was a confining place even without fences.

As though reading Mary Gray's mind, Brown looked at Alice and asked, "Do you need help at your place? You said you're from Halifax. I've been up your way."

"Yes, I could use some help," she ventured.

"I'd do it for free, as long as I got to see my Mary Gray," Brown said, lifting her hand to his mouth and brushing it with his lips.

Mary Gray's head was spinning. Five hours ago she was on her way to a convenience store for groceries, contemplating how many meals she could make with Beanie Weenies, and now she was considering marriage. It was too much.

"I think I'll leave you two to your plans," Jack said, with a bit of wonder in his voice. And then, interrupting his own departure he said, "It looks like we can get the horse loaded tomorrow. Just let me know what time," he said, as left for his bedroom.

"I believe Mary Gray and I have some things to discuss, Brown, if you would let us have a few minutes," Alice said, interpreting Mary Gray's overwhelmed face as a plea for time and space.

"No worries. You two have a lot to figure out. I'll be

A HORSE OF A DIFFERENT COLOR

taking off for my place across the yard," he said, unlatching their hands, and rising from his chair. The women were silent as he walked to the door and pulled on his boots and coat. Mary Gray wondered if he would return and kiss her in front of Alice. He did not. She didn't know whether to feel disappointed or relieved.

"I'll be a stone's throw away," he said, winking at them both, and then exited the door.

"What is going on?" Alice asked with a mix of curiosity and incredulity.

"It's as smack-me-between-the-eyes as it looks. We were a third of the way to the store when the tractor quit, and when he helped me down from my seat, he made a pass at me. I wasn't sure if he was serious. We started walking back here and under the spell of that beautiful moon, cupid shot his arrow. We began talking. Well, actually, he fell on the ice and when he fell down I ended up down on the ground with him, and then he kissed me, or maybe I kissed him. Anyway, here we are. He thinks God orchestrated all these events so that we could meet. He has declared that he wants me to marry him."

"Do you think you will?" Alice asked.

"I have no idea. I'm of six different minds. Is this really even happening?" Mary Gray asked. "This could be a dream."

"Well, if it's a dream, then we're both in it. I'm certainly grateful that God has seen to my finding Sally May. But arranged it all? That's saying a lot. What do you think?"

"I don't know. This is definitely not your ordinary set of circumstances, not in the least. Maybe that's part of the allure. What I should say is, let's see how this goes under more normal circumstances. Let him court me while we live apart. See how much he wants me then. And for that matter, me him. Time will tell the strength of this relationship."

"Do you want us to leave tomorrow?"

"Oh, absolutely. I am ready to get home," Mary Gray said,

A HORSE OF A DIFFERENT COLOR

a small amount of regret catching in her heart.

"Jack and I have a plan and if the weather cooperates, we should be able to get Sally May loaded and be home by dinnertime. She will be glad to be back to safety."

"I'm for that," Mary Gray confirmed, longing for her own home, her own place of safety.

In the early hours of the night Mary Gray tossed and turned. Mary Gray, was on the living room sofa next to Alice in the easy chair. Alice noticed her restlessness.

"Having trouble sleeping?"

"You could say that. I was married once before. I don't want to make the same mistake twice."

"They say all women marry their fathers and all men marry their mothers," Alice proffered.

"I adored my father."

"Where did you grow up?"

"In Vermont. My father was William Walterson from Galveston, Texas. They called him Buck. My mother was Ann Gray from Millidge, Vermont. I was raised mostly by my mother and her two sisters. My father traveled with his job as a mining manager." Mary Gray didn't say that she never really understood what her father did because he wore casual clothes along with his silver-tipped boots yet he never smelled of dynamite or hard labor that she imagined lingered on those he managed. But he didn't wear a suit, either, so she could never figure out what his job really was.

"When he came home from trips he would bring me little gifts, sometimes glass figurines." These were moments she treasured more for his affection than any trinkets he might bring. She would dive into her father's warm embrace and he

A HORSE OF A DIFFERENT COLOR

would rock her and mumble into her hair her favorite, endearing words, "You are my most beautiful daughter," which was only slightly strange since she was his only daughter. His only child.

"How did your parents meet?"

"My father first saw my mother in Millidge on the sidewalk on a warm spring afternoon in 1947. She was on her way to a dress shop and he was headed for a quick dinner. They were both on a street corner when she stopped him from stepping into the path of a careening car. Some rambunctious sixteen-year-old with his buddies was on his way to the quarry for a swim. My father, in his Texas hat and big boots, bowed and tipped his hat to my mother to offer his thanks and then invited her to the nearby diner for dinner. My mother said that eating with him in a town where everyone knew everyone else's business was risky, that their being together would be worthy of a week's worth of gossip. But she said that romance wasn't on her mind, even though she was twenty-eight and did not want to become like her maiden aunts. She insisted that she was simply intrigued by the possibility of hearing stories from another place.

"My father told her he was in Vermont to work for Simcorp Mining which was headquartered in Texas. When she asked him about serving in War World Two, he explained that he had worked in the shipyards near Houston constructing mine sweeps and because of that he was deferred from serving. After that he went to work on a different kind of mine. At Simcorp when the company bought the granite mine outside of Millidge they sent him to run it the Simcorp way. My mother wondered how the locals

A HORSE OF A DIFFERENT COLOR

would feel with this outsider telling them what to do. To his credit, Daddy was not one to bark orders. But, New Englanders are not easily charmed. They often have hard edges and don't mind letting you bump into them. Daddy was softness inside his tall, handsome frame. My mother said that she judged him to be in his thirties. And though he wore no wedding ring she did not take that to mean anything. She said she knew that men, especially traveling men, were known to shed their rings conveniently while on the road."

"Your mother sounds pretty smart. What was she like?" Alice asked.

"Nothing like Daddy. Daddy was tall and had brown wavy hair that never wanted to behave. Maybe that's why he always wore a hat. He had a distinctive nose, too, big but beautiful. It was like him. He was bigger than life. He could tell stories. Whether or not they were true you almost didn't care. He made you want to listen. My mother was the practical one. Lovely, but medium in every way, medium height, medium build, medium brown hair, and middle of the road in all her thinking. I guess you could say that I take after her. Her one becoming feature was her delicate wrists and ankles. Her own mother used to tell her that age brings compression and expansion so enjoy anything slender for it will surely never last."

"That wasn't especially kind to say, even if it is true," Alice said.

"She told me that during dinner when she had trouble cutting her chicken off the bone, he pulled her plate from her, cut her chicken and slid the plate back, all while explaining the operations of mining. She said he seemed

A HORSE OF A DIFFERENT COLOR

comfortable around women, which both pleased and worried her. She figured he had either grown up with sisters, or was married with children, or he was simply so self-possessed that he didn't need to wait on other people's approval to be himself. She said she decided that she liked that about him.

"And then he told her that he was single and at age 39 he wasn't sure if he should just call himself Daniel Boone and start wearing a coon-skin cap. He laughed at his own joke, one she never understood.

"My mother said he ordered coffee for them both and dessert even though he had no idea if my mother drank coffee or ate dessert.

"My mother rarely ate dessert in all the years I knew her. She said he was so easy about it all that she found herself eating and talking like she was someone else, someone relaxed and happy with life.

"She did say that getting a word in was hard, since my father loved to talk. But my mother felt it was important that he know she was not some lightweight he had asked to dine with him. So she told him that she had attended Smith College where she studied Literature and Architecture. She talked of places of interest in Millidge and throughout Vermont. Since she had not heard of any buildings of significance in Texas besides the Alamo, she asked him about it. But he ignored her question, which left her wondering if she had insulted him since Texas was so under-represented with regard to historic monuments.

"She said he was a generous tipper, but that turned out to be true wherever he went, whether it was out of genuine kindness or to ingratiate himself with the locals, it was his

A HORSE OF A DIFFERENT COLOR

way.

"After dinner he walked her to her car looking so handsome and unlikely in that town. She said he took her hand, raised it to his lips, and then placed it on the steering wheel before he said goodbye, and then he shut her car door, tipped his hat, and walked back down the sidewalk with his big boots clicking."

"What a promising start."

"Two weeks later she saw him at a different location on the same street. She said his face lit up when he saw her and he held her eyes so she wouldn't skitter away. He took her hand and brushed it with his lips and mustache. My mother said she thought to herself, this man knows how to work women. He told her that his foremen were coming along nicely and that he expected to be finished in Millidge in another week, and could she have dinner with him that Saturday evening. My mother thought she should say Let me check my calendar; That evening may be difficult; Sorry but no. What she said was yes.

"He chose the nicest place in town with white tablecloths and a piano player. She said that she intended to eat lightly and drink not a single drop of alcohol so she could be in full command of herself. My grandmother and aunts had also suggested as much. But almost as soon as they were seated a steward brought a bottle of champagne that Daddy had ordered ahead of time, and when she saw those amber bubbles dancing in fine crystal, she couldn't resist. And after Daddy refilled her glass, she said his wit grew more humorous, his stories more colorful and his features more handsome. His irresistible charm melted all her defenses and

A HORSE OF A DIFFERENT COLOR

by the time they left, she was willing to say yes to any question he might raise.

"But he did not ask anything of her. He simply returned her to her mother's home, her ancestral home that she said for all its dignity suddenly seemed to her ordinary and provincial. She described him as all light and desiring of everything big and new. He was like a beautifully unmoored ship that could sail anywhere and even make its own wind. He was poetry to her stately prose. She said that she was almost ashamed to invite him into the vestibule of her house with its dark wood and antique furnishings. He took her hand as he had done before, only lingering a moment longer, then bent down and kissed her lightly on her cheek."

"He sounds like he was a real a charmer."

"My mother said that she was over the moon, but since he was leaving in six days she didn't know if anything could or would come of it. But on his final full day she made a point to be on the main street in case he happened by. She said she went in and out of shops feigning interest in the merchandise. She was about to give up when the stores started to close at six o'clock. She made her last stop at the watchmaker's to pick up her repaired timepiece, the last excuse she could use for being in town, and when she came out of his shop Daddy was standing in front of her, large and real as ever. He asked if she was interested in keeping time, indicating the name on the shop window. She wasn't sure if he intended the double-meaning, so she laughed and held up her package. He then clarified, that he was asking if she would keep time with him. She said her heart nearly burst. And as calmly as she could, she told him yes.

A HORSE OF A DIFFERENT COLOR

"Daddy told her that he would be required to return from Texas in four weeks to check on the work of the men he was leaving in charge. He asked if he could write to my mother during that time and would she allow him to take her out again once he returned. She, of course, said yes.

"So, he swept her arm into his and glided her along the sidewalk, past the place she had pulled him back from the racing car, past the original diner, the dress shop, and all the other shops whose lights were now dim. When they reached the end of the pavement he paused, turned her to face him, and peering into her eyes he said that he had not stopped thinking of her since their chance encounter on that very street. He said that he hoped that she would allow him to court her properly but that he understood that a beautiful woman like her must have many suitors. He said that he hoped that he wasn't too late to be a contender and that he would make her very happy.

"And then he kissed her in the open public, which was not done in those days in Millidge. Mother said she worried that others would see them, but then she decided she just didn't care.

"They got married six months later. It was not difficult to choose where since it would have to be in her church and the reception at her ancestral home. Daddy's brother came from Texas as his best man. His parents didn't make the trip due to their health, and his sisters were unwilling to travel such a long distance. It was several years until I ever met anyone on his side of the family.

"When my mother threw her wedding bouquet, one of her maiden aunts caught it. Everyone laughed about who she

A HORSE OF A DIFFERENT COLOR

would find to marry at her age.

"At that time Daddy needed to remain in Millidge at the mine for another year. There had been an accident and the company wanted him there. But he didn't know where they would send him after that year. So my parents started out living in my grandmother's house. They all got along. My grandmother and great aunts loved my father's stories and Mother said Grandma and her sisters just liked having a man around the house. He was entertainment for them all. The only flaw my grandmother could see was that Daddy never wore anything but boots.

"I was born three years later. My parents were still in Millidge because the company kept Daddy on, but by then they had bought a modest home in one of the new post-war housing developments. My mother loved being a homemaker. She got involved in community affairs, women's clubs and church endeavors. She hosted teas and garden parties, and when their little home became too small my mother began angling for a bigger house. Daddy would have said yes, but then my grandmother died quite unexpectedly. So our family of three moved into the Gray ancestral home. By then my grandmother's sisters were gone. So Mother had room for entertaining and she was happy to have her family's heirlooms surrounding her. She said I was a charming little person, curious and bright and a little bit sassy, which my mother said came from my Texas blood. At that age I was still cute, and so she let me get away with more than she should have."

"You don't bear any of that now, Mary Gray. You are as upstanding a citizen as any I've known."

A HORSE OF A DIFFERENT COLOR

Mary Gray smiled. "Here I am rambling. Maybe I'm more like my father than I think. I need to let you sleep."

"It is amazing, though, how our earliest years shape us for the rest of our lives."

Mary Gray continued thinking about her upbringing. If there was one unhappiness, it was that her father liked to drink after work, at the house, which was hard to name as a fault. Her mother said that lesser men would stop in bars and linger through the evening hours. When he came home, after attentively kissing both her and her mother and whirling them both around with compliments galore—which neither she nor her mother ever tired of hearing—he went next to the liquor cabinet. The house had never had a liquor cabinet because no one drank, but her father purchased one and had it delivered to where it sat, and that was his stopping station night by night.

She thought about how her father traveled frequently for Simcorp, trips that took him away for a week at a time, but he never missed the weekends. Mary Gray knew that her father was a man of means, that he had men under him and certain responsibilities, yet he never shirked his duties to the household, the main one being to wash the family car and to mow the expansive lawn. The gardener her mother hired did the planting, weeding, and trimming since her father would not relinquish grass-cutting, saying that a man should be seen in the community as pulling his own weight, never mind that this meant riding atop a lawn tractor.

Mary Gray recalled that fateful Saturday morning while he was outside on his lawn mower. She was twelve years old, at

A HORSE OF A DIFFERENT COLOR

an age of innocence and curiosity. She entered her parents' bedroom and spying her father's wallet on his chest of drawers, she decided to see what mysteries it held. After counting a large sum of cash, she noticed a little interior pocket. Inserting her fingers she slid out a photograph. It was a picture of her mother and herself at seven taken in front of their house five years earlier. Snow lay in piles around them, a picture perfect Vermont scene. She liked that he had kept the picture with him. Behind that she felt something else. Her fingers had to work to coax it from its hold as though something were keeping it from the light of day. As she wriggled it out of its place she had the strange thought, what if it were a picture of another woman?

What she dislodged was a photograph, and it was of another woman, a woman holding the hand of a girl who appeared to be about eight. The figures were small, but clear enough to see that the woman was very tall and slender, strikingly beautiful in a natural way, her wavy hair loose and her face without makeup. The girl, presumably her daughter, was even more lovely, a replica of her mother with the same long waist and a confident smile. Mary Gray realized why the breath left her body. The girl's nose and facial features were identical to Mary Gray's father's. She squinted at the black and white photograph, willing it not to be true. She turned the picture over and to her surprise found script in a woman's hand. *Ursula 1963*. That was this year, Mary Gray had thought. Her heart pumped faster and her thinking became fuzzy. How could this be? She suddenly became agitated that she had gone snooping. She would have to do something, but what? She couldn't confront her father because she would

A HORSE OF A DIFFERENT COLOR

have to admit that she had spied. She couldn't tell her mother and expose her to a heartbreak worse than anything she could imagine.

Mary Gray had searched her mind for a logical explanation. Was this one of her father's sisters? They had made summer trips to Texas to see his relatives. But the name Ursula was never mentioned in the Walterson clan. And who was Ursula, the woman or the daughter? And where was this taken? Mary Gray squinted at the photograph, searching it for any clues. It was in front of a house, as her own picture had been, but this was a simpler house. Nothing showed of the yard or surroundings to be able to guess its whereabouts, even to say Vermont or Texas.

The lawnmower shut off and Mary Gray knew that she had only a few minutes. She carefully slid the photos back in place and then quickly rifled through the rest of his wallet for any other anomalies. A slip of paper was crumpled between two twenty dollar bills. She pulled it out. It was a phone number. Mary Gray decided to write it down. She rushed to her bedroom and returned with paper and pencil and scrawled the numbers. She returned the paper, closed his wallet and left it on the chest of drawers as she found it.

When she returned to her room she felt something she had never felt before: betrayal. Her father had another daughter, tall and very beautiful in a way that she would never be.

Mary Gray lay on the sofa wrapped in now-familiar blankets. She thought about how her father had loved her, but had betrayed her. This had nothing to do with Brown. Or did it? Her feelings for Brown were complicated, but that was

A HORSE OF A DIFFERENT COLOR

because this had developed so fast. She wanted to apply logic to her emotions, and then chided herself for such a silly notion, as if feelings could be ordered to be proper. She was glad for her talk with Alice, and she felt clear that the best answer was to delay a response to Brown's proposal until they could test out their compatibility. She would tell him her decision in the morning.

In the wee hours of the morning, Mary Gray dreamed of Brown and her father, their faces blurring from one to the other. The man or men both told her she was beautiful. She awoke to the toddler's cries from the bedroom. The mother was trying to soothe the child and encourage her back to sleep, but she was having none of it. The two had occupied Jerry Wagner's bedroom when it was apparent that he was not returning from Richmond. Mary Gray, on the living room sofa, stretched her limbs and neck, wondering if she could fall back to sleep. Unable to do so, Mary Gray unwrapped herself and started for the bathroom. She detoured into the kitchen to make a pre-dawn pot of coffee. One was already simmering. A note by the machine read, "Tell me YES today." The *Howdy* mug was next to the note.

She looked around. No one was up. Alice was asleep in the recliner. The mother and daughter were quiet in the bedroom. Jack's door was shut.

Mary Gray giggled to herself re-reading the note. Maybe he really did love her, if someone could truly fall in love in a matter of days. She realized that this was the first time she was seeing Brown's handwriting. It was tightly formed, careful, even academic, the exact opposite of what she expected. She poured herself a steaming mug and took it with her into the bathroom.

If she knew one thing, it was that she was ready for a new set of clothes. She had been alternating between Alice's duds, and her own sweater and slacks that were hastily thrown into

A HORSE OF A DIFFERENT COLOR

a tote back in Halifax, and extracted from the F-250 four days earlier. Fortunately, the house included a washer and dryer which was going day and night when the house had twelve stranded people. Today she would wear her own clothing which felt right, like being back in her own skin. She would need to feel her comfortable, confident self to face Brown.

He came through the door at 7:06, when the sun was just beginning to show.

"Sweet spot," he said, as he knocked his feet free of snow and took off his coat to hang on a peg. At first she thought this was a term of endearment meant for her, and then she remembered his telling her about the lengthening days on the cattle trail.

He came over to her as she stood at the kitchen counter preparing breakfast. He waited.

"I got your note," she said, blushing, not quite looking at him.

"And?" he asked.

"And, I think we need to slow down, take this one day at a time. This all happened so fast. I think we should date for a while." As she said the word *date* she inwardly cringed, thinking this a very old-fashioned, school-girl term. But it was what she felt. She was not ready for any other answer.

"I'll go for that," he said easily. "I'll wait for you," he announced, pulling the *Rodeo* mug from the dish drainer and pouring himself a full cup.

18

WASHINGTON SPRING

Sue wedged her lunch bag into the work refrigerator. Her mind wasn't on her hospital shift, but on Martin. She reached in her smock pocket to touch her cell phone for the dozenth time. Martin had been texting her. The first text had come the week after the reunion, casual, simple: *Great seeing you, Sue.* She took her time replying, urgently wanting to respond yet knowing deep down that to say anything would indicate she was willing to play along with him. She relished having Martin's phone number which meant direct and private access to the man. *You, too, Martin*, she finally wrote. Those three words took her two days as she wrote one sentiment and then another, erasing each possibility until she settled on those three specific words. When he replied: *I can't get you out of my mind,* her belly did flip flops. Sue had not felt more alive than when Martin kissed her on the couch at the Sheraton. It had not been so much of a romantic kiss as a kiss of simple, comfortable affection. There was no harm in that, she had told herself. After all, she and Martin

A HORSE OF A DIFFERENT COLOR

had many shared experiences. They had lived through the same life dramas, at least up until age eighteen, and so why would a kiss of affection not be appropriate? However, her insides stirred just thinking about him. They texted each other secretly for weeks. When the snow storm descended on Parabar Shore, Sandy sat watching the Weather Channel. Sue debated how to answer Martin's text message: *I need to be in Baltimore on business next week. Meet me?*

A HORSE OF A DIFFERENT COLOR

19

RICHMOND

Setting out from Fortune Farms proved to be a series of moving parts before Alice could load Sally May.
Brown had already completed the barn chores when he woke Jack. After breakfast the two men set off. First, they had to get the abandoned tractor left out from the night before. The tractor plow was necessary for digging out Alice's F-250. So the men boarded the large farm truck, and by-passing Alice's truck continued on to the tractor. It remained in the middle of the road from fourteen hours earlier. Brown jumped out and poured fuel from the diesel container into the tractor's tank and started it. Brown in the tractor followed Jack back to Alice's F-250. Between Brown's plowing and Jack's hand shoveling the two had the truck dug out and running in just over an hour. Jack steered Alice's truck from its tomb, and onto the road back to Fortune Farms. Brown got into the farm truck and parked it more or less in the spot where Alice's truck had been. Then he set out in the tractor back toward the farm. Jack reached the farm first, arriving at the house about eleven o'clock. Alice was packing her things.

A HORSE OF A DIFFERENT COLOR

Mary Gray was lining up remaining meals for the day, slim pickings given that she and Brown had never reached the store.

"Ready to load you two," Jack announced. "Brown's on the tractor. He'll meet us at the barn. You've got great weather for driving." It was a sunny, blue sky day.

The women said farewell to the mother and toddler, with Mary Gray offering final instructions for their lunch. Alice was elated to see her truck, like a fond friend. Jack handed Alice her keys, and after loading in their things, the women and Jack set out for the barn.

Sally May acted like a dream. She had been happy to see Alice. Now, smelling the familiar trailer and truck, she was willing to be boarded, as though she knew this was her ticket home.

Alice was tying a stabilizing rope from the horse's halter to the trailer when Brown drove up on the tractor. He hopped down from it and then helped himself to the trailer to survey Alice's work. He squeezed in beside her and checked her knot. Alice chaffed at his testing her and then smiled to herself when he saw that everything was just as it should be.

He patted the pony on her haunch as he jumped down from the trailer. Mary Gray was watching from a distance. Brown walked over to her. "You'll need to take me to the farm truck on your way out," he said.

"Ask Alice. She's the driver," Mary Gray said.

"Jack, I'll fetch the truck," he announced. "Alice, will you take me to the farm truck? I left it where your truck was," he said.

"Sure. I believe we're ready," Alice said.

The women eagerly hugged Jack, thanking him for his hard work that allowed them to be free of their snow prison and safe from the storm. True to his word, Jack refused to take any extra money. Brown squeezed into the back seat of Alice's truck. Mary Gray was aware of his breathing behind

A HORSE OF A DIFFERENT COLOR

her.

Alice accelerated carefully away from the barn. Icy patches remained along the plowed lane where the sun had not penetrated, and she could feel the trailer swaying. She kept her eyes focused on the road. The passengers remained silent. Mary Gray wondered what she could possibly say, even if she had words.

"Ahead there, you'll see the farm truck," Brown piped up.

Alice pulled beside the farm truck and put her truck into park.

"I want to take a picture of this," Alice said. The tomb was still visible, showing the depth of the snow that had buried them. "I bet it measures four and a half feet!" Alice remarked. She snapped a few pictures with her cell phone. Brown climbed out and opened the passenger's door. Mary Gray got out and stood facing him, she a full foot smaller. While Alice remarked on the snow, Brown and Mary Gray lingered in their own world.

"I'll wait to hear from you," she said.

"Oh, I'll call. I'll call you tonight to be sure you made it home safe and dry," he said. He reached down and kissed her lightly. "You will be on my mind," he said. And then he left her standing by the passenger door. She watched him go. She hated being left, preferring that he wait for her to leave first. But he started the farm truck and put it in gear as Alice boarded her own truck. The two trucks accelerated in opposite directions toward the places they each called home.

A HORSE OF A DIFFERENT COLOR

20

HALIFAX

At 5:20 p.m. the women arrived in Halifax along with Sally May. The sun that was now setting behind them had done fair work of drying the motorways. Even the back roads near Halifax were clear enough to drive the speed limit. Upon reaching home, Alice explained to Mary Gray the process of unloading the trailer.

"I need to get Sally May stabled. You can go on home to Parabar Shore if you like."

"Let me make dinner first." Mary Gray laughed. "I'm already in the habit and if it's okay, I can use what's already in your kitchen. We'll eat together. The final meal of our adventure."

When Alice came trudging in from the barn, she was greeted by a mouth-watering aroma. Alice asked if she could wash up. She was bone weary and hoped a good scrubbing in her own bathroom would revive her. Mary Gray nodded then sat down at Alice's kitchen table to wait. While she sat she reminisced about the table they had shared with perfect strangers for four days at Fortune Farms. She replayed the scenes of laughing and going about the routines of life with

A HORSE OF A DIFFERENT COLOR

all these souls, waiting for the one bathroom, sharing the washing machine, the feel of freshly laundered, still-warm bath towels. Simple pleasures. They had cooked enough food for all to feel satisfied. It made her think of the story of Jesus feeding the multitude from five loaves and two fish. She smiled. Was this all some grand scheme on God's part to bring Brown and her together? That seemed very farfetched. She was content to think of the week's adventure as something she could never have predicted. And yet, she had made connections that otherwise would never have happened. That was how she was willing to see Brown, a delightful connection. Whether he worked out to be more than that, only time would tell.

She turned these thoughts over in her mind as the minutes ticked by. On some level she actually didn't want her escapade to end. It had been like summer camp, challenging, unpredictable, and gratifying in a hundred ways.

Coming out of her reverie, she realized that twenty minutes had passed. She turned off the simmering pot and went to check on Alice. As she approached the bathroom door she heard the water running.

"Alice?" Mary Gray asked through the door.

No answer.

"Alice?" Mary Gray asked a little louder and knocked. "Dinner's about ready. What about you?"

No answer.

Suddenly concerned, Mary Gray opened the bathroom door and sucked in her breath. Alice was lying on the bathroom floor, face up, not breathing. Mary Gray dropped down beside her.

"Alice?" Mary Gray's mind fled to the CPR training that she attended years earlier. She couldn't remember which to do first, breathe in the person's mouth or start chest compression. In panicked bewilderment, she opted instead for the telephone and called 911. Mary Gray grabbed a piece of mail

A HORSE OF A DIFFERENT COLOR

from a table where Alice's neighbor had stacked the pile, and told the voice on the end of the line her location and that she couldn't remember how to administer CPR. The answering voice walked her through the steps. Mary Gray went through the motions, but she knew deep down that it was all for naught. Besides, she couldn't apply the amount of force to Alice's chest that was required, which would break her ribs. Mary Gray heard herself telling the 911 operator that she couldn't do it. The operator told her that help was being dispatched.

While she waited, she held Alice's hand, knowing that Alice was gone. She stroked Alice's hair as tears spilled from her eyes. After what seemed an eternity, a rescue squad came bolting up the lane, siren blaring. Mary Gray left Alice to open the back door. Two men entered and she directed them to the bathroom. One of them dropped to his knees, tore open Alice's blouse and started compression with rapid, movements. The other started collecting vital signs and administered a shot. It seemed so clinical, so anonymous. Watching all this jarred Mary Gray after such a solemn time alone with her friend. After numerous attempts to revive the woman, the pair admitted that she had expired. One of the medics said she probably had a stroke and had died immediately. He also explained that a sheriff would need to come out to look over the scene. The other medic radioed the request.

Mary Gray went in search of a blanket to cover Alice who looked vacant and exposed on the bathroom floor. She located a green patchwork quilt soft with age and took it to the bathroom to lay across Alice. She left her head uncovered. The medics packed up their equipment and filled out forms, all of them awaiting the officer. When the uniformed man arrived, he introduced himself and asked questions of Mary Gray and the medical team. Taking out his cell phone, he called the county medical examiner. Following instructions, the officer answered a series of questions. Finally he returned to Alice and the medics who were waiting in the kitchen.

"I'm sorry for your loss, Ma'am," he said to Mary Gray. "I am able to release the body for removal." He made this announcement while adjusting the holster on his belt. He seemed uncomfortable making this particular house call.

Mary Gray let out a breath. Sitting there she had realized the sheriff was deciding whether Alice had died of natural causes or if an investigation was needed.

"Are you a family member?"

"No, a friend," Mary Gray answered.

"I suggest you speak with a family member so they can make the appropriate decisions."

Mary Gray now wished she had paid more attention to Alice's stories. She knew about Alice's grandson, the one who loved Sally May. She thought of Alice's cell phone and the phone numbers stored in it. She could call random numbers and ask if the person knew whom she should call.

"Do you know how to contact Peter, her son?" the sheriff asked.

Mary Gray was startled that he already knew whom to call, but then, perhaps he also knew Alice.

"Did you know her?" Mary Gray asked.

"She was kin to my wife," he answered, adding, "but then we're all pretty well related in these parts."

"I'm sorry," Mary Gray said, now recognizing that Alice wasn't just a woman she had met a few days ago, but someone with an entire tree of familial relations.

"I was going to look for names in her cell phone."

"Start with Peter," the sheriff said, and then left with the medics trailing him out the door.

Mary Gray took a deep breath before placing the call. Peter answered, thinking it was his mother on the line.

"Mom—"

"Peter? This is Mary Gray Walterson. I'm a friend of your

A HORSE OF A DIFFERENT COLOR

mother's. We've had quite a time with the recent snow storm. In fact we got caught in it down in Virginia. The good news is that we retrieved her lost pony." Mary Gray wondered why she was going into all this explanation and not getting to the point. "But now that we're back to her house, your mother. . .your mother had an episode and collapsed. The rescue squad was just here and they believe that your mother has expired." There, she said it.

"Expired?" he asked.

"She died," Mary Gray said.

"My mother died?" he repeated.

"Yes. Completely unexpectedly. I found her on the bathroom floor. The medics did everything they could. They believe she had a stroke and went very quickly. No suffering," she added.

When he was silent she rushed to fill the void.

"We just returned from Virginia two hours ago. Your mother and I drove down with the horse trailer to get Sally May. We got stuck in that god-awful blizzard that dumped four feet of snow. But the men from the horse farm let us stay at their house for the last four days. Today we finally set out. Maybe the strain of driving was too much. She had to concentrate hard to keep the truck and trailer on the road. Thank goodness the roads were basically clear, but it must have taken its toll on her."

"I'm sorry, could you tell me your name again?"

"Mary Gray Walterson. I met your mother at the Halifax library last week. We struck up a conversation and figured out that it was her horse that had shown up in my community, Washington Spring, in Parabar County. It had become like a stray animal that we kept feeding, but our members decided we needed to find it another home. By the time I met your mother, unfortunately, we had just sold it, to a man in Virginia. When your mother and I put two and two together and realized this was hers, we contacted the horse farm. The

A HORSE OF A DIFFERENT COLOR

owner told us to come immediately so your mother asked me to go along. She was so happy to find Sally May."

"My son will be happy to hear that Sally May's alive and home. She was his favorite." He paused. "I am trying to gather my thoughts about my mother. She's gone?"

"Yes, I'm so sorry."

"We will need to come down to Halifax, to the house. Are you staying there?"

"I suppose I can. Do you want me to?"

"That would be good, I think."

"Where are you? And when do you think you will come?"

"My wife and I are in Hazlin Landing, near Baltimore. Tomorrow morning. What about her body?"

"The sheriff was here and suggested I contact you."

"I suppose we'll use Adderon's Funeral Home. Let me talk with my wife and call you back."

The two hung up.

About ten minutes later the phone rang.

"I've called Adderons. They can be over to you in about an hour. My wife and I will come in the morning. We can be there about 10 o'clock."

"Then I'll stay," Mary Gray answered.

After she hung up she stared at the paperwork the men had left where she sat at Alice's kitchen table. It was still set for dinner.

Two men arrived in pressed slacks and dress shirts. Even without a hearse--they brought a van—they had the air of funeral home personnel. The first man introduced himself as Mr. Adderon, and the other man as his assistant. The two went to the bathroom to examine Alice's body. The funeral director returned to Mary Gray and said that they would remove the body shortly and advised Mary Gray to stay in another room while they did their work. She sat back down at the kitchen table and watched as they rolled in a flat gurney

A HORSE OF A DIFFERENT COLOR

with folded sheets resting on top. After a few minutes they returned through the kitchen toward the back door. The gurney now extended to its full height contained Alice's body draped with white cloths, her head covered. Mary Gray automatically stood in reverence for her friend.

After loading the van, the funeral director returned with his paperwork. Mary Gray read and signed it and the two men left, disappearing down the lane.

Mary Gray looked around herself. The house was totally empty of life. It had been a beehive of activity. Now, with silence so potent she could hear the high pitched hum of her own nervous system.

Mary Gray was confused as to what to do. Whom to call. She could call John and share the epic events of the previous five days. She should let Acton know that the horse was safely home. She needed to contact St. James to say that she would miss another week of altar guild duties.

Instead, she reached for her purse and pulled out a slip of paper. It said, "Tell me YES today." She flipped it over. On the back side she had written Brown's phone number.

"Mm-Yellow?" the voice answered.

"Brown?" Mary Gray said tentatively, somehow losing all her nerve.

"Sweetheart! Did you make it to Halifax?" he asked. "I've been thinking of you the whole way."

"We did. Alice got the pony in the barn here and I set out to making us some dinner. Oh Brown. She died."

"The pony?"

"No, Alice. Alice died."

"God almighty! What on earth do you mean?"

Mary Gray explained the events since their return, the medics, the sheriff, the men from the funeral home, and the son who would be arriving in the morning.

"Do I need to do anything for the horses tonight?" Mary Gray asked, now realizing that she had responsibility for the

A HORSE OF A DIFFERENT COLOR

farm.

"I'm coming up to Halifax. Tonight. No sense in you trying to take care of her horses and farm when you don't know a donkey from a mule." She tried not to take that as an insult. What he said was true.

"What about your duties at Fortune Farms?"

"The men owe me time, their gettin' out of Dodge just when the storm rolled in. They was coming back on Monday, but I'm gonna call two of 'em and tell 'em they need to get here tomorrow morning. Give me the address and I'll see you in a few hours."

Mary Gray thought about the man who roared by Alice's truck on the wrong side, racing to the barn with his load of hay. She wanted Brown here. And she didn't. It felt like eons since she had been by herself in no one else's company. Why did she suddenly think she couldn't bear this little loneliness? Maybe because she was in yet another strange house. It had been a long week and what she really wanted was to be home. She sighed.

"I'll be fine here."

"So you know how to feed the horses? What else does she have? Goats, pigs, cows, chickens?"

"I don't really know. I could contact the neighbor who's been looking in on things. In fact, he may show up since Alice may not have let him know that she was back."

"I won't hear of it. I'm getting in my truck now and coming up. What's the address?"

Mary Gray picked up the earlier piece of mail and gave Brown the address.

"You'll be in better hands with me, anyway," he said reassuringly.

She wanted to believe that he was right.

The next days were a straight march of responsibilities. Brown really did know how to care for barn and farm. Mary

A HORSE OF A DIFFERENT COLOR

Gray felt sure she would have been lost without him. Peter and Cynthia arrived from Baltimore. They left their two children in boarding school, not having told them the news.

Peter made funeral arrangements with Adderon's and the Methodist minister. He set the funeral date for the following Saturday. This would allow time for Cynthia and him each to pick up a child on Friday after school and the four to come to Halifax on Saturday for the service. He told Mary Gray that after the funeral they would head home so the children could be back to school on Monday. His plan seemed the model of efficiency.

While he was at his mother's, Peter scoured her drawers for legal papers. The house and farm were all to go to him. He knew that his mother fully expected him to keep the property in the family. The question was, who would live there? He and Cynthia certainly would not. The children might one day want the farm but he could think of better uses.

Peter mentioned casually to Brown did he know if the neighbor could look in on the place?

Brown scowled and said that the farm required a full time hand to look after it, and it wouldn't be fair to put it on a neighbor. Venturing the possibility, Brown said, "If you want someone to run the place, I'm your man."

"I appreciate your stepping in while we're getting all this sorted out, but I don't expect…"

"I mean a real arrangement. I have the qualifications and the know-how from twenty-six years of farm management. I can handle everything from hogs to cows to horses, but I prefer horses. We could work out a deal where you pay me for my day job and I lodge in the house and keep it up, too. If you and your wife and children want to come spend the night, well I can make myself scarce. It would be like your home away from home."

Peter said he would think about the offer and get back to

A HORSE OF A DIFFERENT COLOR

Brown.

Mary Gray watched all these proceedings with hope and dread. Not only would Brown be able to see her, he would be living just a few miles away.

A HORSE OF A DIFFERENT COLOR

21

BALTIMORE

Sue turned into the parking lot of The Four Seasons Hotel. It stood tall and luxuriant before her and all of Baltimore Harbor. Suddenly her carefully chosen slacks and sweater seemed completely inadequate. Anything but Chanel and Gucci would have been. She sagged thinking of all the energy she put into sneaking a clothes bag to her car so she could wear her hospital scrubs like usual when leaving home. The day had the appearance of any other as she walked out the door to her cottage. She hadn't counted on meeting another Washington Spring member. As much as she was interested in catching up, she wanted much more to keep moving.

Keep cool so they won't notice your hurry, she told herself.

She listened to words and heard her own responses, but her mind was elsewhere. As quickly as she could extricate herself, she got in her car and left. The road, so very familiar, now looked like a luminous ribbon whimsically winding its way to the place where she would meet Martin. Branches of

A HORSE OF A DIFFERENT COLOR

bare trees seemed beautiful. The sky, though gray, was a gorgeous gray. And the piles of lingering snow, now smeared with dirt and grime, didn't register in her mind. She felt alive, and perhaps for the first time in her life, happy. But now at the hotel she realized that the clothes she changed into at the interstate rest stop would never do.

She noticed a man and woman walking from their car toward the hotel. The woman's perfect blond hair peeked out from the hood of her fur-trimmed parka. She wore stylish boots. The two laughed as they walked arm in arm toward the lobby door.

Were they married? Sue wondered. Could they, too, be there for a romantic interlude? Is this what the other half of the world did with their days—and nights? And she had only now stumbled upon this secret delight? But then she thought of Sandy. He may not be at all like the man she was about to meet, but he had stuck by her. They had made a life, out of nothing really, except broken dreams. Didn't that count for something? But perhaps loyalty had its limits, she considered, as she heard the laughter of the couple once more. How could it be wrong to be loved? And to want to be loved? Isn't that what preachers always preached? To love one another?

She glanced at her watch. She was exactly on time to meet Martin in the hotel bar at noon. She would go in her nylon snow jacket, blue pants and wool sweater. If he truly did love her, he wouldn't mind what she wore.

A HORSE OF A DIFFERENT COLOR

22

HALIFAX

Peter and Cynthia departed the day they arrived, leaving at sunset in their shiny black Escalade.
"We will be back on Saturday at eleven," Peter told Mary Gray.

Peter had scheduled the pre-funeral visitation for 1:30 p.m. on Saturday, and the funeral service for 3:00 p.m., both to be held at Wesley United Methodist church.

The telephone rang with questions. People had heard that a friend of Alice's was staying at the house. Callers asked if they could bring food. Mary Gray thought that was unnecessary since the son and family wouldn't be staying the night when they returned. As Mary Gray considered Peter and Cynthia's decision, she felt this would be too much for the children to manage in one day, but then, Mary Gray had to admit, she wasn't a parent and she didn't know these children.

The next morning Brown got a call from Peter.
"He said he wants to hire me for caretaking," Brown announced to Mary Gray when he hung up. "I could have

A HORSE OF A DIFFERENT COLOR

squeezed a little more salary from him, but, I didn't want to spoil the stew. Besides, I don't want him here breathing down my neck thinking he needs to supervise what he doesn't' know. He's a city slicker. You can tell he hasn't been in a barn for years, maybe ever. I'll take what I can get just to be near my sweetheart."

After breakfast Brown and Mary Gray both left the farm, Brown, to head to Fortune Farms to tender his resignation, pack his belongings and move. He said that he could do it in three trips if he handled the items himself, or in one, if he rented a towing trailer. He opted for the trailer so he could make the break swift and clean. Mary Gray set out for Washington Spring.

A HORSE OF A DIFFERENT COLOR

23

WASHINGTON SPRING

For the first time since her move to Washington Spring, Mary Gray felt her arrival as a true homecoming. When she pulled into her driveway Sue emerged from her house ready for work.

"You've been AWOL!" she hollered, about to get into her car.

Mary Gray swiftly walked over to Sue, suddenly glad to see her. "It's been quite a time," Mary Gray said, and gave an abbreviated explanation of the week.

"I sure am sorry to hear about that woman's sudden death. My father died without any warning, a myocardial infarction, so I know what that son is going through. He'll have his hands full." Sue pushed up her sleeve to glance at her watch.

Mary Gray mentioned that the son was making arrangements to have someone stay at the house and manage the farm. She didn't say anything specific about Brown.

"And that horse—you mean to say that you retrieved that horse and brought it all the way back here to Maryland, and

A HORSE OF A DIFFERENT COLOR

that woman was its rightful owner? How amazing you happened to be at the library at the same time she was, and for you to mention our horse to her. Have you told Acton yet? Or John? Or Angelika? They will want to know." Sue made to get into her car.

"No, I'm just getting home. I'll talk to them after I get myself unpacked. I'm sure the entire community will want to know."

"By the way, Sue," Mary Gray shouted through Sue's closing car door, "I'm really with you now about the sign-out policy. And we need to get a CPR class on our community calendar."

Inside her house, Mary Gray breathed in the familiar smell and exhaled with contentment. Her eyes fell upon her father's cupboard, her antique lamps, the books on her tables, so many touchstones of her life. At that moment she didn't care that her entryway was carpeted, or that her house was an open floor plan, and that she lived in 1,100 square feet. The thought then struck her that this would be a small space to share with someone like Brown who was not only large in size but in personality. What would he think of her mahogany furniture, books and doilies? She shook her head free of these thoughts and continued with the job of settling in.

Sandy stood in his kitchen and opened a box postmarked from one of his sisters. A note inside said *From Mom's*. Nothing more was written. He sifted through the contents, old comic books and matchbox racing cars. He pulled out six different grade school photos where he and twenty-some other children stood in front of a large auditorium curtain. He could see everyone's progression from first grade through sixth. The boys wore buzz cuts and the girls had pony tails. As he dug deeper into the box, Sandy saw an old photograph of his family at the seashore. It was from the one time they

A HORSE OF A DIFFERENT COLOR

had traveled to Ocean City, New Jersey. The picture was a scene at the beach. Children and families with beach umbrellas were crowded side-by-side all looking very much alike; however, for his family this was the only time they enjoyed that luxury. Sandy was five years old and he remembered his mother warning him not to touch anything at the guest home where they stayed. He and everyone in his troupe had to wipe themselves down and then shake out their towels and shoes before they could enter the house. His mother ordered that they not drag in any sand. He had tried to abide by these rules, but when he undressed in the bedroom, clumps of wet sand fell from him. He stood naked, his bottom exposed to his sisters who laughed at him with a jovial happiness. From that day on they started calling him Sandy. How had he forgotten?

John sat in his cottage and looked through his living room window at the gray light. Eighteen items along with pottery shards had been uncovered, each a clue to the indigenous people who once occupied the land on which Washington Spring was built, exactly where he was sitting. A wave of melancholy and regret swept through him. The artifacts were all lost, but one. The relief he might have felt was overshadowed by guilt. Covering up his findings was not what his wife or mother would have done. He knew that they were right.

The baby rattle with tiny pebbles rested in a nest of cotton. He would place it anonymously in the mail tomorrow to the Smithsonian National American Indian Museum. They would be grateful for the anonymous gift. John sighed and looked at his mother's picture in a sturdy wooden frame.

"Acton?" Mary Gray said from her landline.
"Yes, Mary Gray. Hello," Acton replied.
"I just got back to the Close. I've had quite an adventure.

A HORSE OF A DIFFERENT COLOR

Thank you for giving us the contact information for Jerry Wagner. Alice and I tracked him down, and we located the pony. He told us we had to come pick her up that same day, the day of the blizzard, but we didn't know that such a bad storm was on the way." Mary Gray proceeded to tell Acton the tale of her events.

"Acton, Alice's papers included the bill of sale between Fortune Farms and Washington Spring. It said that we received $50,000. I believe I remember our check being $5,000. Did I get that wrong?"

Acton froze. This was the moment he had been dreading. For all his rehearsals, he suddenly couldn't think of what to say. He had turned this over in his mind a thousand times. To continue covering up the truth would be to keep the lie alive. To tell the truth would expose his embezzlement of the funds.

"Mary Gray, there's quite a bit more to the story," he said, stalling for time.

"What do you mean?" she asked.

"Let's put this conversation on hold. You've just returned and you have many things to sort out. I'll get back with you on the bill of sale, okay?"

He hastily got himself off the phone with a margin of time bought to decide his plan.

Acton took a seat in his living room and looked out the window. A scene of white still dressed the shrubs and ground. If he could only clear his conscience, he thought. The money had allowed him to save face with the art gallery for their annual award. However, that was a small matter compared with his entire future. His family name was now at stake. He had been schooled in keeping the Alexander name unsullied. And now he had stained it over his pride. Acton felt isolated and alone. His friendships back in the city had been built mainly around mutual activities and now that they

A HORSE OF A DIFFERENT COLOR

were no longer near one another, those relationships foundered. He didn't know with whom to seek counsel except for himself. And he wasn't so sure he could trust himself, anymore.

A thousand times a day his thoughts ruminated on his decision about *the transaction*. The bill of sale had been easy to forge with new numbers since Fortune Farms used a standard document that he could reproduce. The signatures were his and one other party. So he took a pen in hand and simply scribed the other man's signature to look nothing like his own. None of it had been hard. That was the weight of it—how easy it had all been. He told John that the check had inadvertently been made out to him, personally, so he deposited it into his own account, and wrote a check from his same account to Washington Spring for $5,000, which matched the amount on the re-constructed bill of sale.

Washington Spring members had no reason not to trust that everything he said was true. And so the exchange had transpired with ease. He could never have imagined that the horse's owner would be located, let alone that someone from Washington Spring would have been involved in its return and have access to the original documents. He was caught.

Acton opened up his checkbook. Slim numbers. He looked at his bank records. Not much there. He went online to see his brokerage account balance. It was slightly above its lowest point given a small rise in the market and some dividends. If he had to return the $45,000 he could order his new investment manager to sell his remaining positions. But he would be broke, totally and completely broke.

He drew a long breath. Would the community press charges for embezzlement? Prison time, what a foreign thought. And would his skin color throw weight on the scales of justice against him?

Forcing his hand to do as his conscience ordered, Acton picked up the telephone and placed a call.

A HORSE OF A DIFFERENT COLOR

"John? This is Acton. May I come over?"

A HORSE OF A DIFFERENT COLOR

24

HALIFAX

Mary Gray returned to Alice's house on Friday, the day before the funeral. She and Brown had spoken each evening by phone. He had succeeded in leaving his work at Fortune Farms on good terms, and now was completely moved in at Alice's, running the farm. Brown asked Mary Gray if she would come to Halifax the day before the funeral, saying the house might use a little touch up before the family arrived. Mary Gray agreed, but in her heart, she was not eager to go. She couldn't identify exactly what held her back. Her heart yearned to be saturated with love for this man, as this man so obviously felt for her. And yet, she could not give herself to him without reservation. He was handsome. He was kind. He was unfailingly willing to do for others. But something wasn't right. She simply couldn't put her finger on it.

When she arrived at Alice's house Brown greeted her with a bear hug and kiss which she welcomed, her resistance falling away when he smiled at the sight of her. He twirled her around like a ballerina.

A HORSE OF A DIFFERENT COLOR

"Stunning," he said, commenting on her beauty. She demurred, looking down at her ordinary self. "I picked up lunch for us," he added heroically. "It's in the Fridgidare. You only need to lay it out. Come on. Let me show you what I've been doing."

He took her on a tour of the outside, nodding toward the horses in the pasture.

"Sally May has settled in." He pointed to the east. "I figure that trotting ring means that Alice did some training. The snow's melted enough that I've had the horses out every day since I've been back. I love this place. The new barn is a good one. I sure hope that Peter-man will see how right I am for this job."

Like a little boy seeking praise, Brown took her around to see numerous projects he had underway. Mary Gray nodded her approval, oohing and ahhing in the right places. After thirty minutes of his showcase, she said she should get on to the house. Brown retrieved her things from the car and carried them inside.

The house wasn't quite the shambles she thought it might be.

"I know you have the magic touch," Brown said. "Just call when you've got lunch laid out."

It was ten o'clock when she started on her tasks. The house needed dusting and vacuuming, the tools for which she found in the storage closet. She saw that he had tossed some blue gel in the toilet, but otherwise, the bathroom needed a great deal of help. Mary Gray wondered how it was that men could live in filth and then think that a little blue liquid swished around would cure it all. She was on hands and knees in the bathroom when the phone rang. She drew herself up and over to the wall telephone.

"Hello. Alice Croft's," she answered.

"Oh—who is this?" a woman asked.

"I'm a friend of Alice's, Mary Gray Walterson, from

A HORSE OF A DIFFERENT COLOR

Parabar Shore. May I help?"

"My name is Desiree Chilton. I used to clean for Ms. Croft. I understand that she passed," the woman said.

"That's right. She died last week."

"Well, glory be. God rest her soul. I was her cleaning lady and I wanted to pay my respects. Is the service tomorrow?"

"Yes, tomorrow. Visitation is at 1:30 p.m. and the service is at 3:00 p.m."

"I realize this may be a little forward of me, but do you suppose someone could pay me for services rendered? I worked for Ms. Croft all last month and would have been paid last week, but of course, God rest her soul, that wasn't possible."

"I'm afraid that I'm not in charge of those affairs, Ms. Chilton. Alice's son will be here tomorrow with his family, but I don't know how attentive he can be to financial matters."

"No, no, of course not."

"Perhaps you could write up an invoice and I could put it with the mail and items being collected for her son?"

"Oh, I don't know if I'm able to do that. I hate to put another thing on the family right now. It's just that..."

Brown entered through the side door, shed his coat and boots, and walked to the kitchen sink.

"Yes, I hear that you will need your money, Ms. Chilton. Is there a number I can leave for him to call you, and perhaps an amount that you're due?" Mary Gray's attention was drawn from the telephone to Brown's hand-washing in her sparkling clean sink. She reached for the back of an envelope on a nearby table, and located a pen.

The woman gave Mary Gray her phone number and a figure.

"Okay, I will leave this word for Peter. Perhaps he will get in touch with you tomorrow. That's really all I can do," Mary Gray said.

A HORSE OF A DIFFERENT COLOR

"I am much obliged," the woman said. "I do plan to attend the service. I've been knowing Ms. Croft since the day I was born, or more like, she's been knowing me since the day I was born."

Hanging up the wall telephone, Mary Gray turned to face Brown. "I guess I got carried away with housework. What time is it?"

"It's nearing one o'clock," Brown said.

"Oh my! I had no idea. I'm so sorry!" Mary Gray said, and scurried over to the refrigerator to see what Brown had purchased.

"I see roasted chicken and potato salad, slaw and…" then standing upright and spotting the top shelf, she continued, "sweet tea."

"Got some baked beans on the pantry shelf."

"I can heat those up fast," she said. Brown helped himself to a seat at the kitchen table. Everything felt reminiscent of their time at Fortune Farms, only now it was just the two of them. He seemed all the more intent on her feeding him. Clearly, he wanted her to be responsible for the inside, and he the outside. If the order were anything different, it would not have felt right to him, although in this traditional arrangement, there seemed to be no regard for her years of intellectual contribution and her education. Maybe this was the problem she was feeling?

"What'd that caller want?" Brown asked, sitting and waiting, while she dashed about, placing items before him and onto the table.

"A woman who cleaned for Alice, says she's owed some money for the work she did last month."

"How much?"

"$200."

Brown whistled. "For a month of cleaning? How often did she clean?"

"Twice, I think,"

A HORSE OF A DIFFERENT COLOR

"That's a hundred dollars a pop. You do that and don't charge at all!" Brown announced.

Mary Gray bristled. This was not the sort of situation she wanted to get herself into, and now she could see exactly how her work at Fortune Farms had set up this man to think that she was prepared to be his Haus Frau.

"I'm not inclined to be a cleaning lady," Mary Gray said.

"You've got this place sparkling to a shine. I said you could perform magic and I sure was right." He was going on as though he had not heard her.

She scooped warm beans into a serving dish and presented it on the table. She sat. He prayed.

"Lord, we thank you for this fine repast that provides us strength for the work you give us this day. Let us be mindful of your tender mercies and loving kindness to us, for your name's sake. Amen."

Mary Gray immediately felt guilty. Maybe she was being too sensitive. After all, this man had given up everything to come to Maryland, and of course he was not able to take care of home as well as farm. If the Lord asked for her to lend a hand, perhaps she could be less selfish and do so. She certainly took a domestic role while at Fortune Farms. Maybe she could find some satisfaction by serving here.

People dropped by with food the next day saying they would be attending the service in the afternoon. Mary Gray appreciated their kindness, but wasn't sure what to do with their dishes and casseroles since she had already made provisions for the family.

The weather was mild for the end of February with a lightly clouded sky. The heat of the sun helped to continue the melting. Many places were completely bare of snow, although big banks of it existed where plows had dumped their load.

On cue, at 11 a.m. the family arrived in their black

A HORSE OF A DIFFERENT COLOR

Escalade. Brown had told Mary Gray that he would show them around the farm. Mary Gray knew that he wanted to ingratiate himself with Peter so that Peter would see his value and keep him on.

Mary Gray reached for her coat to head out to greet them. As she emerged from the house, so did the children from the car. They were older than Mary Gray imagined. In Alice's photos the children were much younger. The boy seemed to be ten or eleven and the girl fourteen going on eighteen. She was as tall as her mother, with long blonde hair hanging to her shoulders. She wore a tight black dress to show off a slim teenage figure. The boy was shorter, stockier, in a suit not meant for him. He wiped his nose and stood awkwardly waiting for his parents' direction. Cynthia was in a black dress and black heels, her own blonde hair swept in a tasteful arrangement atop her head. Peter was in a dark suit with a plain tie, looking like this was his everyday wear. He began ushering everyone toward the house.

Brown appeared from the barn and intercepted the family. Mary Gray could hear his greeting.

She backed off from her own hello, remaining at a distance. Brown shook hands with Peter and bowed graciously with hat in hand toward Cynthia. Brown was every bit the gentleman, Mary Gray observed. He introduced himself to the children offering to take them on a tour, but Peter waved him off, indicating that he and the family should go into the house. Brown's face fell, but then he smiled and tipped his hat, in affable agreement.

Now the four approached Mary Gray who smiled her best funeral-day smile. She didn't feel the need to shake hands or embrace the lot, so before they reached her she said hello and turned to lead them into the house. At that moment she thought that her leading them into the house was quite presumptuous. This was their house, the house that Peter had known his entire life. As they entered, the boy asked if he

A HORSE OF A DIFFERENT COLOR

could see the horses. His mother told him after the funeral he could go to the barn.

Peter suggested they sit in the living room. Mary Gray waited for each one to choose a seat and then perched on a small chair between the living room and kitchen. The little group made idle chit chat. There was no sign of Brown. She expected that he would be in shortly for lunch and to change clothes.

The subject of lunch came up as Mary Gray announced that she had food ready for them.

Peter and Cynthia looked anxiously at one another.

"We thought that we would get something at the town café," Cynthia explained. "We didn't want to trouble you."

"Oh, it's no trouble," Mary Gray said. Now she risked being disappointed as Brown had been. Should she press them to accept her offering? She stood.

"We have hot and cold lunch, either one. Homemade chowder and cornbread for the ones who need their bones warmed, and deli meat sandwiches for those who would prefer something cold."

"Oh, how sweet you are to go to all this trouble," Cynthia said. Then, almost embarrassed, she added, "Angeline's a vegetarian and also gluten-free and Chadwick is cutting back on bread, so I'm afraid that—"

"I'm sure we can figure something out," Mary Gray interrupted, surprising even herself with how desperate she sounded. "You won't get anything to your liking at the café, I can assure you! They have a very basic menu," Mary Gray added, to bolster her argument. "I bet you can find some things here, if you help me," Mary Gray said, indicating to Angeline, a little less edge in her voice.

Cynthia looked to Peter who shrugged.

"Well, kids, see what you can do. Chadwick, please take off your suit jacket and put a towel over your shirt if you're working around food."

A HORSE OF A DIFFERENT COLOR

The children followed Mary Gray into the kitchen. The three were putting a meal together when Brown came through the door. His presence was always felt when he entered a room.

"Isn't she the finest cook in the county?" Brown boomed with pride at Mary Gray who was smiling to see the children setting the table.

The funeral included a graveside burial. Since the cemetery was on the church grounds, nearly everyone proceeded from the church service to the gravesite. People walked in a line following the minister and family, which meant tromping on graves that they otherwise would never have violated. Mary Gray hung toward the back of the procession, Brown following her, holding his ten gallon hat in his hand. The bare soil, soggy from snow melt, gave way under foot. Mary Gray thought about the muddy mess people would later be scraping from their good shoes.

They gathered under a green tent which bore the name *Adderon's*. When the minister finished, he took a shovelful of wet dirt which had been loosed for him and dropped it on top of the small box of ashes, visible in the grave's hole. Then he turned and, one by one, shook the hands of the family members, including the children. Mary Gray noticed the intense look on Chadwick's face whose eyes peered into the face of the minister. Of all the family, Chadwick seemed the most affected by Alice's death.

As people turned to leave, Mary Gray overheard one of the older church women say to another, "Her mother was a gem of a woman; never batted an eye when she had to put her husband into the ground, but then why would she? Him being so derelict. No one will forget that day."

After the events, Mary Gray and Brown returned to the farm. Brown changed from his funeral suit into his standard uniform of jeans and flannel shirt. He also switched out hats, hanging his dress hat on a peg, exchanging it for his work hat. In the kitchen he stood fidgeting with his familiar hat while Mary Gray, still in her funeral dress, dashed about placing the neighbors' food onto the table.

At 5:00 p.m. the family came in without saying much. The boy went directly to the sofa and sank down on it. He had loosened his tie and now tossed its tail up and down. His sister stood by the sofa, awaiting instruction.

"Why don't you go change your clothes, Chad," his mother said. Then to Brown, "Would it be alright for him to use your room?"

"Sure it is," Brown said, then added, "It's as much your room as it is my room. Come on, boy, we'll get you set up to see the barn." Brown indicated the room. The boy looked to his mother for where to find his clothes. She pointed to a duffle bag in the kitchen. He shrugged, went and picked it up and followed Brown. Taking a detour he said, "I'll use this room," indicating the second bedroom where he always slept when he stayed with his grandmother. He preferred to follow his familiar patterns, even if his grandmother was no longer there.

Outside, Brown suddenly becoming a tour guide, showing Chad around as though the farm and barn were entirely new to the boy.

"I know where the hay and grain are kept," the boy mumbled.

"Is that right?" Brown asked. "Are you a seasoned hand, then?"

"I stayed here a lot and helped my grandmother," he said. "I was here when the fire happened."

"So that explains the brand new barn," Brown said. "Tell me about it."

Chad recounted the awful events. He talked while Brown led them through a gate and out into the pasture. The sun

A HORSE OF A DIFFERENT COLOR

was sinking in the sky.

"Let's bring in the horses," Brown said, as Chad finished his tale.

"I want to get Sally May," Chad said.

Chad spotted her at the far end of the field. She was facing away from him, but hearing his voice, she turned her head and sniffed the air. The boy broke into a run, his feet carrying him toward her as fast as he could go. She lifted her head, nodding at his appearance.

"Sally May!" he cried. As he reached her he threw his arms about her neck and buried his face in her mane. The pony let him hold her. As he did, a flood of tears streamed from his eyes. His horse was home. He ached for his grandmother to be home, too.

"Son, you want to ride her?" Brown asked when he caught up to the pair.

"No, I don't ride," the boy answered, trying to hide his sniffles as he straightened to the stranger.

"You can if you like," Brown said.

"What do you mean?" the boy asked.

"There's nothing like the feeling of being one with a horse and the best way to do that is to ride her."

"How do I do that? I've never done that before."

"You see the riding ring? We take her over there and we put you on her, simple as that. You lead her and I'll follow."

They arrived at the ring and Brown instructed the boy to leave Sally May where he could put a saddle on her and place the bit in her mouth. The boy watched as Brown did these. Then he led Sally May to a three-step platform so the boy could mount the pony's back.

"She's ready for you," Brown said.

The boy cautiously took the three steps, and with some effort swung his leg up and around and got himself on. Brown held her tight, and the pony obeyed.

Brown showed the boy how to wrap the reins around his

A HORSE OF A DIFFERENT COLOR

hands and after a few instructions, Brown led the pony and rider away. Soon Brown let go and Sally May continued walking around the ring. For her it was familiar territory. Although she had been ridden by other children, she seemed to know that this child was the most special one in the world.

Chad held the reins just as Brown said. He felt elated. Being so high up he could see for a mile. Through his legs he could feel Sally May's muscles. She walked with purpose. He felt her dignity and his own, as though she were transferring that feeling to him. He looked across the field toward the barn. His sister had come out of the house and was standing by the gate. She raised her hand in a small wave. The boy smiled. This was his place, he now knew. No matter how long it would take, he would work his whole life so he could be here. This was his home.

A HORSE OF A DIFFERENT COLOR

25

WASHINGTON SPRING

"John, what I need to tell you is a complete account of the sale of the horse," Acton began. They were seated at John's dining room table which was the familiar spot for community meetings. John had taken a seat across from Acton so the two could talk more closely than head and foot where they customarily sat. Acton had come in a pressed shirt and polished shoes. The ordinary acts of ironing and polishing had pointed his energies in a positive direction.

"Go on," John said.

"The horse, it turns out, was a Tarpan pony, or a descendant of a Tarpan, a type of wild horse that's thought to be essentially extinct. A few horse enthusiasts in Europe were trying to re-establish the line by back-breeding. Apparently, someone here was doing the same, which made this horse worth more than anyone realized. I figured it out before I sold it, but I didn't disclose it because I needed money and I thought that if the horse were worth more than $5,000 I would take the rest, as a sort of finder's fee. The community

A HORSE OF A DIFFERENT COLOR

seemed happy to get $5,000, which is already a very nice sum for a horse. But this horse was worth more."

"How much did you get?"

"$50,000."

"So you're saying that the horse actually sold for $50,000?"

"Yes. And I took the remaining $45,000 as an undisclosed finder's fee."

"But the bill of sale showed $5,000."

"It did. I created a new one to indicate $5,000. It's not the original. I kept the original."

"I see."

A long pause hung between the men.

Acton had hoped he would feel better for finally admitting his malfeasance, but in that moment he only felt worse. His heart pounded. His stomach churned. He reached into his pocket for a Rolaid.

"You needed the money?" John asked.

"Yes. My niece was managing my investments. She had a good record with my portfolio, so over time I let her have more and more of my wealth. She put me into a company that she had no business investing in, let alone with most of my assets. I don't need to tell you what you can already guess: the company's stock fell to nothing. I could bring charges against her for failing to follow the federal fiduciary standard, but it would ruin her. It's enough punishment that she has left the investment field. I had to come up with funds for an arts award I've been underwriting."

"I can see this put you in a tight spot," John said. "I can imagine your concern about how to keep afloat after such a devastating loss." John sighed. "We have many things to sort out here. One, your decision to mislead our community, two, who should know about this, and three, your ability and likelihood to continue in our community."

Acton nodded slightly. He looked past John to the wall.

"I feel like your action was completely outside of your

A HORSE OF A DIFFERENT COLOR

character, that you would never have done this had circumstances not led you to such desperation. I wish you had come to me, to any of us, to let us know. I realize as I say this, that it is a man's pride at stake, and you more than most, have had a clean record of service, to country and community. Add to that record the obstacles you have no doubt overcome in your life, the difficulty of racism to name just one. Your not wanting to speak out against your niece shows your qualities all the more. These must have made it impossibly difficult for you to come to me. I am sorry, Acton. Truly sorry."

Another long silence fell.

"You have certainly been a good friend to me in launching this project while I turned my attention to caring for Pauline," John said. "Let me ask you this, Acton. If you were able to continue living in Washington Spring, would you?"

"I would be seeing my crime every day in the eyes of the people I live with. Their knowing. My knowing."

"What if they didn't know?"

"I would know."

"Yes. Spoken like an honest man."

"I have a check here for $45,000." Acton pulled it from his shirt pocket, unfolded it and slid it across to John.

"This is your last money, isn't it?" John asked.

Acton didn't move.

"I see." John sighed heavily, and nodded to himself. "Have you freed yourself from your other obligations?"

"I have."

"Will your income cover your living expenses here?"

"Yes, the basics are covered."

Touching the check John said, "I am prepared for this matter simply to be kept between us. You are free to decide what you would like. You are a much-needed and much appreciated resident here." John looked at Acton with hopeful intention.

Acton could not meet John's eyes. His head gave the

A HORSE OF A DIFFERENT COLOR

slightest nod.

John began to get up but Acton interrupted him. "Mary Gray knows," Acton said.

"Mary Gray?"

"She was the one who located the horse's owner and saw the original bill of sale. She knows that the amounts are different."

"I see."

"John, I appreciate your kindness toward me, but this really is a matter for the community to decide."

"Again, spoken like an honest man."

"It's the community that needs to determine a course of action. They may want to press charges."

"I see what you are driving at; however, I believe there are times that call for discretion, and this may be one of those. I have been around long enough to know that men make decisions they regret, and if they are not given the chance to rectify themselves, they turn to abuses and worse. I have seen it happen. I, myself, have been granted mercies by men who knew better than I what I could be capable of, both for the good and for the ill. Acton, you are a good soul. I know it to be true of you. Only a good soul would ask to be considered for punishment. I am not willing to punish you. And I strongly recommend that you do not punish yourself. We need you here. God knows there are fewer and fewer good men anywhere," John concluded.

"Mary Gray." Acton reminded John.

"I will speak to her. You will hear from me after I have talked with her."

Now John rose and waited for Acton to rise also. The men looked at one another across the table. John held Acton's gaze as long as possible before Acton dropped his eyes. He felt anything but worthy, certainly not of the community, or of his own name.

After seeing Acton to the door, John sank into one of his

A HORSE OF A DIFFERENT COLOR

living room chairs. He reflected on the past Sunday's sermon. It had been about not casting the first stone.

26

HALIFAX

Mary Gray said goodbye to the family as they boarded their vehicle. Chad smiled to his sister as they slid into the backseat. The boy had a secret that he was sharing only with her. She smiled back at him.

Brown and Mary Gray waved as the car started down the lane. Brown pulled his arm tighter around Mary Gray's waist and turned her toward him. At his height he gazed down into her eyes. She waited for him to kiss her.

"That boy had never ridden a horse. Today was his first time," Brown suddenly announced, as if this explained why he was looking so fully into her face. "I got him on one, for starters."

"Which one?"

"Sally May."

"That would be the perfect one."

They went inside the house. Mary Gray began gathering her things to prepare to go.

"So you're going to leave a man when he's down on his luck?"

A HORSE OF A DIFFERENT COLOR

"What do you mean?"

"Peter told me he would only be needing me for another two months. He plans to bring in a contractor to turn the property into a housing development. He thinks he can put twenty-four houses on this land. I told him flat out that he was crazy, that the land probably didn't perk and that small farms needed to be preserved and that I was prepared to stay on indefinitely. He said he understood but that he was sending a surveying crew out next week and to be on the lookout for them. I declare that man has nothing but dollar signs in his soul."

"That reminds me. Did he see the note about the $200 owed to the cleaning lady?"

"He took the mail, if that's what you mean. He said he was sorting out matters as quickly as he could. He said his mother's land was in trust, with him as the beneficiary, so they could avoid probate. That means he can do what he wants more or less from the get go."

"I hate to leave you with this bad news, but I need to get back to my house. I have been missing my home." It was true, she had.

"You haven't yet invited me to see it," Brown said playfully.

Mary Gray was alarmed. She had not invited him. In fact, she had said virtually nothing about him to anyone, other than to describe him along with Jack as the heroes who saved scores of people from the disastrous snow. She wasn't quite sure why she hadn't said more.

"All in good time," she said, unsure of what she meant.

"You're saving me for an announcement, aren't you?"

"What?"

"You're saving up to make an announcement to your friends there in Washington Spring that you intend to marry a man you just met. You just don't know yet precisely how you're going to tell them."

A HORSE OF A DIFFERENT COLOR

Was he right? Was she hesitant simply because she didn't know how or when she could talk about this unlikely attachment she had formed with this man?

"Ah, you'll know when the time's right," he said, and pulled her into his arms for a kiss.

A HORSE OF A DIFFERENT COLOR

27

WASHINGTON SPRING

Mary Gray returned to a message on her home telephone from John. He didn't sound anxious to speak to her, so she unpacked her things, her mind working on the problem of why she didn't feel right around Brown. He was sweet to her. He helped her whenever she asked. He gave her compliments galore. She just didn't feel as though she had access to her own mind when she was around him. She didn't know how black holes worked, but it was as though he was a black hole that she fell into where all signals were lost, to the outside world, to her own world, to her own heart. She went to bed and pulled the covers close. She knew so little about herself around him, but she knew everything about herself when they were apart.

Sue texted one word, then pressed send.

It had been a dream come true, Martin greeting her in the hotel bar with the sly smile she remembered from the reunion when he teased her about falling off the horse. Her legs went

A HORSE OF A DIFFERENT COLOR

watery and her heart raced. His eyes could carry her across the length of the hotel if need be. Everyone and everything else was background, a blur as she walked toward him. He was a body in a tweed jacket, but all she really saw were his gorgeous eyes and mouth. He greeted her by brushing his lips against hers, sweet and subtly suggestive. All she had imagined was happening. He handed her a glass, then taking his own in hand, he led her to a table. Others who were lunching in the tavern lingered and talked at their tables, while Sue and Martin said very little and rushed through their lunch. They were coming to his one simple question.

"Would you like to go upstairs with me?"

Her voice gone, she smiled her answer.

Upstairs, they entered his room, champagne on their breath and intentions in their hearts. Sue tossed her items on a chair, then turned to Martin. The moment had come. As it opened before them, Martin's cell phone rang. It buzzed on the credenza with the name Candy flashing. Martin ignored it and instead slipped his hand around Sue's waist. She thought he was pulling her to him until she realized he was maneuvering her away from his phone. He bent down to kiss her, but the spell was broken.

"I think you should get that," Sue said.

"Nothing is more important to me than you," Martin mumbled, now trying to pull her toward him.

"Really?" Sue wondered. "If I am so important, then do as I ask and answer your telephone." Suddenly she felt very powerful. The champagne had emboldened her.

"That's no one I need to talk to now."

Sue reached for the phone and swiped. "Hello?"

"Martin?" a woman's voice answered quizzically.

"This is Martin's phone, yes," Sue said. "Who is this?"

"Is Martin there? Is he okay? This is his wife."

Sue stared at Martin, then thrust the phone at him.

A HORSE OF A DIFFERENT COLOR

"Your wife is calling."

"I couldn't reach my phone. I'm in a coffee shop and some customer reached it while I was getting cream for my coffee." Sue listened to the story Martin was inventing, craftily covering his tracks.

"I need to call you back later." He didn't wait for his wife to respond but simply ended the call.

"Now, where were we?" He reached out his hand to stroke Sue's face, a gesture that moments earlier would have endeared her. Now it angered her.

"Is that how you treat your wife?" she suddenly demanded.

"Isn't this the pot calling the kettle black?"

"You lied to me. You told me that you and Mary divorced."

"We did. That was years ago."

"And you conveniently forgot to tell me you had remarried?"

"Are you married, Sue?"

She was flustered. Of course he was right, but there was a principle at stake here. He had lied to her and she wasn't going to stand for it. She gathered her nylon coat, her winter gloves and purse and stormed out the door.

Days later he was now stalking her by phone. The one word she texted was *NO*. This would also be her last word to him.

"John, it's Mary Gray. I hope I'm not calling too early this Sunday morning."

"Mary Gray. Good to hear from you. Are you back?"

"Last night, yes. I hope you didn't need me to call you sooner."

"No. But I do hope that we can talk. Could you come over later today?"

"I have altar guild clean up after church. How about 2:00

A HORSE OF A DIFFERENT COLOR

p.m.?

At St. James-in-the-Wood Mary Gray felt completely at home. The liturgy pulled her along into the pattern she knew by heart. The music was balm to her aching spirit. And the sermon seemed particularly poignant about letting oneself be loved.

Mary Gray watched as the priest prepared for Holy Communion. He took the wafers from the silver box and placed them on the polished paten. He took the empty chalice and placed it next to the paten. He took the glass cruet and began to pour the dark red wine. He lifted the white linen purificator to dab the wine at the cruet's spout. There was no spill. Mary Gray smiled and silently patted her purse. Super Glue really did have its merits.

As the church service ended and Bryan completed his organ postlude, she took her place in the sacristy for clean up. Everything was in its familiar and right place, like a kitchen she knew from memory, no pulling open drawers hunting for things. She loved the lingering scent of Sunday's flowers and the smell of incense stored in the cabinet. She went about her chores as Bryan poked his head into the sacristy door.

"Hey stranger!" he said. "We didn't know if we would have to perform a requiem mass for you." He pulled her into a little hug. She noticed how comfortable he felt.

"It's been a wild week or two."

"Has it ever. I want to hear all about yours."

"Bryan," she suddenly asked. "How do you know if you're in love?"

"In love? Why do you ask? Are you in love Mary Gray?" he teased.

"I'm asking you because I don't know." She pulled off her white polishing gloves and faced him.

"I see. It's that serious. Hmm. Well, when I met Jimmy there were fireworks that went off in my head and I felt like

A HORSE OF A DIFFERENT COLOR

my spirit was soaring, or maybe that was when he agreed to our first date. Why, do you feel that way?"

"Let's just say the pyro-technicians haven't quite shown up yet."

"Uh huh. And do you want them to?"

"I don't know. Maybe it's a product of being my age. Maybe it's not wanting to upset my routine. Maybe it's that I really don't love the man. He certainly seems to love me."

"Fireworks from his end?"

She nodded.

"Oh. That's the worst. And you're feeling guilty because you aren't looking at the same colorful display. Yeah, I've been through that. And the very sight of the person makes your stomach churn because you want to love them, but you really don't and you think, maybe if I hang on a little longer I will. And then you start justifying the whole thing by saying, well, maybe love is a process and it takes time to really know someone, let alone love them."

"That's it."

"Well, Honey, here's the truth. You either love him or you don't. And you don't. So kiss him goodbye and move on. Your prince charming awaits you somewhere. I gotta go. The choir will be looking for me."

Bryan dashed out the sacristy door. In two minutes flat he had nailed exactly what was going on inside her. Was it that simple? She didn't love Brown? She admired him. She liked him. She just didn't love him. And if that were the case, should she in fact tell him goodbye? She pulled out a knife and held it to the neck of a candleholder to dislodge some errant wax.

"Mary Gray, come in." John welcomed her into his home. As familiar as his cottage was, she rarely sat in his living room, which is where he indicated they should have their conversation. She wondered if this were a social call, or

A HORSE OF A DIFFERENT COLOR

something to do with Washington Spring business.

"I hear you had quite a time while you were gone," John began.

"Well, it was an adventure." Mary Gray proceeded to tell him, keeping her comments about Brown to a minimum.

"I'm glad that you were able to befriend Alice and she you before such an untimely death. You always rise to occasions, Mary Gray. You have the right balance of heart and head to get you through any situation."

She wondered about his comment. She felt short-suited on both sides of that equation. The source of the Washington Spring name entered her mind.

"Alice told me that George Washington used to hunt on these very grounds. She said he visited the Barclays who settled here. He would come for hunting parties. On one of their outings they ran short of water and apparently Washington remembered seeing a spring and led the hunters and horses to it. She said that after that they called it Washington's Spring. Had you heard that story?"

"Pauline and I were told there used to be a spring of water called Washington Spring, but that no one knew where it was. I certainly hadn't heard that tale."

"Alice's pony must've figured out where it was. What a happy coincidence, like coming full circle, from Washington's horses to Alice's."

"So, the horse is now in its rightful place?" John asked.

"Yes, the horse is home. And Alice's grandson is thrilled. There's one fly in the ointment, though. Alice's son is planning to use her land for a housing development. He thinks Halifax County needs more houses."

"I see," John said. Considering his own development debacle, he kept his thoughts to himself. "I want to speak to you about the transaction that involved the horse."

Suddenly Mary Gray's mind zeroed in on the subject. "Yes, I've been meaning to check this with you. Fortune

A HORSE OF A DIFFERENT COLOR

Farms' bill of sale was for $50,000. My memory is that we received $5,000. I have a copy of their paperwork. That's a large difference. What do you make of it?"

"You're right. The initial transaction was for $50,000. Acton had to do a good deal of research on our behalf, and in doing so he learned that the horse was worth far more than the estimated $5,000 we all thought. He had to negotiate hard to get that large sum." John stopped and looked for Mary Gray's reaction.

Mary Gray looked puzzled at his incomplete explanation.

"The discrepancy is what I want to talk with you about. Acton had a little stumble about the fee from Fortune Farms. He initially held onto $45,000 of the original $50,000. He was in a bit of a financial bind right then and acting on bad judgment he delayed turning over the full amount. But he has since paid it to us.

"But didn't the paperwork he presented say $5,000?"

"It did. And this is what I want you to understand. Acton is a valued member of our community and I believe that you would agree with me that we appreciate and need his contributions. And, he has been completely reliable. Do I even need to mention how critical he has been to forwarding Phase II of Washington Spring, or for that matter, how key he was in getting us opened when Pauline was in her final days." John paused. "Acton had a momentary lapse, which he came to tell me, and he has restored the full amount. He is prepared to go before the community about this, but I feel as though that would not be necessary."

"I see." Mary Gray took in this news. She wasn't sure what she thought about giving this man an out. Acton certainly was central to the community and as far as she knew, he had never before done anything to hurt their welfare. A stumble, John said. An interesting word. Maybe she herself was stumbling where Brown was concerned. She could have told him at the start that she really wasn't interested in a relation-

A HORSE OF A DIFFERENT COLOR

ship, that she was perfectly fine in her own life. It was he who pursued her. But she had gone along with it, and as she thought about it, now back in her own community, in familiar space, maybe she had misrepresented herself, led him on, as the girls in high school would say. She had stumbled by not being a person of integrity herself.

"What do you propose?" she asked.

"I think that we don't need to take this before the community. You and I are capable of solving this." He waited.

"Did I tell you that I have the original bill of sale?"

"Yes."

"What do we do with the $5,000 one?" she asked.

"We keep it as a point of record."

"Because the community thinks we received $5,000."

"And the $45,000 becomes an anonymous donation to the community."

"So the community is given the full amount, but the record shows that $5,000 was paid for the pony."

"Do you see any need for another solution?"

Mary Gray could hardly think. Her own judgments were muddled these days. "I suppose not. What should I do with the original paperwork?"

"There's no need for it."

"I see."

"I would like to communicate with Acton in the morning. He's most interested in the right thing being done. I think the right thing is to let this matter simply be closed. If you feel differently, could you telephone me by 8 o'clock tomorrow morning?"

She nodded.

The two went on to talk about the astonishing snow storm. "I think Sue's right about a sign-out policy," Mary Gray said.

"After what you've been through, I can see why," John

agreed. "Let's get that on the calendar."

Walking to her house Mary Gray looked around the Close at the homes of the people she now called friends and decided that she was grateful to live in such a merciful and decent community.

A HORSE OF A DIFFERENT COLOR

A HORSE OF A DIFFERENT COLOR

ACKNOWLEDGEMENTS

I am grateful to my family and friends whose gracious comments corrected and encouraged me and as a result you have a better book in your hands. Thank you all.

ABOUT THE AUTHOR

Robin Arcus is a native of central Pennsylvania and a third generation writer. She is a winner of the North Carolina Writers' Association Rose Post award and her essays have been featured on National Public Radio. Since 1988 she has lived in Durham, North Carolina. A Horse of a Different Color is her first novel.

Made in the USA
Columbia, SC
11 October 2022